Praise for the Novels of Jo Davis

I Spy a Naughty Game

"A masterpiece about danger, action, lost love, and new beginnings with a bit of bondage on the side."
—Fresh Fiction

"It's as if your favorite government agent antiterrorist TV show was X-rated. Each page features either pulse-pounding action or supercharged sex—you don't get a chance to catch your breath."
—*Romantic Times*

I Spy a Wicked Sin

"An edgy and intriguing start to Jo Davis's new series about the mysterious SHADO agency. *I Spy a Wicked Sin* has a fast-paced story line as well as enough suspense and spy games to thrill any mystery lover, but at its core the story centers on the very hot and sensual relationship between assassin Lily Vale and her target, Jude St. Laurent . . . a sexy, riveting story."
—Romance Junkies

"A top pick. I loved it and can't wait for more of this new series."
—Night Owl Romance

"Scintillates with one naughty erotic encounter after the next. The passion is underscored by the mystery. . . . While the wicked games Lily, Jude, and others play ratchet up the heat level, what captured me about *I Spy a Wicked Sin* was the likability of the characters."
—Joyfully Reviewed

When Alex Was Bad

"Davis has done it again . . . a passionate, exhilarating book that will definitely keep a reader's attention. Five hearts!"
—Night Owl Romance

continued . . .

"Davis knows her stuff, and she is a brilliant writer when it comes to romantic suspense. *When Alex Was Bad* had me on the edge of my seat." —Romance Junkies

"From the first paragraph until the last page, Ms. Davis kept me captivated with her erotic wording and sensual play between the characters. The sex is spicy-hot and the suspense will keep you guessing until the very end. Five cups!" —Coffee Time Romance

"Jo Davis sizzles with her debut erotic novel." —Fallen Angel Reviews

"For fans of erotic suspense, Davis serves it up smokin'-hot. . . . Tension builds right to the very end, in and out of the bedroom." —Reader to Reader Reviews

"Wickedly wonton. . . . Take a walk on the wild side and experience an erotic suspense novel not to be missed." —TwoLips Reviews

Trial by Fire

"Romantic suspense that has it all: a sizzling firefighter hero, a heroine you'll love, and a story that crackles and pops with sensuality and action. All I can say is keep the fire extinguisher handy or risk spontaneous combustion!" ——Linda Castillo, *New York Times* bestselling author of *Sworn to Silence*

"Sizzling romantic suspense . . . so hot it singes the pages!" —JoAnn Ross, *New York Times* bestselling author of *Breakpoint*

"A five-alarm read . . . riveting, sensual." —Barbara Vey, *Publishers Weekly*

"For a poignant and steamy romance with a great dose of suspense, be sure to pick up a copy of *Trial by Fire* . . . as soon as it hits the bookstores! Five bookmarks!" —Wild on Books

"Jo Davis set the trap, baited the hook, and completely reeled me in with *Trial by Fire*. Heady sexual tension, heartwarming romance, and combustible love scenes just added fuel to the fire. . . . Joyfully recommended!" —Joyfully Reviewed

I Spy a Dark Obsession

Jo Davis

HEAT

HEAT
Published by New American Library, a division of
Penguin Group (USA) Inc., 375 Hudson Street,
New York, New York 10014, USA
Penguin Group (Canada), 90 Eglinton Avenue East, Suite 700, Toronto,
Ontario M4P 2Y3, Canada (a division of Pearson Penguin Canada Inc.)
Penguin Books Ltd., 80 Strand, London WC2R 0RL, England
Penguin Ireland, 25 St. Stephen's Green, Dublin 2,
Ireland (a division of Penguin Books Ltd.)
Penguin Group (Australia), 250 Camberwell Road, Camberwell, Victoria 3124,
Australia (a division of Pearson Australia Group Pty. Ltd.)
Penguin Books India Pvt. Ltd., 11 Community Centre, Panchsheel Park,
New Delhi – 110 017, India
Penguin Group (NZ), 67 Apollo Drive, Rosedale, North Shore 0632,
New Zealand (a division of Pearson New Zealand Ltd.)
Penguin Books (South Africa) (Pty.) Ltd., 24 Sturdee Avenue,
Rosebank, Johannesburg 2196, South Africa

Penguin Books Ltd., Registered Offices:
80 Strand, London WC2R 0RL, England

First published by Heat, an imprint of New American Library,
a division of Penguin Group (USA) Inc.

First Printing, March 2011
10 9 8 7 6 5 4 3 2 1

HEAT is a trademark of Penguin Group (USA) Inc.

LIBRARY OF CONGRESS CATALOGING-IN-PUBLICATION DATA:

Davis, Jo.
   I spy a dark obsession/Jo Davis.
      p. cm.
   ISBN 978-0-451-23222-9
   1. National security—Fiction. 2. Intelligence service—Fiction. I. Title.
   PS3604.A963I32 2011
   813'.6—dc22   2010039978

Set in Centaur MT
Designed by Alissa Amell

Printed in the United States of America

In loving memory of Hannah Montgomery, my dear friend and second mom for almost forty years. Losing you is proof that there is never quite enough time to let people know what they truly mean to you. So I hope you somehow know all of the things I ran out of precious time to say.

The world just isn't right without you in it. I miss your sweet Southern drawl and your wicked sense of humor. I hope the angels realize how lucky they are to have you among them. I love you.

Acknowledgments

Special thanks to:

My family for supporting me as they always do, with little complaint that I'm frequently here in body while my spirit is running through the woods taking out the bad guys.

My agent and friend Roberta Brown for always being there for me. You are a special lady.

My editor Tracy Bernstein for all her support and confidence.

My dear friend and critique partner Suzanne Ferrell for coming up with the title of this book! Great one, and so perfect for our heroes' final showdown with Dietz.

The Foxes for making what has been a really tough year immeasurably better. I love you all.

Prologue

astian Chevalier gazed down at the sleeping form of Michael Ross, his boss at SHADO—the Secret Homeland Defense Organization. His oldest friend. In years past, his closest confidant. Fellow football fan and beer-drinking buddy.

The only person—man or woman—he'd ever loved.

And you had to go and ruin your friendship by telling him, didn't you? Sent him straight into Maggie's arms. God rest her soul.

Bastian had thought that nothing on earth could equal the pain of watching from the sidelines, heartbroken, as Michael married her. As he spoke excitedly of trying to start a family, while Bastian's dreams crumbled around him.

Elbows on his knees, he put his face in his hands and gave a soft, bitter laugh, thinking how very wrong he'd been. Because nothing could possibly be worse than a world without Michael in it.

No matter how hard he tried, he couldn't shut out the horrible memory of the gunshots. Of Michael's eyes widening with shock, his body jerking, crumpling to the dirty asphalt outside the restaurant. Gunned down by Robert Dietz's assassin and left to die.

And he nearly had. Michael had fought hard for days, struggled back from the brink of death as Bastian went quietly out of his mind. Bargained with God, the devil, whomever would listen and heed his plea for Michael to live. His promise that if Michael pulled through, he'd never again ask for more.

In hindsight, keeping that promise would be the most difficult thing he'd ever done.

"Bastian?"

At the sound of Michael's scratchy voice, his head snapped up and he scooted closer to the bed, fixing a smile on his face that he hoped appeared relaxed and reassuring.

"Hey, man. How are you feeling?"

Michael blinked slowly, processing the question, long, dark lashes feathered against pale cheeks. "Like a building fell on me. How . . ." He licked his chapped lips and took a pained breath. "How long was I out this time?"

Bastian resisted the urge to touch his hair. Just barely. "A few hours. Water?"

"Please."

After raising the bed a little, he grabbed the plastic cup and pitcher and poured some fresh water. He held the cup close to Michael, angling the straw to place it between his lips. "Easy. Just a few sips."

Michael took a few draws before Bastian gently pulled away the straw and helped him settle onto the pillows. Setting the cup on the nightstand, he busied himself checking the IV line, smoothing the covers—anything to keep from getting caught in the brown eyes now studying him. Watching his every move.

Next he rearranged the plants and flowers sent by Michael's friends and agents, all bearing get-well wishes. Tidied the magazines he'd brought for when Michael felt up to reading. Threw away some take-out wrappers from the previous night. Which reminded him that he needed to go home and shower, change clothes—

Michael cleared his throat. "What are you doing?"

"Straightening things up before I go. What does it look like?" He knew he hadn't been able to hide the tension in his voice or his movements. Not from his best friend.

"Bastian. Talk to me."

He froze, fists clenched at his sides. An awful knot was lodged in his throat. It was more than a product of fear, of agonizing days waiting to learn whether Michael would survive. It burned and ached like nothing he'd felt before, throbbed in a pulsing wave that spread to his churning stomach and to every limb. And he recognized it for what it was.

Hatred. Vile, toxic, eating his insides.

Michael waited. Finally, Bastian's resolve shattered and he gave his friend the truth.

"I'm going to kill him," he said quietly, "if it's the last thing I do."

Michael didn't have to ask whom. The seconds ticked in heavy silence before the answer came, sure and steady. "We'll take him together. Promise you'll wait for me."

Don't you know I'd wait for you forever?

But that wasn't what Michael meant, and the reminder tore at his heart all over again. Still, what was one more promise? He nodded. "I'll wait for you to get well, and then we'll take down that son of a whore. You have my word."

Michael heaved a sigh, his expression relieved, and seemed to sink into the pillows. "Thank you."

Their gazes locked, and Bastian's pulse stuttered as for one unguarded moment something more than gratitude shone in those liquid eyes. An emotion more than warmth, deeper than friendship.

Then the connection was broken as his friend's eyes closed, leaving Bastian shaken.

He must've imagined it. Michael was doped on all kinds of meds, including strong painkillers. Whatever he'd seen in his friend's gaze was drug induced and would be forgotten by the time he woke.

Bastian took his seat again as Michael drifted off to sleep. Now that the man was out, he allowed every bit of the love and worry he felt to show once more. Even wrecked, Michael was beautiful. Mussed sable hair poked in every direction, glinting with natural red and gold tints. His full lips were parted in sleep, and Bastian wondered how they would taste, how the muscles of his chest and back would feel under his hands as he brought the man more pleasure than he'd ever known.

"Stop it," he whispered to himself.

He'd wasted enough years longing for a man he could never have, and his feelings had driven a wedge between them. Michael's brush with death seemed to have given them a second chance at friendship, and he wouldn't ruin it this time. He'd take what he could get, for however long he had left in this world.

A shiver trailed down his spine as he thought of Dietz out there somewhere, crouched in a dark corner like a deadly spider. Waiting to strike again.

And when the bastard made his move on Michael this time, Bastian would step right between them.

To hell with the cost.

One

"Dammit, Michael, what the fuck are you doing here? You shouldn't be back at work this soon! SHADO can survive without you for a couple more weeks."

Michael Ross looked up from the file on his desk and at Bastian Chevalier's anxious face. In spite of Michael's CEO and closest friend driving him bat-shit crazy for the past few weeks of his convalescence, nagging him to rest and eat right, Michael's mouth curved into a smile. He should've known better than to think he could hide in his office without being discovered.

"SHADO will survive, but you, my friend, are about to collapse," he pointed out reasonably. "Don't think I haven't noticed you've been running yourself ragged heading the organization and taking care of me at the same time."

Bastian was tired, no question. His thick golden blond hair was disheveled from being finger-combed so often, Michael was surprised the man hadn't gone bald. Dark circles were smudged under bottle green eyes that hadn't lit with laughter in more than a month. No, more like years, if he was honest, at least where Michael was concerned, and for reasons that had nothing to do with last month's assassination attempt.

Yeah, it seemed he'd made an art out of hurting Bastian. His smile dimmed as his friend continued to argue.

"I've been managing just fine, thanks. And this isn't about me," his friend snapped. "I know the doctor hasn't cleared you to come back at all, much less full-time. And are you forgetting his warning that before you were shot, you were flirting with a stress-induced heart attack? Get your ass out from behind that desk. I'm taking you home."

Michael opened his mouth to argue, but the thunderous expression on his friend's handsome face changed his mind. "Fine. It's not like I'll get anything else done today with you hovering and glaring at me." He locked away the file and powered off his computer while his friend waited. Standing, he grabbed his suit jacket off the back of his chair, wincing at the sudden tug on his healing wounds as he shrugged it on. Thankfully Bastian refrained from delivering the smug "I told you so" that obviously hovered on his lips.

"How did you get here, anyway?" Bastian asked in exasperation.

"Simon." Michael paid the older gentleman handsomely to act as his butler, personal attendant, and driver, if needed. The man took his job seriously and did it exceptionally well.

"Figured as much. You're the most stubborn jackass who ever lived," Bastian grumbled, leading his friend out of the offices and into the main hallway.

"But you love me anyway," he pointed out cheerfully. Then he stumbled mentally, wondering why he'd said that. Christ, the last thing he needed was to give Bastian the wrong idea. False hope. Worried, he shot a sideways glance at his friend, but Bastian only snorted, shaking his head.

"I've spent the past month nursing an ungrateful horse's rear end. Super."

"A jackass is a donkey, not a horse."

"Whatever."

"And I *am* grateful. More than you know."

"That's because you'd go nuts rattling around in that McMansion of yours with nobody but an uptight British butler for company." Bastian raised a brow. "Tell me I'm wrong."

"Okay, you've got me there. But that's not the only reason I— Hey, are you fishing for a compliment?" With suspicion he eyed his friend, who managed an innocent expression.

"Of course not. You don't have to say you like having me around for me to know it's true."

"Good. Because I do, you know. Like having you around." Damn, he had a feeling he'd just been played. But any annoyance over the fact vanished when Bastian graced him with a thousand-watt smile that illuminated his friend's sexy face and did really weird fucking things to his insides. Sort of twisted them up and—

Shit, no. The warmth spreading from his belly to his groin was not arousal. No goddamned way.

"Michael, welcome back."

The warm, husky greeting jerked him from his confusing thoughts and his steps halted as he looked around for the source. Their electronic-surveillance expert approached, hand out, a smile on her wide, luscious mouth that he couldn't help but return.

"Katrina. It's good to be back." He shook the offered hand, noting how her strong, self-assured grip belied the soft, pale skin and slender fingers. Gorgeous on the outside, made of tough stuff on the inside. Not butch, but classy and confident. He liked that in a woman. A lot.

"I'll bet. I can't imagine being laid up for weeks," she said, letting go of his hand. "Then there's all the catching up to do. I don't envy you one bit."

God, that voice of hers. Low and smooth, like a palm sliding over his skin. It wasn't like he hadn't noticed how her sexy voice tightened his balls every single time she spoke. Because he had. Just like he noticed that her drab white lab coat couldn't hide the curves on her lovely five-foot-nine-inch body. Or that wearing her hair pulled back into a serviceable ponytail, as she wore it now, couldn't disguise how stunning the fiery mass was when freed from its confines. He'd always thought she looked like a younger, redheaded version of Rene Russo, and he wondered whether she heard that often.

The truth was, Katrina Brandt flat-out did it for him, even if it wasn't appropriate to let on, what with being her boss. *Sexual harassment suit, anyone?* Still, if he was confused before about the heat enveloping his cock in Bastian's presence, he certainly wasn't now. Women turned him on, period. Relief overwhelmed him, nearly knocking him over.

"He's not back," Bastian grumbled, scowling. "He's ignoring doctor's orders, and I'm taking him home, where I intend to punish him. Severely."

The redhead glanced between them, blue eyes sparkling. "Well, I'd pay good money to see that. I might even help, considering that the boss man here turned down my last vacation request."

The three of them shared a laugh, but Michael sensed a peculiar tension underscoring her playful teasing. As though she really wasn't joking at all. He shifted and pulled his jacket tighter around him, hoping it hid his heavy erection. Jesus, he needed relief. Soon, or he was going to explode.

He cleared his throat. "Crime doesn't take the week off, and, as I recall, you asked me at a bad time."

"Is there ever a *good* time in this business?" Her unwavering stare challenged him for a truthful answer.

"You have a point. Hell, I've been out for a month and the place obviously didn't fall apart." *Thanks to Bastian*, but he didn't say that. "Tell you what—drop by my office with the dates you want off and I'll approve them. You've earned it."

"He means drop them off at *my* office," Bastian said firmly. "He's not supposed to be pushing himself just yet."

"Will do." Katrina swept each of them with what Michael swore was an appreciative look filled with sexual heat. "And thank you. Michael, take it easy. Gentlemen, I'll catch you both later."

Watching her walk away, he wondered which of them that predatory look had been for. Surely not *both* of them. It had to have been the lack of sex that had affected his poor, starved body and turned his brain to mush. Otherwise, he wouldn't be entertaining such crazy ideas about one of his own employees. A soft whistle from Bastian interrupted his thoughts.

"Damn, that's one helluva fine woman," his friend said, leering at Katrina's retreating backside.

A stab of annoyance went through him. "I thought you preferred men."

Bastian looked at him in mild surprise. "You know perfectly well I'm bisexual. That means my options aren't nearly as limited as yours, my friend. Come on, let's get you home."

My options aren't nearly as limited. Meaning the man could indulge in the pleasures of either men or women without a care. And Michael might be straight, but he wasn't blind—the man was pure sex and could have anyone he wanted, when he wanted.

Except me.

If anything, his annoyance increased and he couldn't fathom

why. As he eased himself into the passenger's seat of Bastian's snazzy little red Porsche, he chalked it up to being tired. And horny, too, with no outlet except his own fist. How depressing.

As Bastian pulled out of the parking lot and drove past the guard gate, Michael removed his iPhone from the inside pocket of his jacket. "What do you want for dinner?" Every instruction regarding the household went through Simon. The aging butler liked to know ahead of time so he could inform Mrs. Beasley, Michael's part-time cook and housekeeper.

"Nothing. I'm going home tonight."

The calm, quiet statement socked Michael in the gut. "What? Why?"

Bastian gave a soft laugh that sounded sad to Michael's ears. "If you're well enough to ditch me and go against doctor's orders, it's probably time for me to get out of your hair. You don't need me hanging around anymore, cramping your style."

"What an asinine thing to say." *What the hell?* "Just a few minutes ago, you said I'd lose my marbles without you there, and you're right. Who'll watch TV and hang out by the pool with me? Who'll tell stupid jokes and make me laugh? Even Simon almost cracks a smile when you're around."

"I'm sure you'll get by."

"I don't want to *get by*. I want you to stay . . . unless you're sick of me." Dread balled in his stomach at the prospect of Bastian leaving. Before his friend moved in to take care of him following his release from the hospital, Michael had never realized that his sprawling estate was nothing more than a gorgeous prison with a view.

"That's crap and you know it." Bastian sighed. "I'm happy to stay as long as you need me. I just . . . don't want to overstay my welcome."

"Not gonna happen," Michael insisted. "I'm asking you not to go. Please."

A pause, then, "Okay. I'll stay."

The knot of tension left him in a rush, and he sagged in his seat. "So, dinner?"

"Anything. Mrs. Beasley has me so spoiled it doesn't even matter what she cooks."

Giddy with relief, he placed a call to Simon requesting shrimp marinara, and then closed his eyes. He wouldn't have to face his big, lonely house without his best friend, at least not yet. The near miss brought home a startling truth: somehow, in the past few weeks, Bastian's steady hand and unconditional friendship had become like the air Michael needed to breathe. Seeing the man's sunny face each day, brightening his home, his life, had become some sort of critical axis on which his world revolved.

And damned if that didn't scare the shit out of him, more so than any bullet.

A half hour later, Bastian pulled up to the security gate and typed in his personal access code. Each person authorized to come and go from Michael's estate had his own code, and Michael's head of security—who lived on the premises and patrolled the grounds—received a daily report of exactly when those codes were used. Every inch of the property was monitored by video, as well. However unlikely it might be for Dietz or anyone else to breach the estate, the attempt on Michael's life had caused a definite lockdown on security.

Michael let out a breath as the gate slowly shut behind them. "Home, sweet penitentiary."

"Only for now. Once I wipe the scum that is Robert Dietz from the earth, things can go back to normal."

" 'Normal' is relative in our line of work, but yeah. When *we* catch him, we'll be able to finally relax a little."

Bastian didn't comment further on Dietz as he swung the sports car around to the side of the house and parked outside the four-car garage. Michael sensed a major brooding session coming on and headed it off with a suggestion as they got out and started for the house.

"You've been working too hard. Play hooky with me and let's have a beer or three by the pool, take a swim."

"God, you don't know how tempting that is. But I've got reports, purchase orders to place on the new surveillance stuff, a briefing to prepare our agents who are searching for Dietz and more than a dozen other assholes on the FBI's Most Wanted list—"

"You're going to be the one in danger of having a heart attack instead of me if you aren't careful." He unlocked the side door and they stepped inside, Bastian trailing him through the laundry room and into the spacious kitchen. "I'm the boss, and I'm ordering you to take the afternoon off."

"For totally selfish reasons."

"So? Works, doesn't it?"

"Fine, you win. You take any pain pills today?"

"Nope, not a one. Bring it—I'm good."

Reaching into the fridge, his friend pulled out two bottles of beer and twisted off the tops, then handed a cold brew to Michael. "Two is your max," he said in a firm tone. "You're still recovering, and I'll be damned if I put in all this effort getting your ass healed just to have you screw it up."

"Yes, dear."

"I'm being serious."

"So am I."

Bastian took a long draw on his beer, and Michael found himself transfixed by the sight of his lips wrapped around the opening, the strong column of his throat working. The way his position, leaning against the counter, stretched his dress shirt across his lean but nicely muscled chest. *What the fuck am I doing?*

"Um, I'm going to change," Michael said hoarsely, backing toward the nearest escape route.

"Watcha gonna be?"

In spite of himself, Michael gave a short laugh at the lame joke. "Funny. Meet you by the pool. Bring more beer."

Carrying his bottle with him, he practically jogged through the living room and up the stairs to his bedroom. Once there, he smacked the bottle down on the dresser, not bothering with a coaster to protect the smooth mahogany surface from a ring. Nothing mattered at the moment except tearing off his clothes before his body incinerated.

Months of forced abstinence—that's all it was. First because of Maggie's murder and his ensuing grief, and then because he simply couldn't imagine being unfaithful to her memory—though she'd be the first one to object to his self-imposed loneliness.

God, he needed. So fucking bad.

Naked, he stretched out on the bed and spread his legs, cupping his balls. They were full and heavy, ripe for someone's touch. Rolling them between his fingers, he tried to picture Maggie crouched between his thighs, the way her hair had trailed over his lap and her eyes had danced with mischief as she worked him. But using the memory of a dead woman felt wrong somehow, even though she'd been his wife, and the mirage faded, leaving him bereft and alone with his own hand.

He tried relaxing, letting his mind roam as his fingers skimmed his engorged erection. Ripples of delight skittered along his cock and he gripped it, pumping slowly from the leaking head to the base and up again. His bones melted and he became nothing but the heat lapping at his cock and balls as he stroked, increasing the pressure. *Oh, so good.*

Another image formed, this time of its own volition. Not a memory, but a fantasy. A beautiful redhead between his knees, her mass of hair thrown over one shoulder. *Katrina.* Her breasts swayed as she bobbed up and down on his cock, tongue laving the sensitive underside of his dick. She deep-throated him, buried her nose in the curls at his groin, worked him with her throat. Sucked and licked, driving him out of his mind.

"Oh yeah." His hips thrust rhythmically, driving his cock into that hot, wet heaven. Again and again, delicious, driving him higher, until his balls tightened and he felt the warning tingle at the base of his spine.

In the next instant, his release came and he shouted, fist pumping furiously as warm streaks hit his belly. His dream lover vanished and he released his softening cock, staring at the stripes of cum cooling on his torso. One corner of his mouth lifted in immense satisfaction.

Hetero with a capital H. There was the evidence to prove it.

Ignoring the slight pinch in his abdomen from the surgery that had saved his life, he pushed up and padded into the bathroom to clean up and pull on his swim trunks. The pool, beer, and the company of his best friend were all he needed to keep him content for now.

But soon he'd have to do something about making that dream lover a reality, even if it couldn't be Katrina.

* * *

Bastian stood frozen, fist raised to knock on Michael's bedroom door, gaping at the sight that greeted him through the crack. He'd stopped by after changing in his own room to see if Michael was ready and ask about something regarding work. Damned if he knew what the question had been.

Because the sight of the man he loved and lusted after above all others, splayed and jacking his cock, seared through his retinas, into his brain, and left him stupid. When rope after rope of cum streaked the man's broad stomach and chest, he'd have given his soul to be there, lapping the salty-sweet cream from that smooth, taut skin.

Lowering his hand, Bastian backed away from the door and turned, heart pounding and cock painfully at attention, fleeing as quickly and quietly as possible. He didn't know what Michael would do if he knew Bastian had witnessed such a private moment, and he didn't care to find out.

Kick him out? Maybe not, considering how he'd practically begged Bastian to stay. But it would sure make things awkward between them. Friendship was all he had of Michael, and the thought of losing that made him sick.

"Why did I have to fall for a man who's so straight, his spine is made of titanium?" he muttered.

And he knows how you feel about him. Why do you put up with this shit, letting him stomp your heart into the dirt under his polished shoes?

"Because I'm an idiot."

In the kitchen, he stood for a few minutes, willing away his raging hard-on. And not a second too soon. After snagging two more beers from the fridge, he greeted Mrs. Beasley, who'd just come in, huffing and carrying three plastic grocery bags. The plump, gray-haired woman was flushed and breathless, as though she'd been hurrying to complete her errand and get back to her kitchen.

"Hey, gorgeous," he said, stopping to plant a kiss on her cheek. Taking two of the sacks from her, he placed them on the granite countertop.

"Oh, you!" She blushed harder and swatted at him, setting the remaining bag, along with her purse, next to the other two. Digging inside one bag, she began pulling out fresh produce, and nodded toward the bottles. "Not letting Mr. Ross have too much of that, are you?"

"No way," he assured her. "This is his limit. Can't say the same for me, though."

"Humph. The drink will put you in an early grave. Mark my words." The woman kept at her task, putting away the groceries, movements brisk.

"My grandfather drank a fifth of whiskey every week and died at age ninety-seven. He also ate biscuits and gravy for breakfast more often than not."

"He was likely a laborer, not an office man. Things were different then, when a man had to toil all day to make a wage. Kept a man's body fit and his mind clean, and what little rest or nip of spirits he got was sorely earned."

Well, he could hardly refute that. "You're right. He worked in a steel mill, dawn to dusk. Each generation of Chevalier men has definitely gotten softer since then." He waved a bottle at the portly woman. "Are you worried about me, Mrs. Beasley?"

She sniffed. "Of course not. And you're not soft in the least, just a little slow."

He blinked at her. "What? How do you mean?"

"You'll figure it out sooner or later." Facing him, she fisted her hands on ample hips. "Now, what do you boys want for dinner?"

"Michael told Simon he wanted shrimp marinara, I think." Slow? What the hell was she talking about?

"I haven't been around to get the message," she said in annoyance. "Why that old geezer insists on being privy to every little thing, right down to my menu, is beyond me. It would be a lot simpler if Mr. Ross would phone me directly with his requests when he's out."

Bastian shrugged. "You know Simon. He's very old school that way." Or something. Probably just liked to see the woman all riled up.

"An old snoop is what he is," she grumbled. "Always skulking around, getting into my business." As she turned to the task of dinner, Bastian made his escape.

Bastian didn't see Simon, skulking or not, on the way to the pool, though, in truth, his attention was riveted on the lush surroundings. Michael's home was designed to be an oasis, a tropical-themed sanctuary from the outside world, and the pool area was no exception. Built indoors as part of the house, the huge space was covered and surrounded by walls on three sides. The fourth wall, made entirely of bulletproof glass, faced the outdoor patio, complete with a large barbecue pit, tables, and loungers. A door leading to the patio was propped open if Michael entertained, but was normally kept closed and required anyone wishing to gain access to the pool from the outside to enter their code.

In his opinion, no safety measure was too great when it came to Michael. The man was the head of a covert agency, was in close contact with the president, and as such was always a potential target.

Bastian set the beers on a small table and waded into the water on the shallow end, relishing the cool wetness lapping at his over-heated skin. He dunked his head and then floated on his back, try-ing to concentrate on the beauty of his surroundings rather than the memory of his friend pulling on his hard, reddened cock.

Good thing the swim-up bar was only manned during parties, or Bastian would be sorely tempted to imbibe something with a lot more kick than beer. And he still might hunt down a tumbler of whiskey, despite the admonishment from Mrs. Beasley. Anything to help kill this insane longing for a man who'd rather cut off his prick than be with Bastian or any man.

"Look out below!"

At the shout, Bastian's eyes popped open just in time to see Michael running full-out for the edge of the pool, straight to where Bastian was floating. "Hey, don't even—"

His friend leaped and let out a triumphant war whoop, tuck-ing his knees up cannonball style. Bastian scrambled backward, but not fast enough to avoid being drenched when Michael hit the water with a big splash. He came up sputtering, while Michael laughed.

"You shithead!"

"I thought I was an asshole."

"That, too!"

Swiping his face, he drank in the sight of Michael, dark hair dripping, beads of water making trails down his sculpted, lightly furred chest and abdomen. Two bronzed male nipples peaked immediately, no doubt due to the contrast of wetness and cool air. Three puckered bullet wounds—one too damned close to the man's heart and the others on his side and stomach—didn't detract from his perfection. Bastian tore his gaze from them with effort and covered his lapse with a counterattack.

Cupping his hand, he swatted the water, dousing a smug-looking Michael right in the face—and the war was on.

They battled like a couple of teenaged boys, yelling and chasing each other around the pool. Both grappling for the upper hand in an effort to be victorious in dishing out the most dunkings. Bastian couldn't recall the last time he'd had such fun.

Right up until Michael threw him face-first into the concrete edge of the pool.

Pain exploded in his face and he struggled to his feet, draping an arm on the ledge and holding his mouth. "Ah, fuck."

"Jesus, I'm sorry! Shit! Are you okay?" Michael waded quickly to stand in front of him.

"I think so." Already, his lip was starting to throb. But a tentative check with his tongue reassured him there were no loose or broken teeth.

"Move your hand and let me see."

He did, and Michael reached out, frowning. Gently he grasped Bastian's chin and brushed a thumb over his puffy bottom lip. "It's just a scrape, but I know it must hurt. I'm sorry. God, I'm an idiot."

At his touch, Bastian froze. Every cell in his body screamed out for more intimate contact, but he didn't dare move, much less breathe. "Forget it."

"I should've paid more attention to what I was doing." His voice softened. "You know I'd never hurt you for the world."

Michael's eyes locked with his for several long moments, and Bastian couldn't think. Because Michael still hadn't dropped his hand, was still rubbing the pad of his thumb over Bastian's lip.

Because suddenly there was an unmistakable fire in Michael's dark eyes as his friend's gaze dropped to his mouth . . . and not in examination of his wound. Michael angled his body closer, throwing off enough heat to boil the water around them.

The man appeared ready to devour Bastian whole.

Please do it. Please, I've waited so long.

"Sir? You have a phone call. I believe it's important."

Michael jerked away as though he'd been electrocuted, and spun to face Simon. "I'll be right there."

"Very good, sir."

"And find some medicine to put on Bastian's mouth. We had an accident."

"Right away."

Michael couldn't leave the pool fast enough, and didn't look back as he grabbed a towel from the shelf against the wall, quickly ran it over his body, and walked out. Bastian faced the distinguished old butler, struggling to mask his bitter disappointment at the interruption. If he hadn't known better, he would have thought he saw a hint of sympathy in Simon's usually placid expression. The look said that the butler hadn't had any idea what he was interrupting until it was too late, and that he was sorry. The elderly gentleman had a big soft spot for both him and Michael.

For a split second he considered asking Simon for his input on how to deal with Michael. The man had worked for Michael for years and wasn't blind. But Simon was terribly proper and never ventured an opinion unless asked. And on this matter, probably not even then.

"I don't need any medicine, just a little ice for the swelling," he said, proud of how he kept his voice steady.

Simon nodded. "Do you wish to accompany me to the kitchen, or shall I bring it here?"

"Here, please. I'd like to swim a bit longer." And sit in the hot tub. Maybe then he'd be able to warm the chill that had overtaken him with Michael's abrupt departure.

Simon left and Bastian sagged against the side of the pool, letting the misery seep in now that he was alone. *You know I'd never hurt you for the world.*

"But you do, over and over," he whispered. "And it's my fault for letting you."

Somehow, he had to stop loving Michael. And he would.

The day they lowered him into the ground.

Two

∾

"Katrina, we've got a problem with this new pinhole camera."

Katrina Brandt looked up from the vast array of high-tech spy gadgets on her worktable to see Emma Foster striding into the room. The tall, stacked blonde worked down the hall and served as SHADO's expert in the area of makeup artistry and disguise. Their agents depended on Emma to make them blend into the scenery while on assignment, and on Katrina and her team for reliable electronic-surveillance technology.

A failure on either front was not only unacceptable, but potentially fatal.

Katrina skirted the table and held out a hand. "Let me see." The other woman released it into her palm and waited while she examined the tiny device. "Nothing appears to be bent or otherwise damaged. I'll have to check it internally, run it through a video test feed, and let you know if it can be fixed."

"I figured as much." Emma propped a hip on the edge of the table. "Whether it can or not, that thing cost a couple of our agents some vital evidence earlier today. They got their target's confession on audio, but the video was shot. I had to call Michael and let him know."

She stifled a groan. "There goes my vacation I just managed to wheedle out of the man today. How long ago did you call him?"

Emma checked her watch. "It's going on eight, so . . . a few hours ago. If he hasn't called or come by yet, you're probably safe from his wrath until tomorrow."

"Gee, thanks."

But she doubted that very much and knew Emma did, too. When it came to the agency, particularly to costly mistakes, their boss wasn't one to let things slide. If he didn't catch her here, he'd show up at her condo. The one place she'd always wanted to get the gorgeous man, and for something much more pleasurable than a stern reprimand.

She got back to the business at hand. "No problems with any of the other equipment?"

"None."

"Well, that's something." A glint of gold at Emma's throat caught her eye. "New necklace?"

A broad smile lit the other woman's face. "Blaze gave it to me. Do you like it?" She parted the material of her blouse at the neck to give Katrina a better look. A slim gold chain lay snug but not too tight against her neck. A small lock and dangling heart charm rested in the hollow of her throat.

"It's beautiful," she said, admiring it. "You're a lucky girl."

"I am. And it's not a necklace, it's my collar."

Katrina hesitated. "Your what?"

"My sub collar," Emma replied proudly. "Blaze is my master, and in a few months he'll be my husband, too."

"Oh. I had no idea that you and he were . . ." She fumbled, at a loss.

"Into the D/s lifestyle?"

"Yes, that." The topic was so far out of her realm, she had no idea what to say. Then a thought occurred to her. "Wait. Isn't that why you two broke up a while back? His lifestyle?"

Emma nodded. "Yes. I didn't really understand his world, and I'll admit that the prospect of giving up control scared me quite a bit. I didn't get that the lifestyle isn't about humiliation, and it's not some sexual free-for-all where the Dom gets whatever he wants."

"What is it about, then?" The world of D/s would never work for her, but she couldn't help but be curious.

"The master's sole priority is the safety and happiness of his sub. He's in charge and has the final say, but he'll always listen and consider what's best for his sub. Blaze loves me and would never hurt me, and I love and trust him. It works perfectly for us."

"Well, you're certainly happy these days and that's all that matters," she said, patting her colleague's arm. She studied Emma, seeing her in a new light. Here was a woman with an adventurous spirit and an open heart, someone she hadn't gone out of her way to get to know outside work. Perhaps a friend? She really needed to make more of an effort to socialize, and what better time than now? "Emma, would you like to go have drinks after work sometime?"

The other woman's face brightened. "I'd love to! I'd just need to check with Blaze. What day?"

"Tomorrow or the day after?"

"The day after should work. It'll be fun." Emma squeezed her hand and gave her a grin. "I'd better wrap up and get home before a certain grumpy agent comes looking for me."

Katrina laughed. "Yeah, you'd better go. I'll check with you tomorrow and we'll decide on a place."

"Great. See ya."

Once Emma was gone, Katrina straightened her worktable. In her office, she retrieved her purse from the bottom drawer of her desk, rose, and hit the lights on the way out. The drive home took only about fifteen minutes, but it was long enough for her mind to wander toward SHADO's two most eligible men.

Michael and Bastian were her two personal fantasy bookends. D/s wasn't her thing, but threesomes and more? There was a juicy little tidbit she hadn't shared with Emma or anyone at the agency. She might be poised on the outside, but inside . . . she burned. All the damned time. From puberty on, her passionate sexual nature was a part of her she'd learned to embrace.

Wouldn't her oh-so-proper, sexy bosses be shocked to learn that calm, cool Katrina loved a cock down her throat and another reaming her ass or pussy? What would they say if they knew how many times she'd envisioned them fucking her—and each other— in every way possible?

She'd have a transfer to Siberia on her desk within the hour. But the knowledge didn't stop her from imagining the two most delectable men around using their gorgeous bodies to make a nice, sweaty Katrina sandwich.

God, she needed some excitement in her life. Some wild, kinky sex, to be honest. It had been a long dry spell, and she refused to keep hoping for a connection that wasn't going to happen.

That lesson was reiterated in spades when she arrived home to find Michael waiting on her stoop. As she locked her car, gathered her purse, and approached her door, her gut sank to observe the irritation on his handsome face, the restlessness of his posture. He'd come to chew her out, and then go out on the town. The last was obvious by the skintight brown leather pants that looked as though they'd been painted onto his long, muscled legs. And the snug black T-shirt tucked in at his trim waist. His sable hair had been gelled into an artfully messy, just-rolled-out-of-bed style.

No doubt about it—the man was going hunting for someone to roll *into* his bed.

A spear of disappointment stabbed her breastbone, and whatever he was about to dole out paled in comparison to the hurt of picturing him naked with another woman. Which was completely ridiculous, because she had no claim on him at all, and never would. The man was just emerging from mourning his dead wife and wouldn't be searching for a serious relationship. Especially not with one of his own employees.

"Michael," she said calmly, stopping in front of him. "I know why you're here, and I have no idea why the camera failed."

"Not out here." His snappy tone didn't bode well for the rest of the conversation.

"Of course." She bit back a sigh and moved past him to unlock the door. "Come in, please."

Walking inside, she flipped on the lights, setting her purse and keys on the entry table. With a pointed look, she gestured for him to precede her into the living room. Glancing around, he swept a hand at the designer furnishings.

"You have a beautiful home."

"Thank you. And though I appreciate your attempt to be civil, I don't believe you're here to compliment my décor. Sit down. May I get you a drink?"

"No, thanks. I won't be here that long," he said curtly.

So much for his one attempt at civility. "As I said, I don't know yet what the problem is with the camera. It's new and was functioning perfectly before I allowed it to be used in the field."

"You should have tested it again. Your fuckup has cost us crucial video of a terrorist admitting his role in a subway-bombing plot. It's shitty work on your part, and I expect better."

Katrina stared at him, momentarily speechless. In the few years she'd been at SHADO, he'd never spoken to her in anything but a professional manner, even when angry. To come into her home and verbally berate her was unprecedented and unwelcome. Steeling her spine, she returned a glare of her own.

"There was *nothing* wrong with my work on that camera or any other. My team puts all of our devices through the same diligent testing process, and we've never had a single incident before now." His jaw clenched. Refusing to be intimidated, she stepped into his space. "I brought the camera home with me, and I'll use my equipment here to examine it until the glitch is found, even if it takes all night. That is my promise, and if it isn't good enough, that's too goddamned bad. Fire me."

His dark eyes widened briefly, then narrowed. For a few seconds she could have sworn she saw grudging admiration in their depths. And perhaps something more predatory. They glittered at her dangerously, and she almost backed up a step.

"That won't be necessary. I . . ." He faltered, and just as it seemed an apology was forthcoming, the wall slammed down again. "I'll leave you to your work. I'll see you tomorrow when you have your findings."

Without waiting for a reply, he stalked past her and slammed out the door. Locking up behind him, she muttered, "Can't wait."

What the hell was wrong with him? Michael was frazzled,

upset about something more than the camera. Otherwise, he'd have been angry—the loss of the video feed was no small matter—but he never would have spoken to her the way he just had.

She wasn't likely to ever find out what was eating him, so there was no point in dwelling on it. Besides, she had a long night ahead of her and she'd best get started.

Right after she poured a nice, generous glass of wine.

Michael turned the air in his classic Camaro blue with every foul word in his vocabulary, before he started to feel like total shit. In the space of a few short hours, he'd managed to hurt his best friend again and piss off a respected employee. Two people he admired.

And more than that, desired.

There it was, exposed. For a few seconds, he'd been possessed by the insane need to kiss Bastian. He'd wanted to. Wanted to thrust his tongue inside that sexy mouth. Wanted to mark him on his throat, right where any other man would see and be warned off. So badly that his cock pulsed and ached like never before.

Thank God for Simon's interruption, even if he'd fled like a criminal afterward. Confusion had quickly morphed to embarrassment and then terror. He wasn't gay. The phone call from Emma had given him the perfect excuse to shower, dress, and leave. Bastian, he noticed, didn't try to stop him or even persuade him to eat dinner beforehand. In fact, his friend was nowhere around, and he was relieved about that.

Wasn't he?

Michael had killed a few hours shopping for new club clothes, since his old ones were too loose now. Then he debated going into the office, but couldn't bring himself to do it. He ate half a sand-wich alone at a café and wondered whether Bastian was enjoying the shrimp marinara, or if he was miserable, as well. After driving around and wasting more time, and changing into his new prowl-ing clothes, he'd ended up at Katrina's. Where he'd screwed up royally for a second time.

Even while he was bitching at her, he was never more aware of Katrina as a woman. The fact that he found himself longing to kiss her as much as he'd wanted Bastian confused him more than ever. What the hell was going on with his libido lately?

And now? He was running.

Tonight, he planned to escape his staid life for a few hours. He needed to be touched. He yearned for soft feminine lips and hot bodies. To grind them against his to the beat of raunchy, driving rock music.

For the first time in months, he needed to feel alive.

He knew just the place. Daddy's Money catered to a twenty-something crowd, though there were plenty of men in their late thirties, like him, who frequented the club, looking for easy action. Lots of girls went for older guys, and with any luck, tonight would be no exception.

Fortunately, he found a parking spot a couple of rows from the entrance, parked, and got out, ready to lose himself in fun. He wasn't an old man yet and refused to live like one any longer. Though the pistol tucked into one boot and the knife in the other would help ensure that he *got* old to relive his adventures.

Lessons learned, and all that.

Inside, he was met by a pulsing heavy-metal riff and strobe lights breaking up the darkness. Bodies writhed to the beat, people smiling, laughing. Some hung at the bar, trying to shoot the shit above the noise, maybe find some willing company. Every one of them looked to be having a good time.

He headed to the bar first, waded in, and ordered a scotch on the rocks. Leaning against the bar, he sipped his drink and watched the crowd, trying not to appear too eager. Or desperate. Neither of which would get him laid. The trick was to appear coolly interested but approachable, and he was out of practice.

His first nibble came within minutes. A woman in her late twenties or thereabouts sidled up to the bar next to him, "accidentally" brushing his arm with an ample breast.

"Oh, excuse me!" she called over the music.

"No problem."

"Damn, it's crowded tonight, huh?"

"Sure is."

Fanning herself, she gave him a conspiratorial smile. "Makes me claustrophobic. I'd like to find someplace to chill with less people around, you know?"

He did. The girl was ready, willing, and had her sights set on him. Unfortunately, she had a face like a horse and the teeth to match. He didn't wish to be unkind, but he had to nip her advance in the bud. "Good luck with that."

His tone was definite but polite, and, thankfully, she was intelligent. With a nod, she moved off to greener pastures. Any pasture but his was fine by him.

And so it went for the next forty minutes. Michael drinking scotch and making polite small talk, fending off three more advances. He wasn't picky, but none of them were quite right.

She's drunk.

She laughs like Woody Woodpecker.

Her breasts are plastic, and so is her face.

Maybe the alcohol would make them more attractive as the night went on. And he was more tired than he'd ever admit if Bastian were here to hound him. Maybe he should go home. He was just finishing his second drink when his luck turned for the better. Two gorgeous twentysomething brunettes bounced to a stop in front of him, beaming.

"Hi!" one chirped. "Want to dance? We've sort of been—"

"—watching you and you looked lonely so—"

"—we thought we'd ask!"

Gazing from one striking face to the other, his jaw dropped in astonishment. The women were identical, except that the first one who'd spoken had salon-perfect red highlights in her long, chocolate brown mane. Blue eyes twinkled at him mischievously.

Twins! Oh, my fucking God, yes!

At long last, Michael must have been a really good boy to have earned an evening of being a really, *really* bad one. He gave them his most charming smile and held out both arms for the girls to take. "I'm Michael, and I'd love to dance with you lovely ladies."

"I'm Jeri," the first one said. "And this is my sister, Jackie."

"Our dad was convinced we were going to be boys!"

Michael's brows rose. "Missed that one by a continent."

The girls giggled and pulled him toward the dance floor. "Come on!"

Amazing how his fatigue fled with one sister plastered to his front and one to his back. Dirty dancing to a fast, raunchy Nickelback song, the temperature in his body skyrocketing so high, he thought he'd burn from the inside out. Just vanish in a puff of smoke.

Jeri's nipples rubbed his chest as they moved, the little points poking through her miniscule red tank top, making it clear she wore no bra underneath. Same with Jackie at his back, though her top was blue. Groaning, he held on to the belt loops of Jeri's tight jeans, his erection digging into her flat tummy. What sweet torture: two beauties all for him. Jesus, he wanted to do delicious things to them both, then slide inside. He wanted them on top, underneath him, wherever, however he could have them.

After several dances, he'd had enough. His cock was hard as a diamond and he wasn't going to be satisfied with his fist this time around. He needed hard, naughty sex, now. Pulling Jeri close, he brought his mouth down on hers, thrusting his tongue inside. Tasting her. She tasted faintly of some fruity cocktail; not unpleasant. He liked how she arched against him like a cat, communicating her willingness without words. Breaking the kiss, he spoke in her ear.

"Let's get out of here."

Jeri gave her sister a look and jerked her head toward the exit in an unspoken signal they'd no doubt used before. Jackie promptly stuck her tongue in his ear. He took that as a yes.

"Our place?" Jackie crooned, leading him off the dance floor.

"No. Mine." No way would he make himself vulnerable in a strange place with two women he'd just met, considering Dietz's contract on his head. No matter how badly his dick throbbed.

"I don't know." Jeri frowned.

Taking each girl by the hand, he led them outside. With the noise from the club muted to a dull thump, enough so that they could talk without shouting, he drew them both close. "I work for the government and I have to be careful," he began. Shades of the truth, but that was a luxury he couldn't afford. "I have a gorgeous estate not far from here. Follow me in your own car if you'd prefer. That way if you get a funny vibe, you can just drive away. No harm, no foul."

The sisters exchanged a look, then Jeri spoke up and held out her hand, expression serious. "Driver's license?"

"Excuse me?"

"We'll need to see your license and call our brother. He's a two-hundred-thirty-pound former Navy SEAL with a really bad attitude toward anyone who'd hurt his baby sisters. He doesn't hear from us in the morning, and he won't bother with the cops. You get me? We'll give him your info, you know, just in case."

Michael stared at them, stunned. Then he chuckled. "Smart ladies. All right, sure." Digging in his wallet, he thought, *Bastian will kill me.*

No, dammit. This wasn't about his best friend. It was about being himself, cutting loose. Bemused, he waited while Jeri scanned his ID and placed a call to the person she claimed was her brother. From what he could hear, the girl giving his name and address to the guy she called Jake and coaxing him not to make a "huge deal" of her and Jackie going home with Michael, was on the level.

Hanging up, she handed him back his license and grinned. "Okay! Who's ready to party?"

Just like that, the tempting twins were back in action. On the way to their cars, the girls stopped to ooh and aah over his completely rebuilt '69 Camaro Super Sport. Another point in their favor. Women smart enough to hand him over to their big, kick-ass brother and who knew an awesome classic car when they saw one were pretty cool in his book.

Yes, this night was looking good.

They followed him all the way home, and he couldn't help a surge of pride as he let them in the gate and started up the long, stately drive. As he called Simon ahead on his iPhone, he wondered what their reactions would be and wasn't disappointed.

Parking in front, he got out and waited on the steps. The pair emerged from their little Hyundai and stood gaping at the mansion.

"Oh, my God!" Jackie exclaimed. "What the hell do you *do* for the government? Embezzle money from wealthy countries?"

He laughed, enjoying their wide-eyed amazement. "Hardly. I just do stuff a lot of people can't, or won't."

Jeri gave him a slack-jawed look. "Off the record, I'll bet."

That was a bit too close to the truth, so he led them to the door and let them in. "Shall we?" Simon, impeccably dressed though it was nearly eleven, met them in the foyer.

"Good evening, sir. Your outing was a smashing success, then?" To his credit, he didn't even blink to find two women on his boss's arm.

"It was. Could I get champagne, strawberries, and warm chocolate brought to my suite?" He made his request simple, seeing as Mrs. Beasley had gone home hours ago.

"Right away. Will that be all?"

"Yes. After you bring the tray, I won't need you any more this evening."

"Very good, sir."

"Thank you, Simon."

The butler paused and for a second Michael thought he caught a hint of reproach in the elderly man's eyes. Then he turned and strode for the kitchen, dignified as usual, leaving Michael to think he must've imagined the man's disapproval.

Shaking off a wave of irritation, he showed the ladies upstairs. He was a grown man, for God's sake, and didn't require anyone's permission to indulge in a tryst in the privacy of his own home. Which didn't explain why he was vastly relieved that he didn't encounter Bastian on the way to his room.

Pushing aside an uncomfortable feeling very much like guilt, he closed the door to his suite behind them and got a kick out of watching the two go over every square foot of bedroom, sitting area, and bathroom, squealing about this and that.

"A butler!"

"I know! All proper and English, too, just like the dude from that old *Arthur* movie."

"Jeez, look at this shower! A football team could fit in here."

"You would know."

"Oh, shush!"

More giggling. He kicked off his boots, letting them explore to their hearts' content. They had all night. While they were occupied, he stashed his weapons so he didn't frighten them into sending out a distress call to the brother. A soft knock sounded on the door, and he opened it to find Simon balancing their tray of goodies.

"Just put it on the table in the sitting area."

The old man completed the task gracefully and then gestured to the sealed bottle. "Shall I pour?"

"No, I've got it. Thanks." He clapped the man on the shoulder. "I've kept you up too late, my man. Get yourself to bed."

Simon's lips quirked. "I daresay I won't have quite the same enlightening experience as you, sir."

"You old dog," he said, laughing. Simon rarely joked, and when he did, he was funny.

The man lifted his chin, giving Michael an imperious look down the length of his nose. "Indeed. I possessed quite the bite in my day. Good evening."

"Good night."

He shut the door again and locked it for good measure, trying to imagine Simon as a young Englishman carousing in London. The picture wouldn't form.

"Michael?"

He swung his gaze around to see the twins emerge from his bathroom, stripped to their lacy black bras and panties. Thoughts of Simon left his brain along with all his blood—which promptly headed south. His cock revived and his body hummed in anticipation. He was so damned hungry, and right now nothing mattered more than sating himself all night long, until he lay limp and exhausted. He'd go until his recovering body could no longer hold up, and then they'd sleep, hopefully going another round in the morning.

"Gorgeous," he murmured. "Champagne?"

"Please," Jeri said, and her sister nodded.

Uncorking the bottle, he poured them each a flute and filled plates with strawberries and drizzles of warm chocolate sauce. Taking his flute and plate, he walked to the side of the bed and set them on the nightstand while he turned the covers back. "Treats like these were meant to be enjoyed in comfort. Don't you think?"

Eagerly, they hurried to the massive bed and crawled onto it, careful not to spill their drinks or fruit. He didn't bother to tell them they needn't worry—he planned for the three of them to make a very big mess in this bed before their time together was done.

"You're too dressed," Jackie complained good-naturedly.

"Then I'd better fix that." Slowly, he peeled off his shirt, bracing himself for the worst of their curiosity. The women gasped, and Jeri moved to the edge of the bed, reaching out to feel each of the scars on his chest and abdomen.

"Are those . . . from bullets?"

"Yes, they are. I have a dangerous job."

"This one was so close to your heart," Jackie breathed, her questing fingers joining the tentative exploration.

His breath hitched. God, he'd missed a woman's touch, not to mention the attention. "Too close. Actually, the one in my stomach is what nearly killed me. It took hours of surgery to put me back together. I've just recently recovered."

"Ooh, poor baby." Jeri's lower lip stuck out in a cute pout that struck Michael as being completely sincere.

Not only did he lust after these two, he genuinely liked them. "It's okay. I'm much better now." *Until Dietz makes another move.* But he slammed the lid on that intrusive thought.

"We're glad," Jackie said. "And we're going to help you celebrate. Get naked and climb in."

The two sultry beauties made way for him as he peeled off his socks and then his leather pants. He'd worn no underwear, and his cock sprang free, pointing the way to bliss. He crawled between them and propped himself against the headboard, reveling in how they snuggled against each side of him, sipping the bubbly and plucking the strawberries from the plates in their laps to nibble on them.

"It occurs to me that you two are the ones overdressed now," he pointed out.

"We want you to take off the rest," Jeri said. Dabbing one finger in the chocolate sauce, she smeared it over one of his nipples and began to lick it off with leisurely flicks of her tongue.

"Sounds like a plan." He moaned as Jackie gave the other nipple the same treatment. "Damn, that feels good."

Jeri made a low noise of satisfaction. "You like?"

"Hell, yeah."

Jackie piped up. "I'm thinking this chocolate tastes better on him than on the strawberries. What do you think, sis?"

"I believe you're right, for once."

Fuck, yes. I'm in heaven. Maybe I died after all.

Grinning like an imp, Jeri scooted off the bed, and in seconds returned with the small silver bowl of sauce, complete with a small ladle.

And that's when things got very delightfully messy.

Three

I'm in hell. Christ, make it stop.

Bastian rolled in bed and mashed the pillow over his head, trying to shut out the incessant giggling. When he'd heard the muted roar of the Camaro and realized Michael was home, he'd intended to talk to him, to attempt to mend the awkwardness between them. Halfway down the stairs, he halted, glued in place by Simon's greeting and Michael's request for champagne and strawberries.

For one stupid moment, he'd allowed himself to dream.

After hurrying back to his room, he'd listened and had his second-worst fear confirmed. Michael, the idiot who'd gone out without an armed escort, was home safe—but not alone. The knowledge crushed his chest in a ruthless grip, squeezing the breath out of him.

If Dietz wasn't out there somewhere, waiting for another shot at Michael, Bastian would leave. Not just this house, but the state. He'd give up his position working at Michael's side, move away, and never look back. Maybe he still would, after Dietz was put behind bars.

Until then, he was forced to keep his tears deep inside, where they cut like ground glass. Bleeding him slowly to death.

Michael squirmed, beyond excited as Jeri scooped a spoonful of chocolate and began to drizzle the sauce from his chest to his belly. All over his turgid, leaking cock and aching balls.

"Mmm, he makes a nice hot-fudge sundae," Jackie purred. She licked a trail of sauce streaking down his side.

"Banana split," her sister corrected, crawling between his knees to grasp his cock.

One soft pair of lips suctioned a nipple while the other surrounded the spongy head of his cock. He hissed in pleasure as wet heat slid down his shaft, laving off the slick syrup. Two mouths driving him crazy, slender fingers kneading his balls, until he couldn't remain passive any longer.

Gently, he pushed Jeri off his cock, ignoring her whine of protest. Sitting up, he reached around her and released the clasp on her bra, easing the straps forward. Her pretty breasts freed, he tossed the garment aside and cupped them, pinching the rosy nipples between his fingers. She moaned, leaning back to give him better access, and he bent, teasing one with his teeth and tongue.

"Lie back and let's get these off," he said, reaching for the waistband of her panties. She raised her hips and he slid them down, tossing them. "Spread your legs."

Her knees parted to reveal slick, pink pussy lips and a small strip of pubic hair above, sculpted to accommodate her bikini line. Ordering her to stay there, he turned to Jackie and removed her undergarments as she wiggled in excitement. The twins were identical underneath their clothing, and he couldn't wait to taste them both.

Moving between Jeri's slender legs, he reached for the bowl, which had tipped in all the activity, spilling some chocolate onto the sheets. He hardly cared. Grabbing it, he dribbled some on her pussy, the action reminding him of a baker icing a pastry. A treat for him to feast upon. He set the bowl aside and positioned himself on his hands and knees between her thighs. Spreading his knees wide, he bent to her, ass in the air.

"Play with me, honey," he said to Jackie. Then he flicked Jeri's little clit, began to tongue the nub, relishing the smooth flavor of chocolate and woman. Parting the folds, he licked her slowly, hyperaware of her sister scooting on her back underneath him, between his spread thighs. Lining herself up with his cock.

"Fuck my mouth, big guy."

Easing forward, he sank his length into that hot cavern, chills of pleasure dancing along his spine. "Damn! Yes, take it all, baby."

Manipulating his balls, she opened her throat for him like a pro, urging him on. All the way in, her nose buried in his groin, sucking him, throat muscles squeezing. Slowly he fucked her face and ate the sweet cunt spread for him. The decadent noises of them slurping, making little sighs and moans of delight, brought him closer to the edge of orgasm than he wanted to be.

"Not yet," he said hoarsely. "I want to fuck Jeri."

"What about me?"

"Don't worry, honey. You're going to sit on my face while she rides me." Shit, the image had him near exploding already.

"Yes!"

The three of them disentangled and Michael fetched a condom from the bedside drawer. While the pair argued over who got to put it on him, he performed the duty himself, sparing the women bloodshed. "Ready."

Jeri straddled his hips, and he struggled not to come as she sank onto his rigid cock. Beautiful. Her body taking him in, hugging him like a velvet glove. Nothing finer than being buried in a woman's pussy. Except eating it.

She began to fuck herself on his length while Jackie straddled his face. Gripping the headboard, she lowered herself to his waiting mouth. He nibbled and licked at first, teasing lightly, getting her there. It didn't take long to drive her mindless, and soon she was moving, demanding more. He ate her then, sucking the needy flesh, savoring the juices coating his face.

His balls tightened and he thrust up into Jeri with rapid strokes. Flesh slapped on flesh, bodies seeking and taking. Enjoying each other. So wicked and so fine.

The orgasm sizzled in his balls and he couldn't hold off. He shot hard with a shout, pumping furiously into his partner, and she joined him a second later. They rode the waves, and he remembered poor Jackie, trembling on the precipice because he'd gotten distracted. He latched on to her clit, working the nub, and it sent her flying in the throes of her own release.

Drinking greedily, he thrust and sucked until the woman moved off him and collapsed. They lay replete, grinning like fools, covered in sticky chocolate and cum. He hadn't felt so relaxed in days; this was exactly what he'd needed to get rid of that weird tension he'd been experiencing around Bastian. He was simply starved for pussy—nothing more.

"Shower, sleep, and then rounds two and three," he suggested.

They ran giggling for the huge shower, and he followed, feeling pretty damned pleased with himself.

His world—at least the part regarding his orientation—was right again.

Life could go on.

Close to dawn, Michael awoke wrapped in fresh sheets and warm females. They were spooned together with Jackie in front of him, Jeri behind. His cock had awakened first and rode Jackie's ass, and it apparently liked the way she was rubbing her rear against his lap. Half-asleep and not wanting to spoil the spontaneous moment, he carefully reached over her for one of the several condoms he'd left on the nightstand.

Fumbling, he opened the package and managed to cover himself. Smoothing a palm over one butt cheek, he dipped his fingers into the crevice between her thighs, urging her to spread for him. "Come on, sweet thing," he whispered into her hair. "Let me in."

"Oh yesss . . ."

She pushed back and he slipped into her pussy from behind. Gripping her exposed hip, he sheathed himself to the balls and began to move. Fucked her with languid strokes, increasing the tempo until his release gathered and shot from his balls. They shuddered together and went still, basking.

He fell asleep still inside her.

Bastian's ears were bleeding.

Groans, sighs, and *thump, thump, thump.* All goddamned night long. Out of all the people in the house who didn't sleep last night, he was the one who'd had the least fun. One word from Michael and things could get ugly, fast. With any luck, the asshole and his new friends were still comatose.

Shower and coffee. Lots of coffee, the only morning food that mattered.

Dressed in one of his best dark blue suits, white shirt, and tie, he jogged downstairs, a man on a mission. *Fill the travel mug, be nice to Simon and Mrs. Beasley, and get the hell out of Dodge.* Simple.

Would've been a great plan if Michael and two dazzling beauties weren't huddled around the breakfast table, laughing, sipping orange juice, and nibbling croissants, having a splendid time. That Michael wasn't an inconsiderate lover who kicked his bed partners to the curb at sunrise didn't make Bastian feel one fucking bit better.

"Homicidal" is the word of the day, brought to you by the letter H.

Jesus. His attempt to sneak past the alcove where they were gathered was foiled by a friendly chirp.

"Oh, hello! Michael, introduce us."

Bastian stopped in the doorway and faced the group, stifling a snarl.

"Yes, who's your friend? God, he's a cutie!"

So were the women, a fact he'd appreciate so much more were they not adorably rumpled and glowing from multiple climaxes. Bastian skewered Michael with a withering stare, and the man's smile dimmed. Bastian remained silent, content to let him fumble.

"I, um, these are my . . . this is Jeri and Jackie," he said weakly, waving a hand at them. "Girls, this is my best friend, Bastian."

He had to admit, they *were* pretty cute, and gazing at him in open curiosity with guileless expressions on their identical faces.

Despite his hurt, he didn't have the heart to be rude to them. "Ladies, my pleasure."

The one with red streaks in her hair swatted Michael's shoulder. "Why didn't you tell us you had a supersexy best friend in the house? We should've invited him to play!"

Bastian raised a brow at Michael as if to say, *And why didn't you?*

A flush colored Michael's cheeks. "Well, I—"

"Maybe Bastian doesn't like the group scene, dingbat," her sister said. Then she gave Bastian a speculative, hungry look. "Do you?"

Uh-oh. Caught like a three-legged antelope in a race with a lioness. He was in love with Michael, not dead. His best friend looked ready to disappear. . . . And suddenly Bastian was enjoying himself.

He gave her a wicked grin. "Which sister are you?" he asked the one who'd posed the question.

"I'm Jackie."

"Actually, Jackie, I love group scenes. I love sex, period, with both women"—he shot Michael a pointed, heated look—"and men." Let them assume what they would.

Jackie beamed. "Oh, wow!"

"Damn, I'll bet that's hot!" Jeri's wide-eyed gaze bounced between him and Michael, brimming with speculation. And lust. "Can we watch? Please?"

The flush on Michael's face deepened to the color of an eggplant. Bastian turned on the full force of his charm, taking evil delight in his friend's discomfort. He'd feel bad later. Much later.

"Oh, I think our friend here might be a teensy bit shy about that sort of thing. He's still in the closet, you know," he said in a conspiratorial voice.

The girls nodded in tandem. "Hey, no problem," Jeri said. But neither of the sisters could hide their disappointment.

"I'm *not* in the closet," Michael said stiffly. His protest was ignored.

"Perhaps another time?" Bastian suggested in answer to Jeri's suggestion. He glanced at his friend. Was it possible for a person's head to explode?

"Sure!" they squealed together.

"Michael has our number," Jackie informed him.

"I'm sure he does." He gave them a wink. "Unfortunately, I have to run. One of us has to bring home the bacon, so to speak. Until next time?" He blew a kiss at Michael. "Later, sweetie."

The women chorused their enthusiastic agreement while Michael sat in angry silence. And no wonder, with the ideas Bastian had planted in their pretty heads about their living arrangement. Michael was visibly furious that he'd insinuated they not only had sex, but were a permanent couple who played around.

Bastian couldn't care less, especially after listening to those two vocalize their appreciation of Michael's prowess all frigging night long.

Stalking through the kitchen, he bypassed the coffeepot and headed straight out the door. Fuck it; he'd drive through Starbucks. And order a triple-caffeinated, hot caramel mocha with four sugars and whipped cream. He'd stop by the gym after work and attempt to kill the calories, along with his frustration.

Turning out of the gate, he soon lost himself in mulling over the strain of living with Michael now that the man was almost recovered. He didn't know how he'd be able to take another night like last night, but he wasn't about to leave before Dietz was captured or killed. Preferably the latter.

He was so engrossed in his current misery, the vehicle following several cars behind him almost didn't register. A silver sedan, non-descript, too far back for him to see the emblem on the grille or read the license plate—*Wait, there is no front plate.* It had been keeping pace with him for a few miles, never gaining, always leaving cars between them. An innocuous sedan among many, meant to attract no attention. An innocent motorist or a tail?

As planned, he drove to Starbucks, but decided to park and go inside rather than using the drive-through. Under any other circumstances, he might believe he was being overly cautious. The awful memory of Michael bleeding out on the ground cured that notion. If he was being followed, he'd know soon enough.

As Bastian pulled in to the Starbucks parking lot, the silver car turned in to a McDonald's he'd passed about three businesses back, and got into the long drive-through line wrapped around the building. Bastian got out of his car, locked it, and strolled inside, the picture of a regular guy stopping for his daily jolt before heading to the nine-to-five. Not a care in the world.

The Glock resting in the holster underneath his suit jacket told a different story. He hadn't been quick enough to save Michael from the assassin's bullets, and could have just as easily been the one dying because he hadn't seen danger coming. Never again.

Ten minutes later, he walked out carrying his caramel mocha and a small paper bag containing a cheese Danish, and casually glanced toward the McDonald's. The silver car was almost to the pay window, if it was the same one. "Time to boogie," he said under his breath.

Sliding into his car, Bastian set his drink in the holder, the bag on the passenger's seat, and got under way. As he left the parking lot, the silver car abandoned the line, headed for the exit, and eased into traffic, once again keeping several car lengths between them.

"Bingo," he muttered. "Now the question is, Who are you?"

Could be Dietz, one of his henchmen, or anyone. Bastian had dozens of agents working scores of cases at the moment, all of which he was responsible for in Michael's absence. Taking out a SHADO leader would be considered a coup for any of the country's most wanted, not just Dietz, and he'd do well to remember that.

The fact that the general public didn't know of SHADO's existence didn't mean shit. Many who comprised society's underbelly did, and that's what counted.

He was more than halfway to the compound and had turned onto the two-lane road several miles from his destination when the sedan made its move. In the rearview mirror, he saw the vehicle rapidly closing the distance, making no attempt to be discreet now that they were on an isolated stretch with help minutes away. Minutes that could prove fatal.

Whipping out his cell phone, he placed a call to the emergency command center at SHADO, taking some comfort in the fact that those guys were ready to roll twenty-four/seven. The voice on the other end of the line was a godsend.

"This is St. Laurent," the man said in greeting, tense with concern. "Chevalier?"

"Yeah, it's me. I'm about six minutes out, got a visitor comin' up my tailpipe and not in a good way. Silver sedan, no front plates. Must have something special under the hood to catch my Porsche. I need backup, Jude, five minutes ago." The car continued to close the gap, and Bastian pressed hard on the accelerator.

"You got it. Hang on." The blind agent—one of the casualties in Dietz's grab for power and money—exchanged a few brief words with someone on the other end, then returned. "Okay, we've got you on tracking. Stay ahead of the target and our team will intercept."

"Tell them to hurry, man. Things are about to get nasty."

With that he closed his phone and tucked it into his suit pocket—

Just as the sedan rammed him from behind. Cursing, he fought to control his lightweight sports car as it fishtailed. While he had his hands full, the driver whipped to the left and put on a burst of speed, bringing the sedan even with his car. Bastian grabbed for the Glock under his jacket and palmed it. Glanced over to see the other driver already had his hand cannon pointed at Bastian's window.

"Fuck!"

He ducked as the window shattered in a spray of glass. Felt his car get rammed again, jerking to the right. Sitting up, he intended to pop off a shot out the broken window, only to see that he was already on the shoulder of the road, barreling toward the culvert beyond. No time to correct the wheel. Only time to suck in a sharp breath as the car met empty air.

The engine whined and the nose dipped. The front end met the earth first in a teeth-jarring impact, then the back. The vehicle bounced and slid sideways, and he was along for the ride. Tossed by the whim of fate.

He barely had time to register the warm liquid flooding his mouth as the car tilted, rolled. Once, twice. A third time, more glass shattering, metal screaming. His head struck something, but the pain didn't register. Only his desperation to stay conscious, or he was a dead man. Because he had no doubt the driver of the sedan would come down here and pump a bullet in his brain.

The Porsche slid to a stop, resting on the roof. Bastian, heart racing, struggled to remove his seat belt. The bastard would be down here in moments to finish him. And where the hell was his gun? The latch gave and he scooted to an upright position, wincing at the bloom of pain in his ribs and head, searching for the weapon that was nowhere to be found. He had to get out of here or he was going to be slaughtered like a pig.

The front windshield had a bigger opening, so he crawled through on his stomach, ignoring the jagged teeth that tore at his nice shirt. Footsteps crunched through the foliage, easing down the incline toward the car, and he crawled faster. From his assailant's hesitation, he wasn't sure whether Bastian still posed a threat and was approaching with caution.

Free of the car, Bastian sat up and got his bearings. Not easy to do with his head swimming. The car had come to rest in the undergrowth in a wooded area, something he could use to his advantage. Position and the element of surprise were all he had. Hopefully, the bastard would believe he was still in the wreck long enough for Bastian to get the drop on him.

Quickly, careful not to make noise, he limped for a nearby copse of trees and ducked behind a large one. Sweat trickled down his face and he swayed on his feet, wondering when his backup would show. Now would be good.

The footsteps circled his car slowly. Taking a chance, Bastian peered around the tree trunk and saw a big man taking stock of the car. Dark hair, swarthy complexion. Smooth skin. Not Tio, then. Dietz's right hand was an ugly, pockmarked son of a bitch. This guy appeared pretty average, except for his size. And the big-ass gun in his palm.

The man bent to peer in the driver's window . . . and spied a torn, bloodied piece of Bastian's shirt clinging to a shard of glass in the front windshield.

Shit! Before the man could straighten, Bastian launched himself across the distance. The man spun, bringing up the weapon, and fired. Bastian hit him in a flying tackle, slamming him into the side of the car and grabbing the hand with the gun. They hit the ground tangled together, each fighting for control of the weapon. Teeth bared in a snarl, his nemesis struggled to turn the muzzle of the gun on Bastian, but he managed to get some leverage, banging the man's wrist into the hard-packed earth until it gave with a sickening snap.

The assailant howled, releasing the weapon. Bastian wasted no time scooping it up, pushing the muzzle under the man's chin.

"Game over," he hissed. "Who do you work for?"

"Fuck you." The shithead spat in his face.

"You wish." He gave the guy a feral smile. "Dietz send you?"

"Who?" The man's eyes cut away, mouth tightening.

"Lying asshole. We'll see how you like being our guest indefinitely."

A sneer marred his face. "I'll make bail before the tow truck gets that piece of shit you were driving out of the ditch."

Bastian laughed. "You think we're cops? Boy, Dietz left out a few important details when he handed you this job—or you failed to ask the right questions. You're not going to jail, moron. You just disappeared down a black hole, never to be seen or heard from again. Hope you watered your plants and fed the cat."

"What're you talking about?" Bastian yanked him to his feet, spun him, and pushed him face-first into the side of the car. "What the fuck? I have rights!"

"Do us both a favor and shut up unless you have something useful to say."

The sound of a vehicle stopping on the road above, shouts, and many feet tramping down the incline in their direction was music to his ears. He didn't relax until a hand clamped on his shoulder and a low voice growled in his ear.

"Got him, boss."

Bastian moved back, limping, his body beginning to throb, his injuries making themselves known. The man who'd spoken, an agent named Lawrence, jerked the would-be assassin's arms behind his back and cuffed him. As he led their prisoner away, another hand landed on his shoulder.

"Bastian? You okay? We heard a shot."

He turned to see Blaze Kelly, a good friend, onetime lover, and a damned fine agent, frowning at him in concern. "Went wide. I'm fine. Think I'm gonna need a ride to the office, though," he said, waving a hand at the totaled Porsche. His joke fell flat. Suddenly he didn't feel so good.

Blaze steadied him. "Jesus, man, your head is bleeding. We're taking you to McKay, getting you checked out."

"I'm okay, really—"

"Let's go. Just don't vomit in the Hummer."

He gave Blaze a lopsided smile. "No promises."

"That's what I was afraid of." The big agent wrinkled his nose as he helped Bastian up the culvert. "You smell like chocolate and coffee."

"My caramel mocha, which perished in the wreck along with my breakfast."

Food was the exact wrong thing to mention at that moment.

His stomach heaved and he dropped to his hands and knees, retching.

"Well, shit," Blaze sighed.

Indeed. This morning had started out in the crapper and had, unbelievably, gone straight to hell. Definitely room for improvement.

Then again, he was alive. Five points back in the plus column. He'd need all he could get before he brought down Dietz like the rabid dog he was.

Michael was balls-deep in Jeri when the phone rang. He groaned, not paying too much attention to the noise. Either Simon or Mrs. Beasley would pick up, and they knew better than to disturb him when he was entertaining guests.

He'd barely achieved release, emptying himself into her sweet pussy, when a firm knock sounded at the door. Restraining a growl of irritation, he eased out and patted her on the rear. "Go away," he yelled toward the door.

"You have a call, sir," Simon informed him in that steady tone.

"Take a message."

"It's of the utmost importance."

"Damn," he muttered, running a hand through his hair. Knowing Simon, the call *was* urgent or he wouldn't have interrupted. "Hang on."

Scooting from the bed, he ignored his companions' pouts and pulled on a pair of jeans he retrieved from the end. Stalking to the door, he opened it and slipped into the hallway, shutting it behind him. Simon stood with his hand covering the mouth of the phone, worry in his eyes. That alone chilled Michael's soul.

"What's wrong?"

"It's Agent Kelly, sir. There's been an incident." He held out the phone. "Let me know if I can be of assistance."

Michael took the phone and waited until the older man disappeared around the corner before speaking. "Blaze? What's going on?"

"Michael, listen to me. First of all, Bastian is okay—"

"What happened?" he demanded. Christ, his best friend had been gone only an hour. What could have taken place since then?

"He was followed and the guy shot at him, ran him off the road. He rolled the Porsche, but listen—*he's okay*," Blaze emphasized. "Bastian called for backup, but he already had the asshole subdued when we arrived."

"Thank God," Michael breathed. "Where is Bastian now? Put him on the phone."

"I can't. McKay's checking him out. He's got some cuts and bruises, maybe a concussion—"

"What?" he shouted. His knees turned to rubber. "You said he was okay! I'm on my way."

"That's not necessary. I wanted you to know, that's all. The assailant's in a cell, but he's not talking."

"I'll be there in forty minutes or less."

Ending the call, he yelled for Simon. Like magic, the man appeared from around the corner. No doubt he'd listened to every word. He handed the old butler the phone. "Bastian had some trouble on the way to work. I've got to go."

"Will he be all right, sir?"

"I think so. See my guests out, would you? They drove their own car, so they won't need a ride."

He sniffed. "With pleasure."

There it was again, the disapproval. He didn't have time for this. "I'm driving myself to work, and before you say anything, yes, I'm well enough."

"I was going to ask whether that's wise, considering that his trouble might have been calculated to goad you into rushing off alone."

He stared at the old man. "You're pretty smart, you know that?"

"So are you, but you're upset. One of us must retain his wits."

"You're right." His mind scrambled for calm despite his urgency to get to Bastian. "Ring security. Tell them I need the car and an armed man to ride with me. I'll have a shower and meet them out front in ten. And, Simon, thanks."

"You're most welcome."

The old man left to do as Michael asked. Michael returned to the bedroom and gave the ladies a lighthearted smile he didn't quite carry off. "Emergency. I have to go, so you'll need to get dressed. Simon will show you out."

"Aww, I thought we were gonna spend the day together," Jackie whined.

Jeri punched her in the arm. "Shush. Can't you see something's happened?" To Michael, she said, "I hope everything is all right. Call us?"

"Sure." Somehow, he didn't think he would, no matter how much he'd enjoyed their company. "I had a great time. Truly."

They began gathering their clothes and getting dressed. He gave them each a brief kiss, but didn't wait for them to leave before hitting the shower. He made short work of the task, and donned a pair of nice black pants and a white dress shirt. A shoulder holster containing his gun and a jacket over it completed the ensemble, and he made it out front with one minute to spare.

With the attempt on Bastian, all bets were off.

Michael Ross was officially back at the helm, and God help Dietz or anyone else who hurt those he cared for. His gut twisted in cold rage.

"You're going to pay, motherfucker."

Four

Katrina was headed for Michael's office to report her findings on the pinhole camera when the man himself rounded a corner ahead and dashed for the elevator.

"Michael, wait!" She quickened her steps to catch up, reaching him as the elevator doors slid open and he ducked inside. Following him, she blew out a breath. "I was just on my way to speak with you."

"About?"

"The camera," she reminded him. "I stayed up half the night, but I located the problem."

"Oh. That." He looked distracted, and practically vibrated with impatience.

She frowned. "Yes, *that*. You know, the little technical failure you reamed my butt over last night? Seems the unit had a faulty microchip, a manufacturer defect isolated to the batch we recently received. I mailed them all back this morning and they're sending out a new order."

He nodded, expression tense. "Good."

Good? That's it? "Okay, what's going on?" Her gaze strayed to the panel and she noted the single lit button. "Why are you going to the fourth floor?"

"I don't recall making it your business."

"You're obviously upset, and I care," she said softly. "So I made it my business."

The elevator glided to a smooth stop and the doors slid open. As they emerged, Michael grasped her upper arm and gently steered her away from the open doors of the compound's hospital. He glanced up and down the hallway before he spoke, and let go of her arm. "This morning, an attempt was made on Bastian's life," he said in a rough voice tinged with anger that wasn't directed at her.

The blood drained from her face. "Oh my God. Is he all right?"

"Agent Kelly said he was, but I'm here to see for myself."

"Was it Dietz?"

"The assassin is in lockup, isolated from the one who almost killed me, but yeah. I'm pretty sure it was Dietz." He looked as though he would strangle his former colleague with his bare hands, given the chance.

"But why would he target Bastian?"

"Why else? To get to me." He closed his eyes as though in pain. "It never occurred to me he'd go after Bastian. God, I'm so stupid."

"No, you're not." Reaching up, she touched his face. "You don't think like a monster, that's all."

Opening his eyes, he took her hand and held it between them. "I get paid well to outwit the monsters, and sometimes that means thinking like one. Why I can't seem to get the drop on Robert is beyond me."

"You will," she promised him. She believed that with all her soul. "In the meantime, let's go see your friend."

"You'll go with me?"

A wistful expression crossed his face and tugged at her heart.

This man had no one except Bastian, and someone had tried to take him from Michael. "Of course. Come on."

Keeping hold of his hand, she tugged him inside, where a nurse quickly showed them to the cubicle where Bastian lay on a small bed. A butterfly bandage was stark against his tanned forehead, but no other evidence of injuries was present. He looked fine, if a little bored. When they entered, he momentarily brightened, but immediately seemed to withdraw as he watched Michael come in. Katrina wondered again what was going on with these two lately.

"Hey, buddy, how are you feeling?" Michael let go of Katrina's hand and sat by Bastian's bed, unable to hide his worry.

"I'm fine. Ready to get out of here." His attention strayed to Katrina and his face brightened again. "Hey there. Checking up on me?"

She smiled. "Absolutely. I'm so glad you're okay."

"Thanks. Me, too."

Michael interrupted. "Concussion?"

"Mild. I only threw up once." Bastian eyed his friend's suit. "You're awful dressed up for someone who's not back at work yet."

"I am now," Michael said, his tone leaving no room for argument. "This changes everything. I'm here to stay, and I don't want to hear a word about it, other than 'you can count on me to be here at your side.'"

Bastian hesitated, appearing ready to argue, then relented. Probably realized it would do no good. "You always can. You know that."

"Good. Now, this assassin—did you recognize him?"

"No, but he's an amateur."

"How so?"

"Other than the fact that I'm alive with barely a scratch? He thought he was taking out a cop. Demanded to be read his rights." Bastian gave a short laugh and winced, holding his ribs. "Imagine his surprise to learn we don't exist, and now neither does he."

Michael tapped a finger over his lips thoughtfully. "So, not only is Dietz resorting to amateur hit men, but he's withholding crucial details. He's letting his emotions rule, and since we broke up his small army, he's getting desperate."

Bastian agreed. "Before, his goal was the money and power he'd gain from selling the stolen bomb. With those stripped from him, his only goal is revenge. Which makes him even more dangerous."

Katrina couldn't help the shiver that crawled up her spine. "Sounds like you two ought to keep a low profile until Dietz is neutralized."

"That's exactly what we *don't* want to do," Michael said. "If he can't get to us, we can't get to him, either. We need to lure him out of his hole, and that means being seen."

"With backup always on standby," Bastian clarified.

Made sense, but she didn't like it. Problem was, she couldn't tell them what to do. They weren't her men, as much as she wished differently. Even if they were, she silently amended, she still wouldn't be able to order them around.

"Knock, knock." They all looked to see Emma standing in the doorway, concern marring her attempt to appear chipper. "A great big birdie named Blaze told me that our fearless CEO almost got his ass killed. You okay?"

"Not even close, and I'm *fine*," Bastian muttered. Sitting up, he swung his legs off the bed. "That's it. Somebody tell McKay to sign my papers. I'm going to my office, changing my shirt, and getting some work done like I'd planned to do all along."

"You're going home," Michael ordered.

"No, I'm not." Bastian glared back at his friend, and then addressed the room in general. "In fact, I'm having a drink or three after work, if anyone cares to join me. I've earned it."

"Whether you want to admit it or not, you're not going to feel like going out tonight," their boss insisted. "Wait until tomorrow and we'll see if you're up to it."

Emma cleared her throat. "I have an idea." Once she had everyone's undivided attention, she continued. "Katrina and I had plans to have a few drinks tomorrow after work, but in light of this morning's attempt on Bastian, my overprotective man has strictly forbidden me to go out without him escorting me."

This came as no surprise to Katrina, or anyone else in the room, she figured. Just weeks ago, Dietz had kidnapped Emma and held her hostage when he escaped from one of SHADO's prison cells. The bastard had intended to kill her before Blaze and some other agents located and rescued her. Emma posed no more threat to Dietz and he had no reason to harm her now, but that didn't mean he wouldn't, given how unstable Michael and Bastian believed he'd become.

"What do you have in mind?" Michael asked curiously.

Emma went on. "A group outing with the five of us—me, Blaze, Katrina, and you two. I know Blaze will be fine with going, and I'm pretty sure Katrina won't mind having two gorgeous dates."

"Mind? Are you kidding?" Katrina teased. "With these guys along, I'm more than capable of amusing myself if you guys get . . . occupied."

Emma grinned. "Great. It'll be fun! If Bastian is feeling up to it by then, that is."

"I don't know . . ." Michael began.

"I'm in," Bastian said. His smile lit the small room. He smacked his friend on the arm. "Come on, don't be such a stick in the mud. We'll have a great time."

"Some of us more than others." The glare Michael shot his friend could have stripped paint off a car.

Bastian seemed puzzled for a moment, then his face flushed. "You'll have a blast, I promise."

Emma glanced between the two men, a hint of a smirk teasing her lips. "Guaranteed, or your money back."

Apparently, Bastian got the comment, but Katrina was lost. If she didn't get some answers soon about the strange tension between her bosses, she'd scream.

"I, for one, would adore having two hot men on my arm," Katrina couldn't resist saying. Bastian's eyes twinkled as he grinned at her, and Michael gave her a long, searching look, as though he'd never *seen* her before. As a woman. Awareness touched all her nerve endings with delicious heat.

"Fine, I'll come," Michael said, relenting. "A regular club, though, not Blaze's D/s hangout. I don't think the rest of us are into the public scene." Everyone nodded in agreement, and Emma laughed.

"I'll let him know. How about eight o'clock, drinks and dancing at Daddy's Money?"

"Um, the crowd there is kind of young. How about Shakers?" Michael asked the group, and no one seemed to care.

Emma hugged Bastian, careful not to squeeze too hard. "Don't overdo it, and get some rest, okay? See you later."

After she was gone, Michael turned his attention back to his friend. "You still insist on staying?"

"Yep. I'm good." He stood and walked around a bit to

demonstrate, his movements stiff but basically functioning near normal. At least on the surface.

"You're going to be really sore by tomorrow," Michael observed. "Maybe too much to dance."

His friend shrugged. "We'll see. If nothing else, I'll watch. But I'm not about to stay home like Cinderella while you guys shake your booties."

"You mean Cinder*fella*."

"You are *such* an asswipe."

Katrina chuckled, following them out of the hospital area as they continued to bicker like a couple of old men. Beneath all the bluster was a real love that shone through between them, something she wasn't sure they even realized. And she wanted in on that, however possible. Maybe it wasn't going to happen, but bad odds had never stopped her from trying.

Their "date" couldn't get here fast enough.

Five hundred miles away, Robert Dietz paced the dingy motel room, hands clenched into fists to still their trembling. Rage, his ever-present companion these past few weeks, slithered under his skin and expanded, threatening to split him wide open.

It was almost a separate entity, demanding retribution for the empire he'd held so briefly in his hands and lost.

No, it wasn't *lost*, as one would lose a wallet or a set of car keys. It was *taken* by Michael Ross. Starched, uptight Michael. Patriot, law-abiding citizen, everybody's fucking hero. No shades of gray in his narrow world, no room in his tiny brain to understand that sometimes greatness could be achieved only by veering off the path.

Three bullets at point-blank range should've killed the bastard. *By the time I'm done screwing with him, he'll wish they had.*

Maggie's death had been a good start. Robert should've been more patient, played with Michael longer before reaching for the prize. Nothing for it except to rectify that mistake, starting with Bastian Chevalier.

A key scraped in the lock and he spun to see Tio enter, shutting the door behind him. "Well?" he demanded. "What's the word?"

The big, ugly Mexican shook his head. "Our man failed. He's in custody at SHADO, and Chevalier hardly got a scratch on him."

"Goddammit!" The rage exploded, and he swept the lamp and phone from the top of the nearby desk. They hit the floor with a clatter and he stood panting, hands braced on the surface. He needed to destroy something vital, but he was neutered, stuck here in this shithole, hundreds of miles from his target and depending on imbeciles to do his job.

At least he had the money to pay them, thanks to bounty from false investments funneled into his account by his former partners, Augustine Kosta and Ralph Meyer. While the pair had been arrested and a few of the accounts seized, thankfully not all of the money had been traced.

Tio was unperturbed, as usual. "What now?"

He thought for a few moments, reaching for calm, and then slowly straightened. "Continue to have our other contact monitor Chevalier's movements and wait for an opportunity. Then he's to strike immediately, make it look like something it isn't."

"Like a bashing?"

"Exactly. But tell them to leave a special calling card, one Ross won't fail to identify as my work. Understand?"

"Yeah." Tio grinned.

"And, Tio? I want Chevalier dead," he said coldly. "If it isn't done, I'll be forced to take matters into my own hands. And that will get very messy for *everyone*."

Even Tio would've paled, had he been capable. Robert never dirtied his own hands if he could help it.

To chip away at Michael's soul until he begged Robert to end him? He'd make an exception.

"Bastian, wait!"

Bastian stopped and turned at the sound of a familiar, welcome voice and smiled at Katrina, who jogged to catch up with him. "Hey, Red. What can I do for you?" He had a few thoughts on the matter of what to do for her, none of which were appropriate for a boss to entertain about his beautiful employee.

Catching up, she gave him the Death Glare. "A couple of things. First, don't call me Red. The last guy who did that had to get his nose reset."

He wasn't fooled—the touch of humor in her voice betrayed that she wasn't really angry, and he couldn't imagine her striking anyone. But he played along. "Ouch. Wouldn't want to ruin my pretty profile. What's the second thing?"

She grinned, and it transformed her face into a vision that awakened his cock. "Have lunch with me?"

A little burst of happiness lit his previously crappy day, and he warned himself not to get too excited. She was probably already headed in his direction and asked him as an afterthought. "What a coincidence. I was on my way to the cafeteria."

"I know. I stopped by your office to ask if you wanted to grab a bite, and your secretary said you'd just left. I'm glad I caught you."

"Me, too." So she *had* sought him out. Okay, so his entire week was suddenly looking up, and not a moment too soon. "Anything in particular you wanted to talk to me about? Or is the invite purely social?"

"Mostly social, though I did want to tell you that the new shipment of microchips came in to replace the faulty ones in the cameras."

"That's good."

She nodded, then cut him an assessing look. "I also wanted to see how you're doing. You don't seem nearly as stiff as you did four days ago."

"Worried about me?" The idea warmed him all over.

"Of course. If anything happens to you, who'll buy me cheap, fatty lunches at the compound's roach buffet?"

He laughed. "There's an image I needed before I bite into my burger."

"Assuming it is, in fact, all beef. How do you really know?"

"Gross. I think I'll get a salad. Nobody can fake lettuce."

"True." They walked in comfortable silence for a few moments. "How *are* you doing?" she asked, more serious now.

"I'm good. The soreness is almost gone, and I'm ready for our night out whenever it works for everyone else." Truth was, he couldn't wait. Michael had been right to badger him into putting it off, though.

"Tomorrow night?"

"Sounds perfect. I'll check with Michael."

"Great! I'll get with Emma, but I'm almost positive it'll be fine as long as Blaze isn't working."

Bastian thought for a second. "I don't believe he's scheduled for an assignment." And if he was, Bastian would pull him. Selfish but true. He wanted, needed, to get out with his friends for a while, and forget all his worries and disappointments.

Forget that he and Michael were on Dietz's hit list—and on the lists of about a dozen more criminals besides. Cheerful thought.

"Hey, where'd you go?"

Shaking off the dismal mood threatening to encroach on his break with Katrina, he ushered her into the lunch line. "Somewhere a lot more fun than this building," he said wryly, covering his lapse. "I can't remember the last time I went for drinks and dancing with friends."

"No wonder, considering how you've been taking care of Michael for weeks while he was on the mend, on top of running this place." She selected a large salad and a drink from the offerings and set it on her tray.

Following suit, he gave her a sharp look. "I hadn't realized that was common knowledge among the agents and other staff. About my playing nurse to Michael, I mean."

Turning her head, she raised a brow. "Really? Even though you employ a few hundred spies who are trained to find out stuff they shouldn't know and are the best at what they do?"

He sighed. "Well, hell." No telling what else was general knowledge when it came to his feelings for his best friend.

They reached the cashier. He paid for both lunches in spite of her protest, then followed her into the dining area. Of their own accord, his eyes dipped to the sight of her shapely ass gently swinging, hugged by a pair of crisp, tan dress pants as she walked in front of him. God, what a view. And he was too damned starved for hot, willing flesh to drive himself—

Abruptly, she stopped and turned. "It's too loud and crowded in here. Want to go somewhere else?"

He barely kept from running over her. "Let's eat in my office," he said hoarsely. Then cleared his throat. *And let's ditch the food.*

"Okay."

During the brief walk, he wondered whether he was so pent up, sexually frustrated, and starved for attention that any beautiful body would do to help him unwind. The sad answer to that was probably yes, but . . . Katrina was more than a pretty face.

She was intelligent, possessed a sharp wit, and was poised and confident. For the past few weeks he'd noticed she had a way of looking at him, as though she'd like to learn his every secret, that made his balls tighten and his breathing hitch. And he realized he wanted to answer all the questions in those sultry eyes, and do some learning of his own.

This was not a woman to be fucked and forgotten. And why did the idea of any man treating her like an object make him want to punch someone?

Striding past his curious secretary, he led her into his office and closed the door behind them. The large conference table was clear, so he headed for the nearest spot at the end, set down his tray, and took a seat. Katrina settled beside him, at the head of the table, making it easy for them to talk. Cozy.

"Your office is bigger than Michael's," she observed, sticking her straw in a plastic glass of lemonade. "How'd you get so lucky?"

"When Michael gave me the promotion, we ordered the conference table for closed-door meetings, but he didn't want the table in his office. He doesn't like having meetings there."

"And you get to be the one to put up with the foot traffic in and out." Her lips turned up. "Smart of him."

He shrugged. "It's not that bad. I don't really mind, because the meetings are usually scheduled in advance, unless a crisis arises."

"Well, that gives you about ten whole minutes of peace per day," she teased.

"Maybe fifteen. Remind me why I wanted this job?"

"Because it makes you the boss of me? And you've got a great view?"

Taking a bite of his salad, he pretended to consider. "Both very good reasons. Too bad I don't get hazard pay anymore, though."

"Why not?"

"I'm no longer in the field. I'm an office drone."

"That's hardly fair when you're in just as much danger as you were before," she said, scowling.

"I'd get extra money if I went on assignment, but that doesn't happen often in my position." He grinned. "You're pretty when you're huffy. And I shouldn't have said that out loud."

"Hey, you won't hear me complain about receiving a compliment from a sexy man, whether he's my boss or not." She gave him a pointed look, the meaning of which was perfectly clear. "And I shouldn't have said *that* out loud. Do you mind that I did?"

"Not at all," he managed. While his looks wouldn't break a mirror, it was on the tip of his tongue to say he was far from sexy, but he didn't want her to think he was fishing. After picking at his salad for a minute, he asked, "We're friends, right?"

"Of course. We have been for a while, and it's not like this is the first time we've caught lunch together." Cocking her head, she looked at him in open curiosity. "Why do you ask?"

"But it's the first time we've ever eaten alone and enjoyed any sort of privacy. Now I'm wondering why we haven't before."

"It is rather nice, isn't it?" She smiled.

"Very." He hesitated. "Is it just me, or does it feel like something is . . . changing. Between us."

Abandoning her fork, she reached over and laid her hand on his. "I feel it, too. To be honest, I've always admired you. Not just physically, but for your strength of character. How you treat others and how people look up to you. Anyone in this building would put themselves between you and a bullet, and not just because it's their job. Not everyone inspires that sort of loyalty, but you do. And I find that very sexy."

He squirmed inwardly at the praise and thrilled to it, as well. Not that he believed he was so great, but that someone else did. Hell, he was only human—sometimes a man needed to *hear* how much he meant to someone. And be shown. His lonely soul soaked up her words and the open expression on her lovely face. The heat was back in her eyes, too, along with a hint of challenge. His cock leapt, defying his iron control and finally growing to full hardness in his pants, not giving a damn that he was her boss and shouldn't mess around with an employee. Friend or not.

His voice was husky. "All those same things are true about you. Plus you're smart and confident, a straight shooter who goes the extra mile for your friends and coworkers. Look how you came to see me after I wrecked—"

"No," she interrupted, scooting her chair close so their knees touched. "Making sure a friend is okay isn't extra. It's just what you do when you care. And I care about you."

She bent close, and his pulse pounded in anticipation at her clear intent. Their lips touched and he opened himself to the kiss, her sweet taste drowning any remaining inner protests that this wasn't advisable. His blood throbbed and his balls grew heavy, a wonderful ache that he should try to resist, though now he couldn't think why.

"Stand up," she murmured, tugging at his hand.

He didn't think, simply did as she requested. Because he didn't want to talk himself out of what she obviously planned as she shoved her chair back and slid to her knees. Reached for his belt.

The buckle proved a bit stubborn, but she unfastened it and went to work on his pants. In seconds, he was standing over her, cock pointing at her face, flushed and eager. Her lips quirked up and she grasped the base, licked away the little drop. Those striking eyes met his as she brought the head to her mouth, took him inside. The sight of his hard flesh disappearing between her lips almost finished things before they began.

"God, that's good," he groaned. She hummed around his cock in agreement.

He was greedy for her mouth, the silky suction pulling his brain through his cock. He thrust, slowly at first, then with deeper, faster strokes. Gave himself to the pleasure until the tingle at the base of his spine warned him that release was too close.

"Not yet!" Gently, he coaxed her to let him go. "I want to fuck you, come inside you."

"Yes," she rasped, standing. As she reached for the button on her pants, three quick knocks on the door sounded like gunshots.

"Mr. Chevalier?" his secretary called from the other side. "You're needed in the gym right away."

He tried to keep the growl of annoyance from his tone. "What for?"

"Fistfight. Marks and Taylor are going at it. Marks apparently shot off his mouth again about something."

"Goddammit," he muttered, quickly tucking his flagging erection into his pants. Then he called back, "Tell them I'll be right there."

"Will do."

"Sorry about this," he said to Katrina, reaching out to brush her plump lower lip with his thumb. Damn, what rotten timing.

"It's okay. Duty calls." She sighed.

"Rain check?"

She winked. "If you're lucky."

God, he didn't want to leave. "Stay and finish your lunch if you want. And let me know about tomorrow night."

"Okay."

Stealing his resolve, he left before he could change his mind and bend her over the conference table, fistfight be damned.

But there was always tomorrow.

Michael studied his designer-jeans-clad ass in the mirror with a critical eye, gave it a little shake. Not bad for a guy on the long side of his thirties, one entering a new phase of his life.

New phase. How appropriate. He was finally healing after Maggie's murder, and looking forward to being happy again. What would it take to cross that threshold?

And why did it feel like tonight was crucial to crossing it?

Crazy. Just like these weird feelings he'd been having around Bastian lately. And when Kelly phoned the other day to say someone had tried to take out his friend? He'd almost lost his shit. He couldn't get to Bastian fast enough, and nothing equaled the relief of seeing him awake and doing relatively fine—though they ended up putting off their club outing for a few days because his friend was too sore by the next day to move much, as Michael had predicted.

And then there was the gorgeous Katrina. Her comment about having two hot guys on her arm had fired his imagination, sending it boldly trekking where it had never ventured before. Two women? Fantastic. But sharing a woman with his best friend, a man he secretly . . . what? Desired?

Insane. Yet he'd hardly slept the past few nights as a half dozen naughty scenarios involving Katrina and Bastian floated through his mind. Katrina between them, taking them both. One of them doing her with the other watching. To his shock, he'd even pictured Bastian underneath him, Michael powering in and out of his tight channel while Bastian fucked her. . . . And he'd come like a geyser, cock in hand, despite his recent escapades with the twins.

Just a stupid fantasy. It meant nada.

Shoving aside his confusion, he pulled on a dark blue T-shirt and went down to meet Bastian outside. His friend wasn't there yet. His driver, who was one of his private-security men, waited beside the Mercedes limousine that Michael rarely used. That would have to change for a while, since the sturdy vehicle, with its bulletproof windows, was safe enough to transport royalty.

Once they were under way, one of his SHADO agents would follow at a discreet distance, ready in the event of trouble. Michael and Bastian were armed, as well, and wore their guns strapped to their ankles, hidden under their pants. All of this fuss for an evening out. It hardly seemed worth the effort, but maybe he'd change his mind.

The second Bastian exited the front door and started down the steps, he did just that. His friend wore a pair of black leather pants that must've been airbrushed onto his lean body, and a black mesh shirt. As the man stopped in front of him, Michael stared at the broad chest visible through the holes in the fabric. Holy God, was that a . . .

"Are you wearing a ring in your left nipple?"

His friend's grin would've charmed the devil. "You like it?"

He gaped like a landed trout. The man's whole outfit screamed, *Fuck me now!* Damned if his unruly cock didn't take notice, too.

"When did you get your nipple pierced? You've never worn one of those when we've gone swimming." He'd sure as hell remember that, of all things.

"I had it done years ago." He shrugged. "I don't wear it all the time, and normally the only people who see it are the ones I fuck."

The image of Bastian with his shirt off, back arched in ecstasy, the little ring glinting wickedly on his chest, slammed him hard, left him aroused. Shaken. And royally pissed to think of some random hookup getting his or her claws into Bastian.

Michael cleared his throat. "Ready to go? Katrina's expecting us."

"After you."

He climbed in and scooted into the far corner, grateful for the cool, dark interior that hid his steely erection. Needed to get laid again, that was all. Take the edge off, forget about this forbidden craving that dogged him night and day. Only he'd be with friends and playing escort to Katrina, so he couldn't very well sneak off for some action. Or he could, but it wouldn't be right.

"The driver know where she lives?"

He glanced at Bastian, careful to keep his hands covering his lap. "Yeah, I told him. I went by her place the other night to chew her out for the glitch in the new pinhole camera."

"What was the verdict on that?"

"Turns out it wasn't anything she had control over—defective batch of microchips." He chuckled at a sudden memory.

"What?" Bastian eyed him curiously.

"You should have seen her, facing me down. She didn't take any shit from me, just gave it right back."

His friend lifted a brow. "Most of our toughest agents wouldn't oppose you."

"She could teach them a thing or two. Got right in my face, told me to fire her if her work wasn't good enough. She was . . ."

"Stunning? Glorious?"

"Jesus, yes." He sighed, sinking even farther into the plush seat. "Do you have any idea how much it turns me on when someone gives to me as good as they get? No fear, no hesitation? God, what an aphrodisiac."

"Is that what it takes? Wish I'd known that long ago." Green eyes glittered in the darkness. A solid, warm body slid close.

"Bastian . . ."

Strong fingers cupped his face and full, sensual lips descended on his before he could draw a breath to protest. Shock froze him in place as his mouth was taken in a fierce kiss, but when the other man's tongue swept inside, demanding, tasting—

His brain went on the fritz and his entire body melted. Simply opened to the kiss, to the delicious sensations flooding his limbs. How could he feel drugged, yet light enough to fly out the window? The weight pressing into his felt so damned good, so right. Expensive cologne teased his nose, a heady combination of spice and man, and he wanted more.

Without his permission, a needy sound, something like a whimper, escaped his throat, but he was far too lost to be embarrassed. Clinging to Bastian's shoulders, he returned the kiss with months of pent-up passion, loosed the part of his soul he'd kept prisoner in the darkness. It was almost too much, too big, that empty space being filled with light.

Bastian broke the kiss first and moved downward, nibbling his throat. Each small bite made him desperate for more contact, and he wasn't aware he'd arched his back and spread his legs until Bastian laughed in a low, seductive rumble and eased to the floorboards to kneel between his thighs. The man pushed up his shirt and splayed a big hand over his flat stomach, caressing. Then the hand moved lower, palmed the erection straining in his jeans. Rubbed the proof of the feelings he wanted so badly to deny, if his tongue hadn't been stuck to the roof of his mouth.

"Tell me to stop," his friend murmured.

He shook his head, unable to say the word. The one syllable that would prevent his life from being changed forever—if it hadn't already.

His jeans were unbuttoned, zipper lowered. No underwear was present to impede progress, and hungry eyes flashed to his before his jeans were tugged to his hips, cock and balls freed. His only coherent thought was gratitude that the driver had discreetly raised the privacy glass. . . . And then that clever tongue bathed the head of his cock.

"See us? This is me giving to you, and this is you loving every second of it. Let yourself go and experience how good we can be together."

That hot mouth engulfed his shaft, swallowed him into a moist tunnel. Easy, deep-throating him all the way to the base. He gasped, electrified to the core. Jacking his hips, he grabbed a handful of golden hair and started to move.

"Bastian," he whispered. "Oh, God."

Staring at his cock sliding in and out of his friend's sexy mouth, he was fascinated and horrified by turns. It felt so freaking *good*, and it shouldn't. Right? But he couldn't get enough, needed to fuck that gorgeous mouth, to see that beautiful blond head bob up and down over his lap. One of his fantasies in living, breathing color, stripping him bare.

Groaning, he thrust harder as Bastian's free hand rolled his balls. "Yes! Fucking eat my cock. Whatever you want. God, yes, please . . ."

Never anything like this. Couldn't possibly get any better. Or so he thought, until a finger crept behind his balls, parted his ass cheeks. When the pad of the finger began to gently massage his hole, he detonated like a bomb.

"Ahh, fuck! Yes!"

His eyes rolled back in his head and he shot wave after wave of cum deep into the willing throat. Bastian swallowed, working his shaft, wringing every drop from him, greedily sucking him down. Eventually, the aftershocks waned and his softened cock was released. As he came down from the high, a single kiss was placed on the inside of his thigh, a loving gesture that touched something deep inside him. And left him scrambling to deny it.

"I—I—Jesus," he muttered, avoiding his friend's knowing gaze. Briskly, he tugged up his jeans and tucked himself away.

"Look at me." He did, though it wasn't easy. Bastian still knelt on the floor, hands on Michael's thighs. "There's nothing wrong with what we did. Hell, this has been building for a long time, and we both enjoyed it."

"This?" His voice sounded strangled.

"Us. You know I love you, and now—"

"Wait. Hold on." With his brain fully engaged again, common sense kicked in. What had he done? And with his best friend, no less? "There is no *us*, not like that. I'll admit I didn't say no, but this . . . this was a—a heated moment that got out of control. That's all."

Hurt welled in those incredible eyes, stabbing Michael in the heart. Bastian got back into his seat and was silent for a few minutes, gazing out the window at the city.

Almost too quietly to be heard, he said, "You tell yourself that if it helps you sleep better at night. And when you stop running, I'll be here. Just like I always have been."

The words haunted him the rest of the drive to Katrina's condo. Run? That was such bullshit. He hadn't said no to what happened, but he hadn't asked for it, either.

Liar. You begged when your cock was buried in his throat.

No. He didn't prefer men, and if Bastian had been waiting for him to fall in love or some crap? That was his problem, not Michael's.

The car slowed, and he noticed they'd arrived. Katrina was waiting outside, and Bastian opened the door for her. Smiling, she climbed in and brushed her wild red hair over one shoulder.

"Who's ready to party?"

Five

Katrina's cheerful greeting met with two of the weakest smiles she'd ever seen. Both of her dream men looked ready to hurl, and were seated as far from each other as the width of the limo would allow. Obviously she'd arrived in the wake of an argument. Or something.

Each man kissed her cheek and she settled into the seat opposite them, facing backward. Michael seemed to rally first, his dark eyes raking her from head to toe.

"I know I'm ready, especially in the company of a beautiful woman. You look stunning."

"Ditto," Bastian put in. "Absolutely ravishing."

"Thank you," she said, struggling to hide her surprise. Her bosses had never been so overt in their appreciation, and she wasn't quite sure how to respond. Especially in light of yesterday's interrupted play with Bastian. Had the blond god spilled the beans to Michael, causing tension? She should've thought of that before pouncing on the man, but there was nothing to do but make the best of it. "You two are quite mouthwatering yourselves."

Indeed, the pair of them were raw sex. Light and dark, bold and mysterious. Now that she had a chance to study them further outside the work environment, Bastian was as outwardly free and comfortable with his sexuality as Michael was controlled and secretive. The contrast in their attire was subtle, but it was the mesh shirt and nipple ring that put Bastian over the top and made her wonder.

"Can I ask you something?"

"Sure. Doesn't mean I'll answer." His playful tone spurred her on.

"Are you bisexual?" Obviously he wasn't gay, because he'd been really into her at the office. Hell, she'd always been a direct person, sometimes to a fault. Inwardly she cringed, hoping he didn't take offense. But his smile went from stiff to genuine in an instant, whatever had been bothering him pushed to the background for the moment.

"Yes, I am. Does that bother you?"

"Not at all. I think it takes a lot of courage to simply be who you are, with no apologies."

"I appreciate that," he said. He shot a quick look at Michael, who in turn took great fascination in studying his shoes. "I don't advertise at work, but on my time, I live life on my own terms. More people should try it, and put less stock in what others believe is right."

"I couldn't agree more."

Bastian's face lit up, taking her breath away. Yesterday, when she'd said she found him sexy, he didn't look convinced. The man couldn't possibly know how attractive he was, inside and out. An angel. All he needed was a pair of wings.

"I don't care what others think," Michael said defensively. "But I know what's right for *me*."

"Do you?" His friend's voice held a note of challenge.

Katrina's attention bounced between them. "Okay, someone want to tell me what's going on with you two? Whatever it is, you haven't done a good job of keeping it out of the workplace, because I'd already noticed the tension."

For a long moment no one answered, then Michael let out a deep sigh. "Just a difference of opinion. That happens when a couple of guys have known each other as long as we have. Nothing to worry about."

In other words, none of her business. She'd have to live with that, unless one of them saw fit to let her into the inner circle. But given her observations before and the exchange between them just now, she could venture an educated guess as to the crux of their disagreement. If she was correct, her heart ached for them. Especially Bastian.

The limo arrived, stopping under the awning at Shakers. She wasn't easily impressed by wealth, but she had to admit it was pretty cool going out for an evening on the town in such a fine ride. The necessity of the fortified vehicle and armed escort trailing at a discreet distance didn't escape her, but she planned to enjoy herself to the fullest.

Blaze and Emma were waiting just inside the club, and Katrina beamed at them. "You guys look terrific!" The couple was striking in matching leather outfits of deep purple, perfect for a night at the club. While Blaze wore pants, Emma wore a short skirt that showed off her long, toned legs, and a snug tank top.

"So do you!" Emma called, giving her a hug. Blaze kissed her on the cheek.

"Oh, thanks." She felt slightly out of place in her staid black pants, though she'd attempted to make her outfit more fun by wearing a thin, gauzy blouse and black bra underneath. It wasn't as if she went clubbing a lot, so her clothing was more suited to dinner at a nice restaurant.

"Hey, guys!" Emma greeted her bosses, followed by Blaze. "Drinks? We reserved a table in the corner."

"Lead the way," Bastian said.

Blaze showed them to a darkened corner where they could observe the action but were mostly hidden. They took their seats at a circular table, Blaze and Emma on one side, Katrina between her dates on the other. Katrina noted again the chain that Emma called her collar resting at the woman's throat, and wondered what it would be like to be "owned" by a man in that way. Though she liked some kink, the D/s lifestyle wasn't for her. But she'd be really happy to belong to someone special.

Or two someones.

A server hurried over and they ordered a round of drinks, settling into lively conversation. An outsider would never guess that her dates were everyone's bosses; they were so fun to be with— once they decided to let go of their differences for the evening and let their hair down.

Blaze was sort of a nut, which was a far cry from the tough agent she'd infrequently glimpsed at work. While they sipped their drinks, he kept them entertained with stories of ops gone FUBAR, with the other two men chiming in on occasion. With his shoulder-length, dark hair, chiseled face, and muscular build, he was quite handsome. But he couldn't hold a candle to Michael or Bastian.

"You did *not* put a millipede in Ozzie's sleeping bag," Emma admonished her lover, referring to fellow agent Dean Osborne.

Blaze shrugged. "Hey, they're big and ugly, but harmless— unless you kill yourself getting away from one. You shoulda seen the guy dancin' around, screamin' like he was being skewered by Freddy Krueger."

Emma smacked the big man on the arm. "That is so mean!"

"Speaking of dancing." Bastian drained his martini and stood, holding out a hand for Katrina. "Would you like to?"

"As long as you're all recovered from the wreck," she said. A small, flesh-colored bandage on his forehead peeked from under a fall of blond hair. "I don't want you to overdo it."

"Oh, I think we both know how *recovered* I am. Please?"

"What's that supposed to mean?" Michael asked, frowning.

She grabbed Bastian's offered hand and they ignored the other man's question. "In that case, yes!"

As he guided her to the dance floor, she caught Michael's stare. He always appeared so controlled and distant that the fierce hunger in their dark depths surprised her, sent a shaft of awareness zinging through her body. Did he know what she and Bastian had almost done? Would he be angry? Or possibly turned on? Then Bastian tugged her through the crush, onto the floor, and the connection was severed.

The warmth, however, remained. Stoked to arousal as she and Bastian faced each other, they began to move to the throbbing beat of the music. It was a driving number with sexual lyrics, a standard club tune, but there was nothing common about the way her partner's hips swiveled to the tempo. His body swayed with fluid grace, suggestive. Mesmerizing.

The man had missed his calling as a porn star. He had the moves and the beauty, that touch of soiled innocence she found difficult to resist. Had she thought him an angel? Perhaps one with a slightly crooked halo. She'd dearly love to learn just how far he'd fallen from grace.

Her thoughts must've been telegraphed to him somehow, because he reached out and pulled her flush against his body, sealing them together from chest to groin without breaking his rhythm. She'd dirty danced once or twice, but never had she felt as though a man was made to fit against her. His lean, hard muscles were so good under her hands, so right. His sexy mouth was tilted up at the corners, those bottle green eyes shining with amusement, as if he had a wicked little secret and was waiting for her to discover it.

The impressive erection digging into her stomach, however, was no mystery. His desires were clearly communicated, but whether he'd ever finish what she'd started was the question. Maybe he felt funny about playing with an employee. Maybe not.

Returning his look, grinding against him with the beat, she silently gave him her vote.

She had about a dozen queries on her mind, things she'd love to ask him about himself. She'd really love to know more about his bisexuality, his experience. Whether or not he was seriously seeing anyone, though the vibe he was sending off said no. It was just as well that the loud music made conversation almost impossible, because his personal relationships were none of her business. Much as she wished differently.

Just as they found their groove, a hard male form pressed into her from behind. Twisting to see the newcomer, she smiled at Michael and then continued to dance. Nothing fired her blood like being in the very position she'd dreamed of, even if they weren't all naked. Being sandwiched between them felt very right, as though she was a lone puzzle piece that finally found her matches.

One erection rode low on her belly, the other her ass. *Oh, God.* Arousal heated her sex and she wanted so badly for their clothing to vanish, it drove her nearly insane. Michael's hands skimmed her arms and then one pushed her hair aside. Soft lips nibbled her bare neck. She groaned, but neither man could hear.

Body language was more effective than words, anyway. Simpler. Usually, people couldn't mess up a good time by keeping their mouths shut. It was when the mouth engaged that things sometimes went south. She should know.

So she was content to ride the waves of delight swelling higher with every thrust and gyration. Music and sensuality swept her away so that she was hardly aware of Michael maneuvering his way in front of her, edging Bastian to the side, until she found herself staring into dark eyes. Michael's hands molded to her waist, and she twined her arms around his neck, pulling him as close as possible. Which meant they were stuck together like glue.

After a couple more songs, he leaned over and spoke in her ear loud enough to be heard over the music. "Want to get some air?"

Her heart beat a bit faster and she nodded. There was no mistaking the very male triumph on his face as he took her hand and led her through the throng. It occurred to her that Bastian had disappeared from their vicinity, and as Michael led her past their table on the way out, she saw the other man sitting with Emma and Blaze, toying with another martini. When had he left? Guilt assailed her to see him sitting with their friends, yet looking so . . . alone.

But it's not like we asked him to leave us. I certainly would have liked for him to stay.

Maybe he simply hadn't wanted to hang around, or he was more tired than he was willing to admit. He was a grown man, for God's sake, and he could do as he pleased.

The pep talk didn't completely ease the feeling that a piece was missing as she and Michael stepped outside into the night. Still, she basked in the presence of the man at her side, certain that her life was about to change in a significant way—for the better.

Linking their fingers, they strolled along the sidewalk companionably. She noted he kept them to the shadows, placed his solid bulk between her and the street. The reason caused a shiver of fear that threatened to ruin the wonderful mood, and she scanned the surrounding area.

"Michael, this probably isn't the best idea."

"I'm not going to let anything happen to you." His hand squeezed hers, then released it so he could slide his arm around her waist.

"It's not me I'm worried about. You were nearly killed while out with friends just a few weeks ago." Turning her head, she studied him. "In a situation very much like this."

"I wasn't prepared then. I am now." His expression was unreadable. "This very second, we're surrounded by security, though they seem invisible. If Dietz or anyone working for him makes a move right now, he's ours."

The absurdity of the situation hit her, and she couldn't help but give a short laugh. "You romantic, you. Who would've guessed?"

He chuckled. "I try."

They walked a bit farther in comfortable silence, and she wondered at his life. "Is it always like this for you?"

"Like what?"

"The danger," she said softly. "Always having to watch your surroundings. Taking agents along for a simple evening out. Never knowing when one of your enemies might finally succeed in bringing you down."

He considered it for a moment. "I was always cautious before

Robert turned traitor, but it was never like this. I've had security in place at my estate since I established SHADO, but the measures were merely precautionary. The hit Robert put out on me was unprecedented, and once he's neutralized, life should return to normal."

She hadn't missed the harsh emphasis he'd put on the word *neutralized*. "You mean killed or taken into custody?"

"Locking him up didn't work out so well before," he said with a hint of bitterness. "So stone-cold fucking dead works for me."

"Mr. President will have something to say about his punishment, since it was the government's weapon Dietz stole."

"He already spoke. Bastian and I have full authority to stop the bastard however we see fit. And I intend to use that authority to put him in the ground."

"I see."

He frowned. "You don't approve." It wasn't a question.

"I can't *approve* of killing, no matter how badly a man deserves it. But it's not my call, and the idea of Dietz leaving this earth isn't what bothers me most."

"Then what does?" Michael studied her in puzzlement.

"How big a scar your vendetta against him is going to leave on your soul."

"*Mine*? I didn't start this little war, but I'll damned well finish it. Where he's going, *he's* the one who ought to worry about his soul, not that he owns one for the devil to take."

Just like a man to think in black and white, regardless of the personal price.

"Hearing you talk that way . . . concerns me. I'm afraid your hatred will blind you to the danger or affect your judgment, and that scares me for you."

"I don't know whether to be flattered or insulted."

"Neither. It's not a slam against your ability to get Dietz, which I have no doubt you will." She gave him an earnest look. "It's a question of how much of you will survive the bloodshed."

"I never knew you cared about me." He sounded pleased about that idea.

"You miss a lot of signals from those around you," she said, thinking not only of herself, but also of Bastian. "Or you ignore them."

"Is that right?"

"Yes."

As they reached the end of the building, he pulled her around the corner and down the alley a fair distance from prying eyes. Pushing against her, he backed her into the brick wall, placing his palms on either side of her head. He leaned close, his lips almost touching hers.

"Tell me, Katrina . . . am I getting the signal scrambled now?" His eyes were dark pools, his body hot as he pressed close. "Do I need to back off?"

Oh, God. How she'd wanted this. But what about Bastian? "No, but—"

"That's a yes or no question."

Her nipples tingled and her pussy warmed. "Your men—"

"Won't say a word. Yes or no?" Lightly, he brushed her lips with his.

"What was the question?" She was only half kidding. The man made her insane, all common sense drowned in a flood of desire. But he was serious, waiting for an answer. "There's nothing wrong with your powers of deduction, but if you need me to be perfectly clear—kiss me, dammit, before I die from the wait."

He dove in, lips capturing hers hungrily, tongue delving inside. She moaned and leaned into the kiss, reveling in his taste, thinking, *At last.* Every sensitive part of her cried out for his touch, his taste. Sinking into him was like coming home.

Before she could dwell on that feeling too much, rough fingers plucked at her nipples through the thin fabric of her blouse and the bra underneath. Hitching the edge of the material, she took his wrist and moved his hand underneath, placed it on her stomach, nudged it upward. Taking the hint, he cupped one breast, rubbed his thumb over the taut nub through the silk. Then he deftly flicked the front clasp and spilled her into his questing hand.

Arching into him, she marveled at how good it felt to be bared to him. How much better if there was no clothing at all to get in the way. Breaking the kiss, he bent and nuzzled her hair, whispering into her ear.

"Jesus, you're so soft. Are you silky all over?" His palm skimmed downward. "Are you smooth, perhaps hot and wet?" His journey paused at the button of her pants.

"Why don't you find out?" She could barely keep from panting as he undid the fastening, parted the material.

His hand slid over her mound, through the small rectangle of curls to her folds, and he practically rumbled in pleasure. "Mmm. Totally bare except for this little soul patch right here. Damn, I wish I had you in my bed right now."

"We could go," she suggested breathlessly, spreading her legs in contradiction of her words. Opening herself.

"But do you really want to stop right now?"

"No! Please, I need . . ."

His low, sexy laugh curled through her blood, but it was his skilled touch that set it to boiling. Unhurried fingers rubbed her slit, dipped between the folds to discover the moisture there. Evidence of her rising desire. They spread the dewy wetness to her clit and lingered, stroking and teasing the little bud, sending tiny shock waves of delight to her limbs. Then two fingers entered her channel, fucked her slowly. Filling her—but not enough.

"You need more, sweetheart?" His smug tone hinted that he already knew the answer.

"Yes, please." She squirmed, arching into his hand.

"I want to taste you first. Okay?"

She nodded, belatedly realizing he might not be able to see her gesture in the darkness. And he'd asked for her permission every step of the way, something she appreciated.

"God, yes."

Kneeling, he took down her pants and lacy underwear, helped her out of them, leaving her wearing nothing from the waist down but her black heels. "Beautiful," he murmured, kissing her mound. "All mine. I'll bet the men who are watching us are jealous as hell." His tongue flicked her clit. "Does that turn you on?"

Did he mean turned on by having sex in public, knowing his men were playing voyeur, or by his glorious mouth? *Yes to both*, she decided, but her response was lost in a moan of pleasure as his fingers spread her and he began to bathe her slit. He licked her juices as though he'd found a tasty treat, swirling and flicking, the light touch driving her insane.

More. Threading her fingers through his sable hair, she urged him to take more. *Deeper.* Taking the hint, he tongue-fucked her until she nearly melted into the brick wall holding her up—and almost died of sheer bliss when he latched on to her clit and suckled it without mercy.

"Oh! Michael!"

He took her expertly to the edge and then stopped, released her, and pushed to his feet. Cruel man. She made an unintelligible noise of protest, but he just gave a low laugh, turning her to face the wall.

"Spread your legs and brace yourself, beautiful." She did, and a finger trailed down her spine, causing her to shiver. "I'm going to fuck you from behind, hard and deep. Unless you want me to stop?"

"Don't you dare!"

"That's my girl."

How she wished. One steamy encounter didn't mean he belonged to her, and there was his best friend to consider, but she'd contemplate the consequences later. At the moment she couldn't think straight with him behind her, rustling around, obviously getting ready. A telltale crinkle of foil reached her ears, and then he guided the blunt head of his cock to her pussy. Pressed inside, stretching, filling her to the limit. She gasped, thinking she felt him all the way to her toes, owning every part of her.

Slowly, he buried himself balls-deep and held there for a few seconds. She savored the connection, his cock finally where she'd wanted it to be for God knew how long. His body covering hers, he began to thrust in long, tight movements.

"You're holding back," she said, tilting her hips out to meet him.

"Don't want to hurt you."

"You won't. Give it to me hard."

His voice betrayed his surprise. "Like it a little rough, huh? Never knew you were such a dirty girl under that poised exterior."

"You know it now. Do it."

"Yes, ma'am. I like to play rough sometimes, too. Maybe sometime I'll show you my special toys."

And she'd imagined him self-contained when it came to sex! But she couldn't answer because he complied in spades, withdrawing almost completely—then ramming home so forcefully she had to spread her hands wider and grip the brick wall to remain steady. Groaning at the delicious assault, she could only hang on for the wild ride as he gave her what she'd asked for.

So fine, his rod pistoning in and out with abandon. Fucking her the way she loved, with the power few lovers would exert over her, no matter how she begged them.

Sometimes a woman needed tender lovemaking, hearts, and roses. And sometimes she needed darkness and lightning, a storm to wash away the loneliness and longing, to make things new. He gave her that and more, flesh slapping in tempo as he claimed what she offered, made it his. She wished she could turn and see him, run her palms over his muscles, cup his ass as it flexed while he drove into her. *Maybe next time. A girl can hope.*

The familiar tingle in her sex became a spark. Flared and caught fire, unraveling her control. Her orgasm hit hard and she cried out, distantly aware that his agents probably heard. She couldn't care less. The feeling of him riding her through the pulsing waves was too incredible. Suddenly he stiffened and gave one last plunge, cock jerking inside her as he was overcome by his own release.

She wasn't sure how long they stayed locked together, his hot breath wafting against her neck. But after a bit, his softened cock slipped from her and he moved away. Pushing from the wall, she turned and saw him disposing of the condom. She averted her eyes, wondering why the sight should bother her after what they'd done. Somehow his cleaning himself in front of her seemed more intimate than the act itself.

Scanning the area for her clothes, she found them carefully

draped over a nearby crate rather than tossed on the filthy ground as she'd assumed. His thoughtfulness warmed her, but the awkward silence that fell between them stilled her tongue. Now came the doubts and recriminations. The utter stupidity of fucking her boss notwithstanding, she could not possibly have let herself become hung up on a more unattainable man.

Men, she mentally corrected. Because she wanted this with Bastian, too.

As for Michael, he'd been mourning his dead wife for months, and was just starting to come out the other side. Or so it appeared. She suspected the truth wasn't that simple and likely played a large part in his withdrawal now. What other factors came into play, she didn't know him well enough on a personal level to say. And it depressed her to realize that dynamic might not change any time soon.

She pulled on her underwear and pants while Michael tucked himself away and waited. Determined to dispel the unease, she walked to him and cupped his cheek. Brushed her lips against his in a feathery kiss. "Thank you."

He blinked in the darkness. "Katrina . . . Don't thank me. I was selfish, and it never should've happened."

Here we go.

"Because you're my boss? I'm a grown woman and you didn't take advantage of me," she pointed out. "Quite the opposite, in fact, so you don't need to be concerned that I'll cry foul."

"That's not the only reason." Taking her arm, he gently steered her in the direction they'd come.

"Dietz?"

He sighed. "What the hell was I thinking? If he believes I care about you, it could put you in danger. Christ, I'm an idiot."

"And do you care about me?" she asked softly.

His voice was quiet. "Yes, I do. More than I should." He didn't elaborate, but she hadn't expected him to. Letting the matter go, she allowed him to escort her into the club again to find their friends. She told herself he was right, that this had been a onetime thing and it was best that way. It wasn't until they arrived at their table once more that she realized there was another consequence of her interlude with Michael, one she'd pushed to the back of her mind as they'd left earlier.

She recalled it as she saw the pain brimming in Bastian's green eyes.

"Don't you think you ought to slow down on those?" Blaze questioned, brow furrowed in apparent worry.

Bastian gazed down at his third—or was it fourth?—drink and shook his head. "No, I don't think so."

He tried to come up with one good reason to slack off on the booze, but nothing came to mind. What else did he have to do? His best friend and a beautiful woman had disappeared outside, and from the heat sizzling in the air, he knew why.

Michael and Katrina. Two people he wanted more than anyone. They'd deserted him without a thought.

No, he wasn't nearly drunk enough. Maybe there wasn't that much alcohol in the city to deaden the pain. But he could try.

Blaze and Emma shared a look, and she gave a slight nod. Bastian wondered what that was about and then decided he didn't give a shit. Suddenly, he needed to be invisible. To get the fuck out of here and find a place to be alone. He had an empty condo waiting that he hadn't seen since Michael's shooting, and this seemed like the perfect time to return there, despite Michael's having asked him to stay at the estate.

He doesn't need me anymore, so why the torture? I can't stand this. Not one more second.

A hand on his arm brought him out of his dark thoughts, and he looked at Emma. Her expressive eyes set in a striking, angular face regarded him with something very unlike pity. The heat in them got his attention, bringing him, however briefly, out of his morose mood. Reaching out, she traced his lips with one finger, the invitation clear even before she spoke.

"Come home with us tonight?"

The words were like an oasis in hell and he savored them, his plans to be alone turning to dust. He should decline, but he felt a little too desperate. A lot too raw. He needed someone to care, to take his mind and body someplace wonderful, if only for the next few hours. However, the ounce of pride he had left urged him to put up a token resistance.

"I'm not certain that's a good idea," he said, glancing at Blaze. Had his friend ever told Emma that he'd fucked Bastian senseless while she'd been held hostage by Dietz? The dark-haired man gave no indication, but Emma put his concern to rest.

"I know you guys played once," she said with a little smile. "It's totally fine as long as I'm the only *girl* he fucks."

Her blunt honesty startled a laugh out of him. "Really? Well, I don't know. Your man was almost more than I could handle. The two of you together? I might not survive."

"Oh, we're very sure you'll do better than survive." Leaning over, she nibbled the outside of his ear, kissed the sensitive skin behind it. "Trust us and we'll take you on a nice trip, no luggage required."

Crap, he'd have to be dead not to respond, and from his dick's prompt reaction, he was far from his eternal sleep. This evening might be salvaged after all—if he could just get Michael out of his heart and keep Katrina from stealing a bigger piece of it than she already had.

At that moment, his best friend and the woman in question appeared at their table. Hair mussed, faces flushed, clothing not quite put to rights. Agony lanced Bastian's chest, and he thought the punch of a bullet probably hurt less than knowing what they'd been doing.

Tearing his eyes from them, he forced a smile for Emma. "Make that a definite yes. I'd love to."

Michael's voice was tight. "Love to what?"

The coldness of his own tone shocked him as he rose from his seat and leaned in to Michael, speaking for his ears only. "Get my ass reamed again by Blaze's magnificent cock while I eat his woman's pussy, that's what. And I can't wait."

Oh, right there. A direct hit. Michael's jaw went slack, his expression priceless. A big crack in the bastard's unflappable calm. Bastian turned back to his companions.

"Ready when you are."

With that, he made his way through the crowd, trusting the couple to follow. And he didn't look back.

Six

His cell phone trilled a greeting, and Dietz glanced at the display. His contact knew better than to phone with anything less than spectacular news, and his gut tightened. He picked up on the second ring.

"What do you have?"

"Got something on Ross. Looks like he's snared himself a new woman."

His eyebrow arched in surprise. This was one piece of news he hadn't been expecting. "Who is she?"

"Some gorgeous redhead he called Katrina."

His pulse quickened, his mind already working this to his advantage. "Brandt?"

"Don't know, but I'll find out. Ross and Chevalier showed up at Shakers tonight to party with the woman, an armed watch in tow, of course."

He resisted the urge to roll his eyes. Did Michael believe him to be that stupid, to make a move at the most obvious time? "And then?"

"They went inside, and Ross came out with the woman a while later, took her into the alley, and fucked her brains out." He chuckled nastily. "I beat off like a house afire, and my dick will still be hard for a week."

"That was more information than I needed."

"Hey, sorry." He didn't sound contrite at all.

"This is an interesting development. Keep me informed so I can decide how to best use this against him."

"Will do."

Dietz snapped his phone shut and sat thinking for a very long time.

Yes, he would use this to his advantage, if necessary.

Right after Chevalier was dead and buried.

On the sidewalk, Bastian waited for Blaze and Emma to catch up, using the few moments to get a handle on his runaway emotions. Trouble was, he wasn't an expert at compartmentalizing, as Michael was. He couldn't tuck those pesky, inconvenient feelings into labeled boxes and shove them deep in a closet. Like when Bastian confessed his love to Michael, and the man married Maggie almost in a blind panic.

That's not fair. Maggie's death nearly destroyed him and he grieved for months.

Okay, so maybe it was just Bastian's issue. Michael couldn't express feelings he didn't have, and Bastian couldn't let go. *I have to. Somehow, I've got to move on.*

Blaze joined him on the sidewalk, Emma close behind. "Michael called the team and they're sending a couple of agents to trail us and watch my house while you're there."

Bastian grimaced. "God, I hadn't even thought of the danger I'm putting you two in by going with you. I should go home."

He'd been thinking with his cock, and had also been focused on striking out at Michael.

"Forget it," Emma said. "We've got a date and we're not letting you wimp out."

"It'll be good for you to unwind for a while." Blaze's golden gaze pinned him. "To forget. Besides, Emma and I are already on Dietz's hit list because we destroyed his plans for the weapon he stole, and the money we cost him as a result. You're not bringing any more trouble than we've already got."

He gave a shaky laugh. "Yeah, you're right. Let's go."

They climbed into a sedan Bastian assumed was Emma's, because Blaze drove a snazzy Viper. Bastian settled in the back-seat and tried to shake off the feeling of being the perpetual fifth wheel. Which was ridiculous. He would relax and enjoy tonight, whatever it took.

"I take it Michael still hasn't come around," Blaze said, pulling out of the parking lot.

Bastian snorted. "Are you kidding? He—Wait a second. I told you I was in love with someone, but I never said with whom." Before Michael was shot, he'd made the confession to Kelly in a moment of weakness, leaving out his friend's name. He thought he'd been careful, but apparently not enough.

"Reality check: it's so obvious to everyone within a ten-mile radius, you might as well put up a billboard. I guessed a long time ago."

"Shit."

"Don't sweat it. We're not going to say anything to anyone." Emma voiced her agreement.

"I know. It's just that I feel . . . pathetic. The man is so straight, his ass cheeks play 'U Can't Touch This' when he walks."

His friends cracked up, and Bastian couldn't help but laugh. He hadn't meant it as a joke, but the visual was pretty funny. And it went a long way toward lightening the mood as Blaze drove them to his house, the one he now shared with Emma.

Twenty minutes later, Blaze pulled into the drive and parked. Bastian tried to ignore the headlights of the car that followed them and parked on the street, and forget the reason the two agents were protecting them. He'd like to believe Dietz had called off his vendetta and skipped the country, but knew the odds of the asshole giving up so easily were slim.

They went inside, Blaze locking the door behind him. He looked at Bastian. "Can I get you something to drink?"

"Beer?"

"Nope. You've had enough, and besides . . ." He leered at Bastian's crotch. "Too much alcohol has a negative effect on the equipment."

Damn. "You're right. No, I'm fine."

"If you're sure."

"I am."

"Good. Now, the first thing we're gonna do is some loving therapy to release all that tension in you, before you break in half." He gestured to a door that Bastian knew hid a stairwell. "In my basement."

Bastian swallowed, excitement flooding his veins at the memory of his initiation into Blaze's world as a hard-core Dom. More like a taste, really. Bastian could never live that lifestyle on a permanent basis, but he'd discovered that every now and then, he enjoyed putting himself in a Dom's capable hands. Letting his worries slide into oblivion, knowing he was safe in Blaze's realm of rules and clear-cut expectations. All he had to do was place his trust in this man, just *be*, and the rest would take care of itself.

They descended the stairs, Blaze in the lead. At the bottom, the other man turned to him. "Have your needs changed since we made your contract?"

No one did a scene with the Dom without a contract, no matter how infrequent he saw the person. They'd agreed on one together the first and only time Bastian had accompanied him here. Bastian shook his head.

"Good. Safe word?"

He had to think a few seconds before he remembered. "Sable." The color of Michael's hair. *God.*

"All right. Strip." The Dom looked at Emma, a glint in his eyes. "Both of you."

Bastian couldn't help but stare at Emma as she complied, and took notice of her toned, athletic body. She wasn't his usual type, if he even had one, with her short blond hair and kick-ass attitude to match her physique. But she intrigued him. Aroused him. It still amazed him to see the woman turn to butter when Blaze so much as crooked his finger. Bastian had to admit his friend was a lucky guy.

Quickly, Bastian removed his clothes and folded them neatly, then placed them on a nearby chair. He faced the other man and stood with his hands at his sides, resisting the urge to ask what came next. Blaze would tell him.

Bastian's cock, already half-hard, rose to full mast when Blaze came over and thumbed his nipple ring. Took it in his fingers and twisted, sending an arc of delight coursing from the tortured tip to his groin.

"Just one pierced? Too bad the other one isn't done." He bent and licked the nub, then took it and the ring into his mouth, suckling.

Bastian sucked in a breath, unable to recall the last person who'd played with it, which was a shame. His nipples were one of his erogenous zones, and he loved this.

Blaze straightened. "Emma, bring me that leather strap from the equipment table."

"Yes, sir." She hurried to get it and returned, holding it out for his inspection.

"This will do perfectly."

For what? He didn't have to wait long to find out.

The Dom addressed Emma again. "Use the strap to bind our boy's cock and balls properly."

"Yes, sir!" She knelt, putting her face tantalizingly near Bastian's crotch.

His heart sped up. He had a pretty good idea what the binding involved, but he'd never experienced it before.

"The binding will keep you from coming until I'm ready," Blaze explained, as though he'd sensed Bastian's unspoken question. "You're wound too tight, and your body needs this. You can't reach your zone if you're worried about your cock and coming. I'm going to take that worry from you. Do you understand?"

"I think so." He wasn't sure he did, but he trusted Blaze to show him.

Emma went to work, her clever fingers gently weaving the strap around and between his balls, separating and lifting them. It felt strange but not painful. Definitely erotic, the sight of the thin black leather crisscrossing up the length of his turgid shaft. Being restrained and artfully presented at the same time.

"Finished, sir."

"Excellent work." To Bastian, he said, "See that padded bench over there? Go bend over it and stand with your legs spread, a bit wider than your shoulders."

"Okay."

His eyes narrowed. "The correct response is 'Yes, sir.'"

"I'm sorry. Yes, sir."

"Good boy. Now get going."

He did as he was told, excitement building, sharpened by a sliver of fear. He knew Blaze wouldn't injure him, but this was new territory. He wasn't used to giving another man total control over his body, and every instinct he possessed as an agent screamed out against being restrained. His more passionate side, however, the one that sometimes craved a darker brand of loving, arched like a cat being scratched.

At the bench, he bent over, turned his head to the side, and rested it on the padding, and spread his feet as he was told. He was hyperaware of how the position exposed him to whatever Blaze wished to do. He wondered how the binding, this scene, was supposed to help him relax and find his zone, as the man called it.

Blaze came up behind him, smoothed a palm over his shoulders and back. "These knots in your muscles are like boulders. You've been under a terrible amount of stress since Michael was shot, haven't you?"

"Yes, sir," he whispered. "I feel . . ."

"Tired, wrung out, unappreciated?"

Fuck, that about summed it up. He could only nod.

"We're going to help you with that," his friend returned softly. "Trust us."

"I do."

"Then let's begin. I'm going to bind your wrists to these rings at each end of the bench. Emma is going to kneel behind you and do some prep work for our session."

Prep work? Sounded ominous. Excitement battled with nerves

as the Dom tied his wrists to the rings, leaving him thoroughly trussed. As Blaze stood off to the side, a hand skimmed over his hip and buttocks. Emma, getting ready to *prepare* him. Jesus.

His ass cheeks were parted, and he flinched as cold gel dribbled over his hole. As she smeared the stuff and then inserted a finger into his channel, lubricating him, he tried to concentrate on relaxing. On the glide of the digit working his hole, stretching him.

"Lord, he's tense," Emma commented, adding another finger.

"Finish stretching him, baby, and then choose one of these to fill him. We want him to really feel what's going to happen next."

Fill him with what? A plug or a dildo? If anything, he tensed even more in spite of his arousal. He didn't know how to surrender and simply enjoy himself, and frustration made his chest ache.

Finished with the lube, Emma withdrew her fingers. After a moment, they were replaced with the blunt end of something slick and cool. Metallic? She began to guide the instrument slowly into his hole, past the ring of muscle clamping down on the invader in self-defense.

"Easy," Blaze said, touching his back. "If you don't relax a little, she could hurt you with the plug. It's probably a bit bigger than you're used to."

Taking a deep breath, he concentrated on letting his muscles go limp. He pictured himself opening for her, a vessel for her to fill at her whim. It helped some and the plug inched inside, spearing his flesh, until it finally slid all the way in and the base fit snugly at his entrance.

"How does it feel? Are you uncomfortable?" Blaze asked.

"Yes, sir, a little. But in a good way," he added. "I'm so full."

The other man gave a husky laugh. "You'll be more than that very soon." Retrieving something from the table, the Dom went to stand behind Bastian, switching places with Emma, who now watched. The man rubbed something flat over Bastian's ass cheeks. "Do you know what this is?"

"A paddle?"

"Exactly. A wooden one, in fact. Do you know what I'm going to do with it?"

"Um . . . spank me?" *No fucking way.* He pulled at his bonds, suddenly wanting to be loose.

"That's right. I'm going to turn that sexy ass of yours red, paddle you until you scream. Until you break free of the pain and sadness, just let it all go. I'm going to make you fly."

"What? No! Let me up!" Anger, black and unreasonable, bubbled in his veins. It didn't make sense and he didn't know where it came from. He knew only that he wanted away from here. He didn't have to do this, expose his soul.

"Can't do that unless you say your safe word. That's how it works." He gave Bastian's ass a light smack, experimenting. Or getting Bastian used to the feel of the plug stimulating his hole.

"Let me up!" he shouted.

"Nope, sorry. Use your safe word." He waited, as though knowing Bastian wouldn't use it, but giving him time anyway. And dammit, the bastard was right. "We both know you need this. I'm going to help you. Trust me."

Another smack, this one with a bit more sting. He writhed, cursing, yanking at his bonds.

"Go ahead," Blaze encouraged. "Let it all out. Get rid of the anger."

Another whack and another, stronger, with a real bite of pain that was probably reddening his ass, as promised.

"I don't want this!"

"Yes, you do. You need it, and I'm here."

More hits, coming regularly now, shooting electric currents of pain and pleasure to his poor, bound cock and balls. He started to pant.

"I'm so fucking pissed!"

"Yes."

"He hurts me every goddamned day!"

"I know."

"He doesn't love me!" His agonized shout reverberated off the walls.

"He does. Give him time," Blaze said firmly. His hand remained steady, delivering the blows, heating the tortured flesh.

"Nooo . . ." Tears streamed down his face, but he was hardly aware of them. His body seemed to rise and float.

Can't do this. Can't . . .

And then something broke inside him. Cracked wide open like a ripe melon, and all the tension, rage, and pain flowed from him like blood from a wound. Drained through his feet into the floor. He let the tidal wave of ecstasy wash over him and became nothing but willing flesh. A slave to the delicious torment of the blows that drove the plug to graze his prostate, making his cock and balls swell to near bursting in their confines.

So good.

"Oh, oh yes," he moaned. "God, yes."

After a few more swats, the blows stopped. "I believe he's there."

"He is, sir."

Deft hands released his wrists and helped him to straighten, guided him to a lower, wider padded bench and urged him to lie on his back. Scooted him to the end so that his rear was accessible. He needed, so badly. Where were they?

His thighs were parted, and through a red haze he saw the Dom kneel between his splayed knees. The man grasped the end of the plug and slowly fucked Bastian with the toy, prolonging the torture until he whimpered, unable to form words.

"So pretty. In just a minute, that's going to be my cock splitting you open, making you writhe and beg." With that, the Dom carefully withdrew the plug, set it aside. Then he rustled a small packet, rolled on a condom. He cupped Bastian's ass in his hands and raised him, pressing the large, blunt head to the opening. "While I fuck you slow and easy, driving you insane with the need to come, you're going to eat my sub's sweet pussy until she comes on your face. Got that?"

Beyond speech, he nodded.

The head, much bigger than the plug, breached his hole. He groaned helplessly as the huge dick pressed inside, owning him. Long, toned legs straddled his head and Emma's pink pussy lowered to his mouth.

Obediently, he lapped the sweet petals of her sex, eager to bring her pleasure. He hoped she enjoyed what he was doing, because much of his attention was captured by the burn of Blaze's big cock taking possession of him. The long, slow slide made him shiver, his desire almost too much for his body to contain. Once the man's cock was seated deeply, fully to the hilt, it held there, letting him drink in the sensation of being owned. Under another's control.

Bastian moaned, continuing to lick and suckle Emma's pussy as Blaze began to fuck him in easy strokes. Just enough to keep him on edge, straining toward an orgasm he couldn't achieve until the Dom released his bound shaft and balls. Decadent torture.

Above him, Emma started to wriggle and murmur little words of encouragement, her release obviously near. He tongued her clit, lashing it with fervor, and she shuddered, crying out. He ate her honey, catching every drop, until she was spent and climbed off. Distantly, Bastian heard her voice as Blaze began to fuck him with more force.

"God, that's hot. Fuck him hard, sir!"

"Goddamn, he's tight. So fucking perfect, so beautiful. How could anyone not want to snatch him up, keep him forever?"

Emma's reply was lost as the man rammed into him without mercy. Fucked him hard, fast, and deep, heavy balls slapping against his ass.

"Please," he begged. "I need to come!"

"I need to come, *sir*."

"Please let me come, sir!"

"Soon," the man growled, never ceasing his pace. A few more powerful thrusts and the Dom stiffened, plunging deep, cock jerking.

Heat filled Bastian's ass as his own cock stabbed the air, seeking release. At last, Blaze eased out of him and began to undo the leather strap, freeing him. Tossing it aside and gripping Bastian's cock, he said, "Come for me."

With a cry, he spasmed. Pumped ropes of pearly cream onto his own abdomen as Blaze fisted his shaft. Milked him of every drop. When the last of the shudders faded, his eyes drifted closed. He was so heavy, melted. Couldn't move if he wanted to.

"Poor baby is exhausted," Emma said, kissing his cheek.

"He's dealt with too much these past few weeks. I think he needed this, and that it helped him at least a little."

Bastian tried to agree that it had, but his lips refused to work.

"Can we keep him?"

"I wish, angel," Blaze said. "But his heart belongs to someone else."

"I know." She sighed.

He couldn't stay awake, but the real regret in their voices brought him a measure of peace and warmth as he fell into his dreams.

The limo wove through the streets toward Katrina's condo at a sedate crawl. Michael's mind churned, thoughts tumbling one after the other.

You know I love you.

When you stop running, I'll be here. Just like I always have been.

And then he'd gone home with Blaze and Emma. To get his ass reamed *again*, as his friend put it. Sure, the very night of the shooting, Michael had figured out that Bastian had been with the experienced Dom. But tonight was different. Tonight he'd gone with the couple to escape from Michael.

And that knowledge caused a strange, terrible ache in his chest.

"How long have you loved him?"

Michael started and peered at Katrina, who was seated next to him. There was no sense in pretending he didn't know who she was talking about. "I don't love him, except as my best friend."

"Right. That's why you look like you've just lost that best friend for good," she said softly.

"He's a grown man and can do as he likes, and so can I. We don't hold each other back. We're solid."

"Michael—"

"I don't want to talk about this," he snapped. Instantly, he regretted being short with her, and relented. "Look, I know you're concerned and only trying to help. So I will say that I know how Bastian feels, and he knows I can't return his affections in the way he'd like."

God, that sounded cold.

"Can't you? Your reaction when he left with Blaze and Emma communicated something very different. Frankly, you looked like he'd just punched you."

He'd felt like it, too. But he didn't acknowledge it aloud.

"Well, he wasn't very nice about it. He was deliberately trying to get a rise out of me." That was the truth, though he knew he was avoiding the issue. Bastian had been cruel because he was lashing out in pain. *I deserved it.*

"He knew we were together, and he was hurt. You can't imagine how guilty I feel for adding to his misery. I like Bastian . . . a lot."

Something wistful in her tone caused him to study her face more closely. "You say that like you mean it more than as casual acquaintances."

She was silent for a moment, then nodded. "I do. You should know I'm extremely attracted to him as well as to you. Actually, we almost had sex recently, but we got interrupted," she confessed. "And I'm not certain what, if anything, to do about it."

Christ. He wasn't sure what part of that to tackle first. She'd almost had sex with Bastian? And she was attracted to *both* of them? Curiosity about her last thought got the better of him. "What *would* you do about it, if you could?"

Instead of answering directly, she countered with a question. "Have you ever been in a ménage relationship?"

His lips turned up. "I've had three-ways, but never anything resembling a relationship. And definitely not with another man involved."

"Even Bastian, your *best friend*?"

"Of course not," he said warily. "Why would I?"

"But you've known him for years, and you two are close."

"Yes. What's your point?"

She turned in her seat to face him, warming to the topic. "It just seems that two sexually charged men who've shared a big part of their lives together would have, at some point, shared a woman. Especially since you two are obviously close."

"Well, I'm not comfortable with the thought of being . . . in a sexual situation with Bastian," he said defensively.

"Exactly. And why is that, I wonder?" She sounded satisfied, as though he'd made her point.

He stared at her in the dark interior of the car, processing what she meant. "You're implying I've avoided having a ménage with Bastian because I'm afraid I'll develop feelings for him."

"Or you're afraid the feelings you already have, the ones you keep under lock and key, will out themselves."

"That's ridiculous." But the protest had sprung from his lips too easily, and his voice had wavered. His heart pounded and his palms felt clammy. "Anyway, what are you trying to get at? You want a ménage with me and Bastian?"

Her voice lowered, her reply husky. "Would you be willing to consider the idea if I did?"

"I don't——" He started to refuse. What stopped him, he wasn't sure.

Taking advantage of his lapse, she scooted close, reached out, and placed a hand on his chest. "I'm a pretty direct person and I'm used to just coming right out with what I want or feel. Yes, I want to be with both of you at the same time."

Even though he'd braced himself for the words, they still knocked him for a loop. "You—you want a ménage with us."

"Yes." Her smile was wicked, those gorgeous eyes sparkling, her touch searing him as her hand moved south. Down his belly to his crotch and the hardness that had come back to life there. "Picture me naked between you. Me, on my hands and knees, sucking his cock while I take yours from behind."

"God," he rasped. He could picture it just the way she described. Her pretty lips stretched around his friend's shaft, wild red hair tumbling around her shoulders, Michael pumping her with long, glorious strokes.

Still rubbing his erection through his jeans, she leaned over and nibbled on his jaw. Kissed his temple. "Tell me where's the harm in three people enjoying each other, Michael. I think Bastian would be game, and part of you is very much willing."

Two orgasms tonight and his cock throbbed like he hadn't had sex in a week. The picture she'd painted fired his blood and his imagination.

"You wouldn't even have to touch him if you don't want to," she continued. "Many ménage relationships work just fine without the men having sex."

"I . . . I let him blow me earlier," he blurted. "Right here in the limo, on the way to get you." Jesus, what had made him confess that?

She pulled back, eyes round. Then her mouth curved into a knowing smile. "So that's why you two were acting weird. You loved it, and that scared the hell out of you. Am I right?"

He sighed. "Yeah. My best friend—a guy—sucked me off, and I fucking loved it. What am I supposed to do about it? I didn't react well, and I said some cruel shit to him. He probably won't forgive me after tonight."

"He will. The man loves you. Anyone can see that."

"He deserves better."

"Then be the one to give him better. It's easy."

"I don't know if I can," he said honestly. "How do I explain? I'm *not* homophobic. I believe everyone has the right to love whomever they choose and I don't have a problem with alternative lifestyles."

"Then what's the problem? What frightens you so much about being with Bastian?"

"I don't know!"

"Michael . . . I think you do."

"What, you're a psychiatrist now?" He scowled.

"Simple deduction," she said calmly. "You're the most self-assured man I know, with the exception of your feelings for Bastian. I believe you haven't let yourself recognize what's holding you back. Would you like to come in?"

The limo slowed to a stop and he looked out to see that they'd arrived at her condo. "I would. Thanks."

After helping her out, he gave the driver instructions to take the car home. He'd get a ride home later from one of the agents watching Katrina's place. He fielded a brief pang of guilt for having his men stay out late to accommodate his evening, but reminded himself they were earning damned good hazard pay to do so.

As he walked Katrina to her door, his mind turned to her assertion regarding Bastian. What *was* holding him back? It wasn't as though he had a terrible family history to blame. His parents were very open-minded, wonderful folks. No bad sexual experiences in his past, with a man or a woman, that he could point to as the culprit.

Quite simply, he was a straight man who was attracted to his best friend. Might even *love* him. And yes, goddammit, love him like *that*. Even in his head, he couldn't put a finer point on the term.

So the issue was Michael's and no one else's. It was his internal struggle with the black-and-white man he'd always prided himself on being, and the man he was becoming. One he didn't know at all, who was beginning to recognize that shades of gray could filter into a man's life—and that maybe it was okay.

He had no clue how to handle the barrage of emotions. Not the least among them was the guilt that haunted him because he hadn't loved Maggie the way she deserved. Not with the undying passion everyone believed. She was a good woman and a good friend, but the marriage had been a mistake. Her loss hurt so much because she'd deserved a husband who spent more time thinking about her than about repairing his strained friendship with Bastian.

In the end, he'd wronged them both.

"Are you coming in?"

Blinking, he realized he'd been standing on her threshold and she was holding the door open, waiting with a bemused expression. "Sorry. I was woolgathering."

"Thinking about Bastian?"

He stepped in, and she closed and locked the door behind them. "And me."

"And did you come to a conclusion?" Stepping close, she wrapped her arms around his waist.

"I think it comes down to an old dog and new tricks. Or something along those lines."

"You're not old, but I can help with the new tricks," she whispered into his mouth.

He groaned, his musings put on hold. She was going to kill him. "Why don't you show me?"

"My pleasure."

Oh no. It's all mine.

But he wasn't about to argue.

＊ ＊ ＊

Bastian woke and gazed into the darkness, disoriented. As his eyes adjusted, he remembered. Turning his head on his pillow, he could just see Blaze spooned around Emma in the moonlight on the other side of the huge bed. For a long moment, he stared at them, his throat suddenly burning.

Why couldn't he have that for himself? Not just the mind-blowing sex—great as it was, sex could be had anywhere—but the intimacy. Love. Because even in sleep, love radiated from the couple, in the way they snuggled tight, unwilling to ever let go. He didn't begrudge them their happiness in the least, and knew he would never be more than a fond playmate for them. Which was okay, because he felt the same where they were concerned. But he wanted, needed his *own* lovers to—

God, he needed to leave. Right fucking now.

Slipping from the bed, he gathered his clothes as quietly as possible, glad he'd thought to bring them up from the basement playroom when they roused him to come upstairs. Not wanting to wake them, he padded into the living room to dress. In less than a minute, he was ready, and had pulled out his cell phone to call the agent outside when a deep voice startled him.

"Leaving so soon?"

He spun to face Blaze. The man stood in the darkness, a huge form, black hair spilling over his shoulders. "Yeah. I need to get going."

"You're welcome to stay, you know."

"Thanks. I appreciate it, but . . ."

Moving forward, his friend gave him a brief hug. "I understand, believe me. Just know we're here for you. Give us a call anytime." His smile slashed the darkness. "For any reason."

Despite the ache inside, he couldn't help but smile. "I will."

Blaze saw him out and waited with him on the porch while Bastian made his call and stayed until the agent's car pulled up. Once he was safely ensconced in the vehicle, his friend waved and headed back inside.

"Wild night, huh?" Agent Chapman commented. The older man sounded tired, but his voice held no real rancor.

"You could say that." He paused. "Thanks for taking me back to the estate."

"No problem." The man yawned. "Gotta say, I'll be glad to hit my own pillow, though."

Bastian agreed. Only the bed at Michael's estate wasn't really his, was it? As much as he wished differently, his best friend's place wasn't his home.

When he let himself in a short time later, turned off the alarm, and stood in the darkened foyer by himself, the reality hit him hard. Michael wasn't here, was probably off with Katrina. The two of them having a great time.

Once again, I'm on the outside. Always have been where he's concerned. Always will be.

This wasn't his home, and he didn't belong here. He couldn't stay one second longer than necessary. It just hurt too fucking bad.

Jogging upstairs, he grabbed a duffel from the closet and shoved as many of his clothes in it as possible. Next, he gathered all his suits, leaving them on the hangers. He'd need those for work. The toiletries in the bathroom and anything else he'd left behind, Michael could toss out.

Slinging the bag over one shoulder, he picked up the stack of suits and took one last look around. The burning started again, the lump in his throat the size of a grapefruit. He couldn't breathe.

He fled down the stairs, pausing only long enough to set the alarm and lock the house again. When he went in to work on Monday, he'd return Michael's spare house key. Outside, he unlocked his rental car, threw in his stuff, and jumped into the driver's seat. As he sped out of the gate, he told himself he wasn't running. He was being realistic, taking himself out of a painful, futile situation.

Nobody's going to look out for you, Bastian, old boy. You have to do it yourself.

This was self-preservation, and he had to go.

And if he had tears running down his face? Nobody would ever know.

Or care.

Seven

〜

Humming, Michael walked into the house. Given the previous night's activities, he should've been exhausted. But this morning, he felt energized. Hopeful. The extra spring in his step and the adjustment in his attitude could be attributed to one person. Well, make that two.

Katrina. God, what a revelation the woman had turned out to be. Beautiful, with a streak of kinkiness under her classy exterior and an open-minded outlook that surprised him. Ever since she'd planted the suggestion of a ménage in his brain, the wheels in his head had done nothing but churn.

A threesome. With a woman he admired and who was rapidly getting under his skin, and the best friend he . . . loved. Yes, loved. Even though he stumbled over precisely which definition of the word to apply to him and Bastian. In any case, after a lot of soul searching, he had no problem envisioning the scene Katrina had described of the three of them together. On the contrary, the idea made his cock twitch in anticipation, though it couldn't manage much more than a nod of agreement after last night.

This really could work. And as she'd said, he and Bastian didn't have to have sex for the three of them to enjoy being together. It would be perfect. As for the fact that he'd let his friend blow him in the limo? A moment of weakness—that's all. Bastian would understand once he explained how good things could be.

Tantalizing breakfast smells were coming from the kitchen, as Mrs. Beasley was no doubt fixing something spectacular. He decided to head upstairs first, see whether Bastian had made it home yet and was conscious. They needed to talk—the sooner, the better. At his friend's door, he knocked lightly.

"Bastian?" No answer. He tried again, louder. "Hey, Bastian?"

The man never locked his bedroom door, so Michael turned the knob and eased it open a crack. If the guy was still asleep, their talk could wait. Peering through the crack, he blinked at the sight of the perfectly made bed, and pushed the door all the way open. He walked inside. Empty. Which meant he'd never come home, or had come back and left early.

"Damn, you must've had some wild night if you never came home." And hell, that thought sat in his gut like a rock.

As he turned to leave, something stopped him. He scanned the room, struck by a sudden sense of the space being completely devoid of life. As if the emptiness was more than Bastian not being here at the moment. Stalking to the dresser, he yanked open the top drawer and stared.

Where socks and underwear should be neatly folded, there was nothing. Next drawer, same story. No T-shirts or shorts.

"What the fuck?"

Heart lurching, he moved to the bathroom. A razor and shaving cream sat on the counter, and there was a bottle of shampoo in the shower. That meant Bastian hadn't necessarily left for good. Right? Hurrying to the closet, he stepped inside, flipped on the light.

Gone. Every damned suit, shirt, tie. He'd cleaned his shit out of Michael's life almost as though he'd never been there.

In a fog, Michael walked to the bed and lowered himself to sit on the side. "Why? Was it because of last night?" Stupid question. Obviously, it was.

He'd screwed up by allowing what happened between them in the car. Had set some sort of expectation on Bastian's part about where their relationship might go. And then he'd pulled the rug out from under his friend not once, but twice. First by shutting him down after the incredible blow job, and then by whisking Katrina right out from under the man's nose to have her for himself.

Okay, Michael was a selfish bastard. But he could fix this.

Fishing his cell phone from his pants, he speed-dialed his friend's number. The call went immediately to voice mail, and Michael took a deep breath. "It's me. We need to talk. Please don't shut me out." He paused. "Okay, I'll try your landline."

Ending the call, he waited a couple of minutes, then dialed Bastian's number at his condo. On the fourth ring, he got the answering machine. After Bastian's taped greeting and the beep, he spoke more urgently. "Please pick up. Come on, don't do this to me. Dammit, I know you're there."

Nothing. *Well, shit!* He'd have to go over there, because this tactic wasn't getting him anywhere. Hanging up again, he pocketed his phone and bounded down the stairs, yelling, "Simon!"

The older man was hurrying through the living room as Michael reached the bottom of the stairs. "I say! Whatever is the matter?"

"Bastian's gone!"

The butler hesitated, uncertain. "Perhaps he had a pressing errand—"

"No, I mean *gone*. As in packed his stuff and left." Frustrated, he ran a hand through his hair. "I guess that means you didn't see him go."

Simon stiffened, appearing affronted. "Of course not, sir. I would have phoned you straightaway had I known."

"Damn, I'm sorry," he muttered. "I know you would have. I'm just worried. I didn't expect him to take off like that." Though the guilty little voice in his head whispered that he should have.

"Really?" Was that a note of censure?

Michael didn't have the inclination to listen to Simon's pearls of wisdom, or a lecture on how he took Bastian for granted. Besides, that wasn't true. "Yeah. Listen, I'm going to look for him. If you hear from him, call me."

"Immediately." The butler eyed him sharply. "And I do hope you can convince him to return. The estate won't be the same without him."

The truth of that statement hit Michael hard as he headed for his Camaro. He tried to imagine the house without Bastian's teasing, his sunny smile, his laughter. The absence of that special light was a depressing prospect.

"Hey, boss?"

Car keys in hand, Michael stopped and turned to see his head of security bearing down on him. A man on a mission. "John?"

The man halted a few steps away, frowning. "I've been waiting for you to get home. Thought you should know that Mr. Chevalier tore out of here in the wee hours this morning. One of your agents trailed him and—"

"Why didn't you call me?" he snarled.

"I tried," the man replied evenly. "Kept getting one of those out-of-service messages."

"I didn't notice any glitch in my cell service. But, then, I was occupied for a while. When did Bastian leave?"

"The gate records show he arrived at five fifteen and departed at five forty-two, with one of your agents—Thompson—right behind him. Thompson tried to notify you, as well, but when he couldn't reach you, he called me. Mr. Chevalier went straight home and hasn't emerged since."

Michael nodded. "Thanks. My phone seems to be working fine now, so call me if anything else comes up."

"Will do." With a wave, the man walked off.

Michael got in and started the car, grateful that his men had his wayward friend under tight surveillance. Thinking of the danger Bastian had placed himself in by moving off the estate, Michael's blood began to boil. By the time he arrived at the man's first-floor condo, his head pounded from being torn between thanking God he was safe and the desire to bitch him out. Stepping from the car, he resisted the natural urge to look for Agent Thompson's sedan, which would give away his location to the bad guys, should there be any lurking.

At the door, he let his fist fly, not caring if he disturbed all the neighbors with the commotion. "Bastian!" *Bang, bang, bang.* "Open up! Let me in, goddammit!"

Silence. *Bang, bang.* "Let me in right now, or I swear to God I'll break in this fucking—"

The door rattled, swung open. Bastian stood there scowling. "Jesus, I was asleep. What the fuck do you want, Michael?"

"What do I—" He heaved a breath, attempting to gain control. "You cleared your shit out and left without so much as a note, and you ask what I want? What the hell do you *think*? Tell me why, dammit!"

But he pretty much knew why, didn't he? Which didn't improve his position. He'd have to do better to reach his friend.

Bastian's lips twisted in a bitter parody of a smile. "You'd better come in before we give a free show to the neighbors."

Fuming, Michael followed the man inside, and, without waiting for an explanation, began with the strongest argument. "Are you crazy? You're not safe from Dietz here, especially now. You're a rabbit in a hole, waiting to get torn apart by his rabid wolves."

"Thanks. Your vote of confidence warms my heart."

"Don't give me that crap! Are you forgetting I nearly died after the hit he put out on me?"

Bastian's face paled. "If I live to be a hundred, I'll never forget. I was the one begging you not to die, remember?"

As if Michael didn't feel like a big enough pile of dung already. "Then we both know firsthand what he's capable of," he said, softening his tone. "Come home, where you belong. Where I can protect you."

The other man barked a humorless laugh, shaking his head. "You're a real piece of work, you know that? Tell me, who's supposed to protect me from *you*?"

His fists clenched, but he forced himself to remain calm. "Okay, after last night, I deserve that. For what it's worth, I'm sorry."

"Mighty big of you to admit. I'll mark the calendar."

"But you'll also recall that you looked right into my eyes after I'd been shot and admitted I'd never once lied to you about my feelings."

"Yes. I said you had nothing to apologize for, and you don't," he said in a clipped voice. "But that doesn't change what you mean to me and always will. I can't turn off how I feel like flipping a switch. You think I wanted to fall in love with my straight best friend? What a joke."

Michael swallowed hard. Bastian hadn't said those words since the day he'd driven Michael into Maggie's arms by uttering them. He hadn't been able to run fast enough. And now? God, he was so confused.

"It's not a joke. Your feelings could never be funny to me."

"Good to know." Cocking his head, he studied Michael, hope flickering briefly in his green eyes. "Tell me something else—besides the danger from Dietz, why should I return to the estate with you? Because my plans for today are to catch a nap, take care of some personal stuff around here, then move to one of the empty living quarters on the SHADO compound until he's caught. I'll be safer there than anywhere."

He's testing you. Don't fuck this up.

Meeting his friend's gaze, he said, "Come back. Because I need you. Because my whole world is off-kilter without you there, and I want to protect you." The hopeful light dimmed, changed to sadness, and his gut flipped. "What?"

"There was a whole lot of 'I' in those sentences. What about me?"

"I don't get you! What do you want me to say?"

"Nothing you don't mean." He started to turn. "Go home, Michael. I'm tired."

His hand shot out and he grabbed his friend's arm, yanking him around. "For God's sake, give me a clue!"

"No. If I have to tell you, the words will never hold any value. And I'm not talking about 'I love you,' either. Though I'd be the happiest bastard alive if you said and meant them."

"Then I must be an idiot, because I don't understand what else there is."

This was not going according to plan. What more did the man want? He tried a different tack.

"You said you can't turn off how you feel like flipping a switch? Well, I can't come to grips overnight with how I feel."

"About?"

"Us."

"You made it crystal clear last night there is no *us*," he whispered, shaking off Michael's grip. "Why are you doing this to me? Ripping my heart out two, three times isn't good enough for you? You want blood?"

"That's not completely fair to me. You can't expect me to change on a dime," he repeated. "But I think I *am* changing. Something's happening to me, Bastian. I look at you and I have these weird, overwhelming feelings. I get feverish, like—like I have the flu or something. I picture my home without you in it, and I can't breathe. You confuse me, and I don't know what to do."

The hope he'd glimpsed before flashed again, but Bastian shook his head. "I'm not going to be your guinea pig while you figure out why I make you sweat. I'm my own man, I have a shred of pride left, and I'm done."

His mouth fell open. "Done. With me?"

"I'll always be your friend, but I have to distance myself from you for my own good. For a while, anyway. I think it's for the best."

"And if I do figure it out? What then?"

"I may be here . . . or I may not. I guess that's the chance you'll have to take," he said softly. Walking to the door, he opened it, the message clear. "See you at work."

Michael found he could barely speak. "Okay. If that's the way you want it."

"I seriously doubt it was ever a question of what *I* wanted. Good-bye, Michael."

As soon as Michael stepped outside, the door shut and locked behind him. He stood for a long moment, completely stunned. And more bereft than he'd been since Maggie was killed.

As he walked away, he thought he heard a sound like a muffled sob.

But it was probably his imagination.

Bastian leaned against the door. Hung his head and tried to stifle a sob, and didn't quite succeed. "Oh, God."

That had been the hardest thing he'd ever done. *If you love something, set it free. . . .*

What total bullshit. He'd probably just made the biggest mistake of his life. Now Michael would happily retreat back into his nice, safe hetero world with his virtue mostly intact—the ill-advised, experimental, guy blow job notwithstanding. Katrina would no doubt be glad to help scrub the memory from his brain.

But Bastian remembered the man's passionate kiss. The raw desire on his face as he watched Bastian's lips slide up and down his cock. A man couldn't fake loving the sex.

No way was Michael faking the pain on his face a few minutes ago as he'd tried to bare his soul to his best friend. *And you shut him down, practically kicked him out.*

His heart screamed at him to go after Michael, call him back. Tell him that he didn't mean any of it, that he didn't want any distance between them.

His head advised that would be the exact wrong move. Deep down, he knew Michael needed this time to work out whatever was going on in that head of his.

But he would not allow himself to sit around and mope. And

wait. He had a life to resume, and, fuck it all, that's exactly what he was going to do.

And if Michael didn't like it? He had the power to make Bastian his . . . if he got his mind and his heart on the same page.

Katrina tied her silk robe more securely around her and padded into the kitchen, flipping on the coffeemaker. Thoughts of Michael, Bastian, and last night chased around in her head as she fished in the pantry for a package of plain bagels and set them on the counter next to the toaster. Next, she grabbed the cream cheese and strawberry jam from the fridge.

Last night with Michael had been wonderful. Exciting. Almost perfect. But something was missing, and—

A knock at the door dispelled the thought and she glanced at the clock. Her neighbor was a few minutes early, which was unusual. The girl was a butterfly, flitting from one flower to the next, and a concept like being on time, much less early, was totally foreign to her. Leaving the breakfast items on the counter, she made a beeline for the door and yanked it open, grinning.

"You're early! I'll alert the media—Oh. Michael!" She frowned. "You look awful. Aren't those the same clothes from last night that you wore home this morning? Good grief, come in."

She stepped aside, noting the shadows in his dark eyes, the defeated slump of his shoulders. Trailing him into the living room, she gestured for him to sit. "What's wrong?"

He flopped onto the sofa with a groan and ran a hand down his face. "I think I just lost my best friend. Isn't that a shitty cliché?"

"Oh no." She lowered herself to the sofa beside him and laid a hand on his arm. "You were going to talk to him when you got home, right? What happened?"

"He'd moved out, went back to his apartment. I drove over there and tried to reason with him, but he practically threw me out," he said miserably.

She had a sneaking suspicion that Michael's idea of "reason" differed a great deal from Bastian's. "Did you run the idea by him of the three of us getting together, seeing where things go?"

"The conversation never got that far or I would've brought it up." Leaning his head back, he stared at the ceiling. "We must've sounded like a couple of thirteen-year-old girls with all the whining about *feelings* and shit, and I just wanted to jump off a bridge. God, I'm such an ass."

The picture he conjured of their emotional talk made her want to smile, but she knew her humor would not be welcome at the moment. "So how did you leave things between you?"

Michael snorted. "He pretty much tossed me out of his life. Told me he wasn't going to be my guinea pig while I got my act together."

"Sounds reasonable."

"What?" He whipped his head around to stare at her. "Whose side are you on, anyway? I need him and my world isn't the same without him. I told him as much, and I got kicked in the teeth for it!"

"Is that the way you told him?" she asked pointedly. "*I* want, *I* need . . ."

"Hell, yes! But what does . . ." He frowned. She waited for him to get it.

He was male, so the wait took a tad longer than normal.

Finally, his eyes rounded. "Oh. Oh, fuck."

"Bingo," she said wryly. "I'm guessing the results might've been exponentially better had a few of those statements started with 'you,' followed by the qualities in him that you love."

"But I thought that's what I was saying!" He heaved a deep sigh. "I really *am* an ass."

"No, you're trying to find your way, just like the rest of us." Leaning into him, she nuzzled his neck, spread a few light kisses on the smooth skin. They'd showered this morning, so he smelled fresh, like her herbal soap.

Scooting to face her, he captured her mouth with his, slid a hand under the edge of her robe, seeking the naked flesh underneath—

And a knock on the door interrupted what might have been a very nice interlude.

"My neighbor," she said with regret, pushing to her feet. "We made plans for coffee. I didn't know you'd be back."

"I can go," he offered. But he didn't look like he wanted to leave.

"No, don't. Actually, you might enjoy meeting her. She's kind of a whirlwind, and that's putting it mildly."

"If you're sure."

"Absolutely." Crossing to the door, she let in the whirlwind and barely opened her arms in time to catch the enthusiastic hug. "Hey, you made it."

"Sorry I'm late! Jesus, maintenance took *forever* to fix our dryer, and then I didn't think my nails were *ever* going to dry, and—Oh, my God!"

Katrina tracked her friend's openmouthed astonishment directly to Michael. The pair was gaping at each other. "I take it you two have already met?"

"Michael!" Her friend squealed and dashed across the room, hitched her extremely short skirt, and straddled the man's lap. "What are you doing here? Did you bring strawberries and chocolate sauce?"

He shot a panicked look at Katrina. "Um, no, I—"

Whatever he was about to say was lost as Jeri checked the state of his tonsils with her tongue. Stunned, Katrina stood motionless as her lover quickly succumbed to the kiss with a low sound of pleasure. Jeri and Michael were acquainted in the biblical sense, apparently. She didn't know whether to be annoyed or intrigued by the revelation.

Intrigue won out, hands down. As she crossed to sit next to them, Jeri pulled back slightly and beamed. "Cool outfit, but I liked the brown leathers and black T-shirt better."

Michael met Katrina's gaze desperately, and it clicked into place. That's how Michael had been dressed the other night when he stopped by here to chew her out for the faulty camera, before going cruising. And he saw Katrina put two and two together. Katrina gave him a wicked smile.

"I like those pants, too."

"He looks sooo yummy in brown," Jeri enthused. She glanced at her friend, curious. "How do you guys know each other?"

"We work together," Katrina said. "He's my boss. You?"

"Oh, he picked up me and Jackie the other night at Daddy's Money and took us to that *huge* house of his! Fucked our brains out all night long, too! Such a beast." She sighed in fond remembrance.

"Don't I know it?" She was thoroughly enjoying watching Michael squirm. So *that's* why the man hadn't wanted to go to that particular club when Emma had suggested it.

Jeri, who was sharper than people gave her credit for, blinked at Katrina. "Uh-oh. Are you guys, like, *exclusive*? Because you know I don't poach, girlfriend. Ever."

Fondly, Katrina brushed a lock of red-streaked brown hair from her face. "I know you don't. No, this—whatever *this* is—is new. Seems we have an interesting situation here," she commented, smirking at Michael. Who looked like he'd swallowed a bug.

"Mmm, I'll say." Jeri wiggled on the man's lap. "He's hard as a freaking rock."

"What should we do about that, I wonder?"

"It would be a shame to let a perfect boner go to waste." Jeri pouted at the possibility.

"We should probably help him out."

"Out of these jeans, you mean."

"A fantastic idea."

"Actually, I don't think that's a good plan," Michael said with a lack of conviction.

Jeri began to yank at his shirt, tugging it over his head. "But you should hear the *whole* plan before you decide, right? What do ya think, Kit-Kat?" The shirt went sailing.

Michael's brows rose at Jeri's pet name for her, and Katrina gave a husky laugh. "I think we should get him naked."

"Ooh, definitely!" Her friend began to work on his fly.

"And then we should eat his balls and cock until he's begging for more."

"Make him burn."

"Yes. And then I have a special toy I'm going to use on his ass while he fucks you," Katrina purred, loving the flush of arousal on his face. The tautness of his male nipples, the heavily veined cock as it sprang free of his jeans. The weighty balls underneath, cradled in Jeri's hand. She went supernova hot, all over.

Jeri made short work of the jeans, then crouched between his knees and gave his shaft a slow lick. "Mmm, as tasty as I remember. Girl, you have the best ideas."

"Do I get a say in this?" he croaked.

"Sure you do. What would you like?" Katrina eyed his physical perfection, mouth watering.

"First of all, I feel stupid being the only one naked."

"Easily remedied!" Jeri chirped. She unzipped her skirt and stepped out of it, revealing that she wore nothing underneath. Her skimpy top went next, showing off her pretty, bare breasts.

Katrina simply untied her robe and let it slide off to puddle on the floor. "Okay, we're even. What else?"

"After we've done things your way, I get to use a toy on *you*," he said, eyeing Katrina like a starving wolf.

"That can be arranged, since I have plenty to choose from." He seemed surprised by that, and she smiled. "Still waters, and all that."

"I'll say." He gasped as Jeri sucked down his cock. "Oh, shit."

Indeed. Watching her friend work him, the hard flesh splitting her plump lips, made her instantly wet. His confession of the blow job Bastian had given him came to mind, and she wished she could've seen them together. She held out hope that eventually they'd all be together. But she had this now, and it was damned good.

With Jeri still kneeling on the floor at his feet, Katrina scooted back slightly on the sofa so she could bend to Michael's lap. Jeri pulled off his cock and gave her room, and then they both began feasting on the straining shaft and his balls. He groaned helplessly, burying each of his hands in their hair, bucking his hips. A time or two, Katrina's tongue dueled with Jeri's, and once they shared a deep kiss, nearly causing Michael to lose control right away.

"Oh, fuck. That's beautiful. Shit, yeah."

They broke the kiss, and Katrina winked at him. "You like the show? Maybe you'll see more later—if you're a good boy."

They went back to licking and sucking him until he was mindless, completely theirs. Sitting up, Katrina whispered she'd be right back, and hurried to her bedroom for lube, condoms, and the promised toys. Back in the living room, she paused at the delicious sight of Jeri bobbing over his lap and Michael splayed with his head back.

"That's enough. We don't want him to come yet," she said, joining them again. "Let's lay him on the floor, where we can get to him better."

Standing, Jeri took his hand, tugged him up, and led him to the middle of the room. She pulled him down again and he went willingly, eagerly waiting for whatever they had in store. Katrina grabbed a throw pillow from the sofa and tossed it to her friend.

"Here, put this under his butt." Next she grabbed the lube, a condom, and the toy she was going to use on Michael. After his rear was elevated, she told him, "Spread your legs for us, honey."

He complied, looking a little nervous, though his erection hadn't flagged one bit. "What are you two doing?"

"You'll see." Jeri giggled. "Well, actually, you won't *see*. But you'll sure as hell feel it. You're gonna go off like a rocket."

He looked at Katrina. "Do I want to know?"

"Probably not. Just relax and enjoy."

Jeri spread his ass cheeks while Katrina took the lube and squirted a generous amount on her fingers. Next she smeared the cool gel on his exposed hole, rubbing in slow circles. He flinched and sucked in a sharp breath, but didn't protest. She kept her touch gentle, letting him get used to the odd sensation of someone touching him in his most private area. Owning him.

Gradually, with each pass, she deepened the strokes. Worked her finger inward, teasing the rim of the puckered opening, dipping inside. Just a bit, to the first joint. Then more, caressing his inner walls, stretching, adding another finger. Farther still, locating the small bump of his prostate and grazing it slightly.

"Oh, God," he moaned, spreading wider. "I've never . . . It's so good. Don't stop."

She had him now. "I'm going to replace my fingers with something much better. You'll feel a slight burn, and you'll be full. And the toy will do wonderful things to this spot. Trust me."

Withdrawing, she retrieved the amazingly lifelike rubber phallus and coated it with the lube. Then she pressed the head to his hole and carefully began to work it inside. She'd half expected some fight on his part, but he opened to her, panting phrases that either meant he was a devoutly religious man or was turned on beyond coherence. She'd bet the latter.

She pushed the dildo to the hilt, watching him writhe like a worm on a hook. Eventually, turnabout would be fair play, but for now she'd relish this power to reduce him to a mass of quivering desire. At her mercy. She fucked him faster, harder, certain by his loud cries that she was nailing the all-important gland.

Jeri stroked his red cock. "Oh, he likes that!"

"He does. Who knew the great Michael Ross was secretly a dirty ass slut?"

"Let's get him ready. I can't wait to ride him."

Twisting the phallus deep, she left it buried in his ass and retrieved the condom, tearing the packet with her teeth. Holding his shaft steady, she rolled the rubber down over his scorching flesh, coated it with lube. Amazing that a man who was so together, even aloof, in his dealings with people could be so incredibly sensual and receptive during sex.

Jeri held his cock steady as she climbed aboard, straddling him. She sank down, taking him inside, and Katrina swore she felt the electricity ripple through all three of them. Michael spanned her friend's waist with his hands and began to thrust, expressing his pleasure at such a volume, Katrina wondered whether the neighbors might hear. Not that she cared.

She stroked his chest, plucked at his nipples. "That's it. Drive into her tight pussy, honey. Split her with that big cock."

"Oh yeah," he panted. "Fuck, that's sweet."

"Look so fine, her riding your cock, my toy in your ass. Fucking yourself while you do her."

"Shit, yes!" The naughty talk spurred him on, and he drove into her faster, more noisily.

Jeri cried out and ground her pussy into him, swept away by the force of her orgasm. This triggered Michael's and he stiffened with a shout, holding her in place. Spasmed until he lay limp and sated.

"Jesus, that was fantastic," he breathed.

Jeri climbed off. "I'll say!"

Michael pinned Katrina with his dark gaze, mouth curving into an evil grin. "And now there's the matter of a toy I get to use, and a show I was promised."

Katrina's sex throbbed in need. "Let's go to my bedroom."

"After you, sweetheart."

Eight

As Katrina carefully withdrew the dildo and set it aside, Michael knew his ass would be sore for a week. Christ, it felt like the entire cast of *Queer Eye for the Straight Guy* had completely redecorated in there and bought him a new wardrobe to boot.

The problem was? He'd loved every second of getting his hole plowed.

Who knew the great Michael Ross was secretly a dirty ass slut? No shit.

Standing to follow the ladies, he eyed the rubber monster that had occupied such a small space and brought such ecstasy. He decided he could make peace with the unexpected joy because, one, it was an inanimate object, and, two, it had been wielded by a woman.

Still, the inevitable question snuck past his defenses. Would the real thing cause as much pleasure? Maybe. Might even bring more. Which, come to think of it, could send him into cardiac arrest.

An image of Bastian behind him, the wet tip of his dick breaching his hole, inching inside, made him shiver. It was normal for his mind to go there after what just happened, right? Just because it might feel good didn't mean he was going to let his friend or any other man spank that monkey. Ever.

Katrina's bedroom was light and airy, the centerpiece a big canopy bed draped with gauzy beige and blue material. The thing looked like it should be sitting in the middle of a meadow in a fantasy book, awaiting a prince and his princess. He knew it was cozy for sleeping, if that's what a body had in mind. Perhaps much later, when they were all so wrung out, they couldn't walk.

He still couldn't believe Jeri was a friend of Katrina's. He'd about died when the younger woman rushed inside, straddled his lap, and revealed his romp with her and her twin with not a hint of embarrassment. That Katrina hadn't thrown him out by his dick, and had instead seized the opportunity to play, made him the luckiest SOB on earth.

"Are you waiting for permission?" Katrina asked. She was reclining on top of the comforter, glorious red hair spilling around her breasts. Jeri lay beside her, cheek propped in one hand.

"I suppose not." He hurried to join them, but stopped as he remembered something. "I seem to recall that it's my turn to use a toy, so if you'll show me where you keep them . . ."

"Over there." She pointed to a top drawer of her dresser, and he strode over to inspect the goods.

He eyed the contents, unable to put a name to some of the items. Damn, she had quite an assortment, and he thought she was spot-on with her comment about still waters. It was true— some of the most sophisticated people he knew had a private thing for kink, preferred sex a bit wild and dangerous. Katrina's hidden naughty side both surprised and thrilled him.

Inspecting the gadgets, he riffled through a colorful assortment of plugs, clamps, straps, bottles of oil, and a squishy, rectangular, jellylike thing with beads trapped in it and a hole in the middle. He did a double take at that last toy. *What the hell is that?*

Continuing his search, he also ran across a small, battery-operated toy with little arms or something on it. Sort of like an evil robot. "Damn, baby, you have some weird shit in here." He held up the squishy jelly thing with the beads. "What the fuck is this?"

"It's a fake pussy," Jeri supplied.

"A *what*?" The women giggled at his expression. And no wonder, since he was staring at it like it was venomous.

"It's a vagina," Katrina said between snickers. "You stick your penis in the hole and the beads stimulate you."

He snorted. "Why the hell would I want to fuck a plastic jelly pussy when I can have a real one?" Sometimes the female mind eluded him.

"Because," Jeri said, drawing the word out and rolling her eyes as though he were hopeless. "It's something different. It's the yum factor of your lover playing with you. Pleasing you."

"Okay, I get that. Maybe next time, huh?" He put the thing back in the drawer—and found what he wanted. Grinning, he lifted out a string of pink anal beads. "I think this will do nicely."

Snatching a small bottle of vanilla-scented oil, he carried the beads to the bed and climbed in, putting Katrina in the middle. "I take it you enjoy using the beads, since they're yours?"

She touched them lightly. "Actually, they're new. I ordered them online a few weeks ago, and, sadly, I've been without a partner to help me try them."

"You're an adventurous lady," he commented, smoothing a palm over Katrina's hip. "I like that. Roll onto your stomach. I'm going to get you ready and then fill that pretty backside of yours. Here, let's put this pillow under your hips."

Jeri scooted closer. "What do I get to do?"

"For now, just watch. You've got an important part coming up." He winked at her, and she smiled happily.

With Katrina settled and spread for him like an offering, he wished his recovery time was faster so he could go another round. Plunder that pretty ass of hers, so firm and plump. But he'd gladly wait, because the goal here was to make her forget her own name, not indulge his cock. Truthfully, he couldn't wait to be the master of her pleasure.

Spreading her cheeks, he drizzled a bit of the scented oil on her hole. "To make things easier. Just relax." He began to work in the oil with one finger, massaging into her entrance.

"Mmm."

Not everyone liked ass play, and until today he'd never fully appreciated how good it could feel. Now he prepared her with extra care, making certain she was stretched just enough that the toy would stimulate without discomfort. When she began to make needy sounds in her throat, her muscles limp on the bed, he figured she was ready and picked up the beads.

"Here we go," he said, placing the first one at the tiny opening. He gave it a gentle push and it slipped easily into her channel, disappearing. "God, that's wicked." Beside him, Jeri agreed, eyes wide.

He kept working, pushing one after the other into her hole, fascinated by the pink orbs being clasped by her flesh, then vanishing one by one. She began to writhe, moaning, and he smiled. This was almost as much fun for him as it was for her. "Just a few more, baby. You can take it; don't worry."

"So full! I need . . ." She started to reach underneath her, between the bed and her body, going for her pussy.

"Uh-uh, no touching," he warned, taking her arm and moving

it to her side. Finally, the last bead was in, and he nodded at Jeri. "Now for your part. How would you like to drive our poor Kit-Kat wild with your mouth? If it's okay with her."

"Yes," Katrina begged, wiggling.

"Ooh, I'd love to!"

"Go for it, honey."

Jeri crawled between Katrina's spread thighs and lay on her stomach, moving close, her face a mere breath from the slick pink pussy awaiting her attention. The lift from the pillow under Katrina's hips was just enough to allow Jeri to feast to her heart's content—which was exactly what she did.

Despite coming a short while ago, Michael's dick took notice of the girl action and perked up a bit. He rubbed Katrina's bottom as Jeri got into her task, licking the pouty little clit and the wet slit. The girl couldn't have enjoyed an ice cream cone more than she loved eating her friend's cunt, and Michael urged her on.

"That's it, girl. Give her a tongue-lashing she won't forget."

When the whimpers and moans from the women began to reach a fever pitch, he reached for the end of the string and prepared to drive his lover over the edge.

Any second, she was going to detonate. Arousal was building at warp speed toward impending orgasm, her skin too tight, the sensation too big to contain. Too hot. Overwhelming.

Katrina moved her hips, trying to fuck her friend's face, get more of the clever tongue and mouth to bathe her, making her vibrate from head to toe. She was a slave to what they were doing to her, and she loved every second.

Then another sensation joined the mix. A gentle tugging at her hole. One by one, the beads began to pull free, slipping away. The stimulation, the fire quickly burning out of control in her asshole and pussy, was not to be believed. Much less endured. She couldn't hold out under this dual assault and didn't want to.

Without warning, her body began to jerk as though electrocuted, the orgasm washing over her in a red tide. "Oh, God! Fuck, yes! Give it to me!"

Distantly, she heard her own hoarse cries and Michael crooning his approval. Jeri moaning into her cunt as she lapped the juices. Everything became a haze of desire as they owned her, brought her down. Left her boneless, sated.

"Thank you," she whispered.

Michael and her friend snuggled on either side of her and the pillow was removed from under her hips. "Sleep," he said, rubbing her back.

And because she couldn't do anything else, she let exhaustion carry her away.

In theory, Bastian's plan to distance himself from Michael had been a good one.

But working for the man made avoiding him damned near impossible. Katrina, too, since the two of them had been joined at the hip for days. They arrived together, took lunch in his office, left together at the end of the day. Bastian and everyone else in the building would have to be blind and stupid not to notice how they glowed in each other's company, the lingering looks filled with lust. God, it hurt to be on the outside.

Sometimes Bastian caught them glancing at him, their expressions reflecting sadness and . . . pity? And he would turn away and find something pressing to do, because pity he absolutely could not fucking take.

He'd rather plunge a knife into his heart.

Rolling his chair forward, he attempted to focus on the reports on his desk from their agents in the field, and their computer surveillance experts—aka hackers—as well. Neither of Dietz's henchmen who were cooling their heels in the basement prison were saying much that SHADO didn't already know.

The hit men didn't know Dietz's whereabouts, but gleefully claimed he must be close, ready to make his move. Bastian agreed, but his agents couldn't get a handle on where Dietz and Tio were hiding. It was like the earth had swallowed the fuckers whole, though he knew they'd never be so lucky. Those two were waiting, biding their time in the darkness like a couple of vampires. Ever since lackey number two had tried to off Bastian the other day, he'd been careful.

Maybe . . . too careful.

The idea took root and began to grow, and Bastian sat tapping his pen on his desk, considering how the plan would proceed. There were several drawbacks, but the reward far outweighed the risk. Mr. President wanted Dietz captured and eliminated, whatever the cost. If Bastian could lure the government's most-wanted criminal into a trap, the agency would earn a fat bonus. And everyone would have peace of mind.

If only he could put his plan into action without Michael's approval, but whatever their personal problems, the man was technically his boss. For the time being, anyway. Bastian knew the FBI would take him back in a heartbeat, and he'd been giving a lot of thought to calling his old director. For now, he had a job to do.

Pushing from his desk, he walked the short distance to

Michael's office and knocked on the doorframe before stepping inside. Michael looked up from his own mound of papers, happiness briefly lighting his face before he seemed to catch himself, face blanking, his welcome cool and professional. Bastian wondered whether he'd imagined the fleeting joy in the man's eyes.

"Come in. What's up?"

Bastian closed the door behind him and took a seat. "I need to talk to you about something important. An idea I have."

Michael leaned forward, elbows on his desk. His voice softened, sounding hopeful. "I'd love to hear it."

He hesitated. Surely the man didn't believe it involved something personal? Like he was here to bridge the canyon between them? No, that was wishful thinking on Bastian's part. "I have an idea to draw Dietz from hiding."

"Oh." Michael blinked, looking deflated. "Okay, let's hear it."

He nodded. "You and I have been extremely careful not to be caught unaware since the attempted hits on us both. We've battened down the hatches too much."

"Explain." His friend frowned.

"We're not accessible, so neither is Dietz. We know he's close by. He's waiting for an opportunity to move, which so far hasn't come along. I propose we give him that opportunity."

"You want to set up a sting."

"Yes." Here came the part Michael wasn't going to like. "With me as the bait."

"No fucking way." Sitting back in his chair, he shook his head. "Find someone else. Get Emma to make up one of the agents to play your role. We'll find someone your height and build, put him in a blond wig—"

"Which is exactly what Dietz will expect us to do. But if I go out to a club on my own, supposedly to pick up some action, he might be confident in making a move."

"I'll have to pull the men back way too far to make him believe you're really alone," his friend said in a low voice. "It's too dangerous."

"What's the alternative? We let him remain at large indefinitely, and just hope that we somehow get lucky and our computer guys or someone else accidentally gets a lead?" He paused. "I've gotten three calls from the president this week, demanding to know how close we are to catching this asshole. How about you?"

"Five."

"What choice do we have, Michael? If we don't do something, Dietz is going to reorganize what's left of his men, and when he does, we're all in deep shit," Bastian insisted. "We're not going to catch him without risk. It isn't possible."

The defeated slump of Michael's shoulders signaled his capitulation on the matter. "I wish the bait didn't have to be you."

"Well, it has to be one of us, and it makes more sense for it to be me. I'm the one he went after last, and I'm sure he wants to hurt you by getting to me. We'll make him think we've relaxed our guard, that I've gone out with no agents trailing me for protection, and I'm positive he'll move."

"That's what worries me. The physical distance that will be between you and our men is problematic. If he goes after you, you'll be alone for as much as five minutes before backup arrives." He paused, thinking. "You'll wear an audio device and one of the pinhole cameras."

For all the good those would do when their enemy put a bullet in his brain. But Bastian wisely kept the opinion to himself. "How soon can we do this?"

Michael was silent for a long moment. "Dietz is keeping tabs on us somehow. I'm willing to bet he has a contact keeping him in the know. Not one of his soldiers, but a local snitch, one he's paying off. Someone who works in the background near us. This person could be a bouncer, bartender, or one of our cleaning personnel here at the agency. Hell, it could even be Mrs. Beasley." At Bastian's arched brow, he grimaced. "Just sayin'."

"Okay, he has a snitch. So?"

"So we let Blaze, Emma, and some of our agents who are more active in the underground community spread the word that you're not happy in your love life. You've suffered a devastating breakup. You're going to have fun, nail every piece of ass that will hold still long enough."

Bastian's heart ached at the version laced with shades of the truth. But Michael would never be devastated on his behalf, he was positive. The man had barely blinked when Bastian shoved him out of his life. "This will take more than one night. He'll watch first, make sure I'm really doing what the rumors said."

Meaning, Bastian would have to make the pickups real. And Michael didn't even flinch, or show an ounce of remorse. He could have wept.

"Do what you must. We'll start tomorrow night. Like you said, he won't move the first night, so we'll have you go fishing again Friday night, Saturday if necessary. If he still doesn't try for you, we'll set up a predictable pattern—one weeknight plus Fridays and Saturdays. Three weeks with no results, and we'll scrap the op and come up with something else."

"Fine. But I don't think that will be necessary."

"Me, either. Stop by and see Katrina before you leave and get the equipment you'll need to wear in your clothing."

Oh, goody. That meeting wouldn't be awkward at all.

"Will do. I'll leave my condo at nine tomorrow night to go out. Not many people are hanging at the club before then."

"Fine."

Bastian took his cue to leave and stood. As he reached for the doorknob, Michael's voice drifted behind him.

"Please be careful."

Briefly, he closed his eyes. "I always am."

If only that concern meant something deeper. But it didn't, and never would. That depressing knowledge dogged him all day and had more than a little to do with his putting off going to see Katrina as long as possible. He might have avoided the errand until tomorrow if he hadn't answered the phone on his desk just as he was wrapping for the day. Not thinking about much except heading to his temporary quarters for the evening, he picked up the handset.

"Chevalier."

"Hey, it's Katrina. Are you coming by to get the equipment you need for the op? Michael said to expect you, and I'm about ready to go home."

Crap. He hadn't realized she'd be waiting for him. "I'm sorry, time got away from me. I'll be there in a couple of minutes."

"Okay, see you."

Hanging up, he buried his face in his hands. "Damn. Okay, stop being a pussy and face her like a man. She already knows that you want her as much as you want her lover." Hell, she'd wanted Bastian, too. Had that changed?

And as a result, seeing her and Michael spending every waking moment together cut twice as deep. After tidying his desk, he shut down his computer and walked out, thinking that a call to his former director was in order. He'd stick it out here until Dietz was caught, and then he'd move back to Virginia or wherever the hell they wanted to send him. Alaska would work.

Or maybe the president would be so pleased, he'd agree to send Bastian overseas as an agent so deep undercover, his real identity would cease to exist. Maybe he'd be like James Bond, breaking hearts all over Europe until he either vanished into a cozy retirement in the Mediterranean or got his ass blown up by the enemy.

Stifling a sigh, he walked into Katrina's office to find her shutting down for the day, as well. She brightened when she saw him and crossed the few feet to give him a warm hug.

"Hey, stranger." Pulling back, she studied him. "Haven't seen much of you in over a week."

"I've been busy protecting the world from heinous criminals." He shrugged. "You know how it is."

"Unfortunately, I do. How sad is it that those criminals keep us employed?" Her eyes twinkled.

"Very. You have a couple of gadgets for me?"

"I do." Scooping them off her desk, she placed them in his outstretched palm. "I don't have to tell you how these work. I just want to point out that the audio device is disguised as a nipple ring. You can wear either a mesh shirt or a solid one and it won't interfere with the sound. The camera was trickier, but Emma and I came up with a solution by disguising it as an earring."

"Neither of my ears is pierced, though."

"Doesn't matter. See this? It's one of those magnetic-button things, no piercing required. The angle won't be as good as if the camera was fixed on your shirt or somewhere it could point straight on, but it'll be okay."

"What about a necklace?"

"Didn't think of that, but we'll design something for Friday night. Come to think of it, changing up the accessories will be good. Less suspicious."

"All right. Guess I'm good to go."

She hesitated, biting her lip. "Bastian, please be really careful. I haven't trusted Dietz since the day he accepted the job as Michael's right hand. He's evil, not stupid. Whatever we've thought of, he's already there."

"Gee, thanks," he deadpanned. "Maybe I should just wear my T-shirt that has the red bull's-eye on it and stand in the middle of the road."

"That's not funny."

"Agent humor. What can you do?"

She considered him a moment, obviously chewing on something. "Why did Michael originally pass you over for the CEO's position and give it to Dietz? I'm not the only one who's baffled by that, either."

"The truth is, he *didn't* pass me over. I turned him down. The gory details, Michael can fill in for you." He was surprised she hadn't asked him already. "Gotta run. Thanks for the gadgets."

"Wait. About the other night—"

"What about it? We're all adults. You and Michael have a thing, and I get that." How calm he sounded. Not at all like his guts were being ripped out. "I've got no claim on him, or you for that matter, as much as I—Forget it. I have to go."

She grabbed his hand. "Bastian . . . I still want you. Do you still want me, too? This is important." Her earnest expression arrested him, those big blue eyes begging him to be honest. He could fall into them and never emerge.

"I'd give anything to be with you *and* Michael. But I fail to see how. I can't have either of you, regardless of how I feel," he said painfully.

"What if you could? Would you have both of us?"

What a fucking question. He stared at her, wondering what game she was playing. "You want to know? Fine. Yes, I'd have you both. And I'm getting too old to play for kicks—with you two I'd play for keeps."

"Then do it." Stepping close, she cupped his face. Gave him a soft kiss that deepened into something strong and passionate. It didn't last long, but it shook him to his toes. Awakened his groin. "Put your money where your mouth is. Finish what we started in your office."

He groaned. "Katrina—"

"What do you have to lose?" She slid a hand to his balls, manipulated them through his pants. Rubbed, stoking his desire.

Everything. He stood to lose it all, but right now he wanted her so badly. "We can't. You're with Michael."

"He and I haven't set any rules yet. Besides, as long as the other man is you, he won't mind." Leaning in, she nibbled on his neck, sending little chills through his body.

"I'm not so sure about that."

"I am." She moved on to his ear. "Trust me."

"I don't have any protection with me."

"I do, in my purse," she said, gesturing to where the handbag sat on the counter behind her desk.

"Oh, shit." Fire licked at his groin, the flames demanding to be fed. He was screwed. Taking advantage of her victory, she turned and dug in her purse, and triumphantly held up the small packet.

Placing it on the desk, she went to work on his zipper.

Flashbacks of the other day in his office teased his brain, shooting little ripples to his eager cock. Bad idea or not, there was no denying that his body craved a replay, but one that ended in satisfaction for both of them.

She opened his pants and his erection sprang free, pointing the way to bliss. When his shaft slipped between her lips, a helpless moan escaped his throat and he threaded his fingers through her soft hair. Urged her to take him deeper.

"That's it. Suck me," he rasped. "Harder."

Grasping the base, she did as he asked, tightening the suction and even using her teeth to lightly scrape the sensitive flesh. He shivered, loving the slight edge of danger, being so firmly under her control. Because there was no doubt that although she was the one on her knees, she was in charge. At the moment.

Just when he couldn't stand the torment any longer, she pulled off him with an audible pop and reached for the condom. "Ready for me?"

"Do you have to ask?"

Smirking, she tore the package with her teeth. Slowly, she rolled the latex onto his sensitized cock, and he found himself wondering whether this was how it went down between her and Michael at the club. Instead of jealousy that she and Michael were together, the idea heightened his lust, driving it to an almost unbearable level. Bastian not only approved, he longed to be a part of them.

A wave of doubt rose and he squashed it ruthlessly, determined to make the best of his time with Katrina. He wouldn't ruin it by overthinking their future—or lack thereof.

Helping her to her feet, he crushed his mouth to hers, fingers working on her zipper. Breaking the kiss, he shoved the pants down, undies and all, sliding them to her ankles. Her shoes were in the way and he lifted each foot, yanked them off, then tossed the pants aside. Cupping her face, he gave a bit of rein to the aggression boiling in his blood. He barely recognized his own voice, low and snarly.

"At the club the other night, how did Michael take you?"

Her eyes rounded. "What?"

"How. Did. He. Fuck. You?"

She licked her lips. "With me facing the wall in the alley, legs spread. Why?"

He gave her a feral smile. "Good. Because I'm going to fuck you differently. Not in the dark, but in the light, where you can't hide." Sweeping his arm across her desk, he sent pens, pencils, and papers clattering to the floor. Then he eased her onto her back on the surface, spread her knees, and stepped between her legs. Rubbed his cock on her mound. "You're going to look into my eyes while I bury myself deep in your hot pussy and fuck you until you can't see straight. Sound good to you?"

"God, yes!"

Reaching between them with one hand, he parted her folds and slipped a finger into her channel, making sure she was nice and wet. Ready for him. Satisfied, he replaced his fingers with the head of his aching cock and pushed inside, sliding all the way to the hilt.

"Bastian," she said hoarsely, eyes wide. Hazy with desire. "Fuck me."

With great pleasure. Hooking her legs over his shoulders, he grasped her hips and readjusted, settling into the cradle of her heat. Withdrawing, he paused, then pushed home again. And again. Reveled in the snug clasp of her pussy walls massaging his dick, making him damned near cross-eyed with pleasure.

"More! Harder!"

"Christ, baby."

He complied, giving it to her strong enough to shake the desk, fingers digging into her pale skin as he drove inside. Pumped her with abandon, her little cries of ecstasy spurring him on, calling to him on a deeper level than he'd ever experienced with any woman. Even in the throes of white-hot lust, one word emerged in his mind, defining the feeling that went deeper than sex.

Connection. He felt connected to her in a way that was almost spiritual, a bond he'd yet to achieve with Michael, as much as he wished for it. But Katrina was wide open to Bastian, trust and something more shining in her blue eyes, accepting what he had to give with everything in her. No hesitation or shame.

The realization drove him over the edge and he exploded with a shout, pulsing his release into her. Distantly, he was aware of her clinging to his shoulders, spasming around his cock, finding her own reward. They held on to each other as the tremors subsided, coming down from the high. All too soon, reality intruded, and with it a ball of guilt that sat heavy in his gut.

He'd fucked his best friend's lover. Would Michael forgive him? Despite Katrina's earlier assurance that Michael wouldn't mind, Bastian wasn't so sure.

Despair joined the guilt, vying for first position on the top-ten list of stupid shit Bastian had done lately. Kissing Katrina's neck, he withdrew carefully and straightened, reaching for a box of tissues he'd knocked to the floor. Quickly, he removed the condom, disposed of it, and cleaned himself, not meeting her eyes. He put himself back together while she did the same, and then stood awkwardly, wondering what to say next. *Thanks* seemed a little strange.

Stepping in front of him, Katrina hugged him around his

waist, snuggling into his chest. "Thank you," she said with a contented sigh. "I've been wanting you forever, it seems."

Funny, coming from her it didn't sound strange at all. Still, the complications of their situation weighed heavily on his mind. "What about Michael?" The tightness in his voice belied his anxiety.

Pulling back, she stared earnestly into his face. "Michael, too. I've wanted you both. And now I don't know if I can give up either of you. Maybe I won't have to."

He stared at her, trying to assimilate what she was saying. "I don't think my best friend is the type to willingly share a woman with another man."

"I'm not talking about just you two sharing me. I'm saying . . . what if the three of us could be together, for real?"

Hope soared for a few seconds, until he pictured Michael's reaction to such a suggestion. The man's withdrawal after the blow job in the limo had been painful enough. His spirits plummeted. "Honey, if you think he'll go for a happy threesome with me involved, you're deluding yourself," he said sadly. "And I've had enough of him hurting me to last a lifetime. Even if I—No. There's no point in discussing this any further."

"You might be surprised. Do us all a favor and don't give up."

"What if you had to choose between us, sweetheart?" he asked quietly. "What if it came down to him or me? Which one of us would it be?"

She didn't answer. Or couldn't. Her eyes filled with tears, and his chest felt like it had caved under the pressure of agony so horrible, he wanted to run. Hand in his resignation right then and keep walking.

Which he would do, immediately after the job with Dietz was done.

*   *   *

Showtime.

"Okay, guys. Going in," Bastian said for the benefit of his backup. "And if anything I do ends up on the Internet? Remember, I take notes on you idiots, and paybacks are a mother."

The other agents snickered. Michael wasn't amused.

"He's going to get his ass killed." Michael would have paced like an animal in a cage, but in the surveillance van, there was nowhere to go. No room to maneuver.

"He'll be fine, boss," Ozzie said, giving him a sharp look. "Give him some credit."

The unusually sober comment from the normally outgoing agent gave Michael pause. He needed to be careful about expressing worry in front of his men. They might take it as doubt about Bastian's abilities, which wasn't true. "You're right. He's my friend and I'm concerned—that's all. He's not used to being in the field anymore."

"It's like riding a bike," Agent Willis said, trying to placate him.

Not really. Every case was different, took on a life of its own. There was no such thing as a normal or routine case.

As Bastian entered the club, they all fell silent. Ozzie adjusted the sound to mute the roar of the crowd and the music, and they watched the monitor as he pushed through the crowd. The video feed wasn't terrific, but that was due to the dark interior of the estab-lishment. They could make out faces, barely, and could pause the video and snap still photos if they spotted Dietz or one of his men.

This particular club wasn't one Michael had ever frequented, but it had a rather rough reputation. Dark, a little careworn, any poison could be found here. Stout drinks, a pill for every color of the rainbow. Anything-goes sex to be had for those in the market.

He wanted to storm into that shithole and drag his best friend out by the hair.

However difficult he'd imagined it would be to watch and listen to Bastian get into his role as a spurned lover on the make, the reality was far worse. He sat riveted, unable to do a damned thing as the man worked his magic.

People were attracted to Bastian, no question. Michael had always known that, but it was a rude awakening to see men and women putting the moves on him. Smiling, groping, fawning over his golden beauty. Each hoping to be the one he chose for some down-and-dirty sex in a back room somewhere. Frankly, it was humbling.

Why does he love me when he can literally have anyone he wants?

On the screen, Bastian worked the bar for a while, then the dance floor. An hour later, he was at the bar again when a new male voice came through the feed.

"Hi." Shy, hesitant. "I'm Cory. Can I buy you a drink?"

The camera panned to the right, showing a cute little blond twink smiling hopefully at the object of his interest. Michael snorted. As if the squirt stood a chance.

"Sure, Cory. I'm Bastian," he replied. Male interest returned in kind.

What the fuck?

"What'll you have?"

"Scotch on the rocks."

The bartender was signaled, the order placed, along with a beer for the twink—who didn't appear to be anywhere near legal.

Michael made a mental note to call one of his buddies in Vice and have them plan a raid.

"Do you come here often?" Cory asked.

Michael curled his lip. What a stupid line.

"Not nearly often enough, angel."

Angel? He needed a Tums.

"Problems at home?"

"Home, work, sleeping. Name it. But, hey, who doesn't have garbage they need to toss?"

The drinks appeared. "Here's to tossing our garbage!"

"A fine idea," Bastian said. Was that a tinge of bitterness?

They toasted, and Michael started to feel sick. More than a Tums could handle. The two enjoyed their drinks and made small talk. But it was the natural progression of events to the inevitable conclusion that almost made him open the door of the van and hurl. He would have if his eyes weren't glued to the screen as though he were watching a train wreck.

"I have to know something. . . . Is that mouth as sweet as it looks, angel?"

"I don't know," Cory said shyly. "I've only done it twice."

Little stinking liar. Surely Bastian didn't fall for that.

"Why don't we find a more private place for you to practice?"

The crowd parted, the camera moving again. To the back of the place, down a hallway. Into a small, dark room. A door closed. The shadowy form of the twink moved up to Bastian, too close, blanking out the picture. Sounds of kissing reached their ears, and then the younger man slid to the floor, out of sight, giving them a view of the wall. A zipper was lowered.

Bastian's groan echoed through the van. Nobody breathed.

The kid must've been good, because his friend fucked the

twink's mouth for all he was worth. Flesh slid wetly, noises of pleasure rose, and Michael's dick hardened in his jeans. He wanted to be the one in that room with Bastian, wanted to slide to his knees.

He wanted to tear Cory the Angel's pretty little head clean off his shoulders. Rip out his heart and spit on it.

Finally, a shout of release, followed by another. For a few seconds, only heavy breathing cut the silence.

"Can I see you again?" Cory asked.

A pause. "Be here Friday night. We'll hook up then."

"Cool." The twink was happy.

Michael wasn't. He was in hell, and the kicker was it was all his fault.

And he had no clue how to make things right.

Dietz looked up from his laptop as the door rattled. Tio came in, pockmarked face stoic, as usual. "Well?"

"Seems like Chevalier has let down his guard. Hooked up with some kid tonight, got his rocks off. If it's a setup, his team is watching from Mars or some shit. Can't find a trace of 'em."

"Oh, they're watching," he said thoughtfully. "I'm sure of it. The trick is to beat them at their own game."

"How?"

"By practicing patience." Quickly, he outlined his plan. "By the time Michael figures out I'm one step ahead, it will be too late."

Soon, Bastian would be as dead as Maggie Ross. And this time, there would be no mistaking who dealt Michael the blow.

Nine

〜〜

"Go home, boys. This op has been a huge bust," Bastian said under his breath, loud enough for the team to hear. Three weeks, and nothing. Not one sign of Dietz. The man just wasn't going to bite, and they'd all have to come up with a different way to get him.

He'd think about that tomorrow. Right now, he was off-duty, and his primary goal was to get a piece of Cory's pretty little ass. It wasn't love, and they both knew it. But it was hot skin and breathy sighs. A way to not be alone for a few hours, with someone who understood what it meant to be on the outside looking in.

Using the key card, Bastian let them in to the motel room he'd rented for the night. Since they'd been hooking up, he hadn't invited Cory to his condo. That wasn't about to change, no matter how sweet the kid might be. Taking him home would imply a progression in their relationship that wasn't going to happen.

But he fully intended to enjoy the lithe, compact body he shoved against the wall when they got inside. The gasp, the innocent, wide blue eyes, went straight to his dick. He pressed himself into the smaller man, letting him get a taste of his arousal. His erection pushed insistently into Cory's belly, demanding satisfaction.

"Get naked," he told the younger man.

"Back atcha."

Bastian stripped, not concerned about the camera or the sound feed. His colleagues would have called it a night, not being eager to hear or see more than they possibly had to, especially Michael. The man had done some major avoiding these past three weeks, as though Bastian had a disease and it might be contagious. Bastian had told the man he needed some distance, but if Michael really cared . . .

He wondered whether Katrina had told Michael about her and Bastian's steamy interlude in her office. Neither of them had let on, and Bastian hadn't asked. *I guess I really don't matter that much to either of them. Not enough to fight for me.*

Whatever. Tonight he was going to lose himself in a hot, willing lover. No expectations, no fear, no broken heart. Just forget his own name and drown in wicked sensation, no promise of tomorrow.

Undressing, he laid his clothes on a chair and hid his backup weapon among the folds of his jeans. Cory had glimpsed it once and though it had made the kid nervous, he'd seemed to accept Bastian's highly edited story of being in law enforcement. He'd even made the requisite joke about handcuffs. Maybe Bastian would bring some next time—if he continued to see Cory.

The younger man climbed on the bed and turned his head to glance at the digital clock on the nightstand before spreading himself on his back. His cock was only at half-mast, but Bastian planned to fix that in a hurry.

Removing a condom and lube from his jeans pocket, he joined Cory and laid the items on the bed. He crawled between the younger man's legs, wanting a taste of the silky, salty flesh. Cupping his hands under the firm bottom, he lifted his lover slightly and enveloped the thin shaft. Under the skillful stroking of his tongue on the sensitive underside, Cory's cock hardened and the kid made a helpless sound, thrashing some.

Since he loved being in control almost as much as he loved the actual fucking, he sucked until Cory was babbling mindlessly, skirting the edge of release. Then he pulled off and flipped the kid over, hauling him to his knees. Quickly, he ripped into the small packet and sheathed himself, then spread some lube over his shaft. He prepped Cory, working a finger into the tight ring of muscle, loosening him.

"Come on, fuck me," he said hoarsely. "Just do it."

"I don't want to hurt you." He frowned. Cory loved ass play, usually liked for him to linger there, and most of the time begged to be rimmed.

"You won't. Fuck me, please."

"Okay, if hard and nasty is how you want it, fine by me."

Bastian gripped Cory's slim hips, lined up, and pushed inside. So tight and hot, just the way he loved it. The inner walls clenching around him, squeezing his cock as he slid in to the balls and out to the tip. Plunged in again. Out.

"Damn, so good. You like being my dirty slut? My whore?"

"Y-yes! Harder!"

He obliged, pumping hard and fast, enjoying the staccato slap of their skin. Their balls smacking together. The friction sent him higher, little shocks rippling along his cock. Already close. Reaching around Cory's hip, he grasped the other man's cock, surprised that it had lost some of its hardness. He stroked it in time with his thrusts, bringing it to life, hoping to bring Cory as much pleasure as he was getting.

His orgasm hit hard, and he released Cory's erection. Buried himself to the hilt and emptied his balls into the kid's ass. When the last shudder went through him, he carefully withdrew and removed the condom. Tied it off and tossed it in a nearby trash can. Climbing back onto the bed, he saw that Cory was stretched out on his stomach. He turned the kid over and arched his brows.

"You never came."

Cory flushed, not meeting his eyes. "Sorry."

"Don't apologize. Happens sometimes. I'd be glad to finish sucking you off." He grinned and licked his lips suggestively.

The younger man glanced at the clock. "N-no, I . . . that's okay."

"You have somewhere you need to be?"

"What?" Those baby blues were startled. Guilty.

"You keep looking at the clock. If you've got somewhere to go, I won't keep you."

"N-No. I mean, y-yes." Cory closed his eyes.

"Is this thing we have going becoming too domestic for you?" he asked. "If you're ready to move on, just say so, kid. I'll be sorry because I really like you, but I'll wish you nothing but the best."

"You like me?" he asked in a small voice.

"I do. You're sweet-natured, cute, adventurous in bed. What's not to like?"

"Oh, no." Cory's face paled, his eyes enormous.

And with that, the warning bells that should've gone off about twenty minutes ago began to clang in his head. "Cory," he said calmly. "Tell me what you've done."

"I think they l-lied to me. They s-said you were a d-dangerous criminal. But you've been so nice to me. Nothing at all like a criminal."

Ah, fuck. "Who said this?"

Cory sat up, wringing his hands. "A couple of men. They claimed to be undercover FBI. But they weren't, were they?"

"Unlikely. *I'm* the one who's undercover, and you got played. Get dressed and hurry." Bastian jumped from the bed and reached for his jeans, removed the gun, and laid it on the chair close at hand. He began yanking on his pants. "Was one of them a big Mexican with a pockmarked face?"

"Yes," Cory whispered, pulling on his own jeans.

"Shit. What did they offer you to lure me here tonight?" He tried to keep the betrayal and bitterness from his voice. He wasn't lured, precisely, but was a willing participant in his own downfall. Cory was a victim also, too innocent for his own good.

"Five thousand. I wondered about that, but they claimed the FBI could expense the cost of paying me. But the real FBI couldn't do that, could they? Jesus, I'm so stupid!" Hands shaking, he pulled on his shirt.

"How much time do we have?" He jammed his feet in his shoes, palmed the gun.

"Five or ten minutes. They said they'd take you into custody, then pay me the money." Cory swallowed hard. "But they planned to just kill us both, didn't they?"

"That's exactly right." Digging his phone out of his pocket, he placed a call to Michael, cursing when it went to voice mail. "It's me. I'm at the motel and things have gone FUBAR. They got to Cory and set me up, but he got suspicious of their story and confessed to me. We're going to try and make it to the compound, but it could be too late to make a clean break out of here. Could use some backup. See you."

He pocketed the phone and dug a card from his wallet. Handed it to Cory. "If we get separated, you find a place to lie low and call that number. One of our men will pick you up and take you somewhere safe."

"Thanks. I don't deserve that much."

"We'll discuss who's the bigger idiot later. Let's go."

Easing the door open, Bastian peered into the night. Nothing moved in the dim light under the awning that covered the row of rooms, nor in the parking lot. He waved at Cory to follow, and stepped out, half expecting to be greeted by a hail of bullets. Even that scenario beat being trapped in the motel room, though, like pigs waiting for slaughter.

Grabbing Cory's arm, he took a couple of steps toward his new car—and two forms rounded the corner not twenty feet from them. Both men were big and carried guns. One of them jogged wide, cutting off his route to the car. *Tio.*

"*Run!*" Bastian shouted, shoving Cory in the opposite direction. Bracing his feet, he brought his arm up, knowing in his gut that he was so fucking dead, but someone was going with him. Making a split decision, he fired at the closest man, the one under the awning, as the pair fired back. A bullet whizzed past his face to embed in the stucco of the motel wall, and a punch hit his thigh, burning. The man he hit went down, a dark stain blossoming on his chest.

As Tio fired again, Bastian turned and bolted in the direction he'd sent Cory. Rounding the corner of the building, he spotted Cory hauling ass across the lot next door, heading for the shadows. Bastian had to buy the kid time to find a hiding place and make the call for help. Using the wall as cover, he lunged around the corner and popped off two shots at Dietz's favorite lapdog, gratified when the man dove for the ground between two parked cars. If he hadn't hit the bastard, he'd at least slowed him down.

Bastian took off, the pain in his leg beginning to register. With every step, agony ripped through his thigh, but he pushed on. Across the street, into an alley next to a dry cleaners that was closed for the night. Emerging from the other end, he limped more than ran across the next street, into another alley, footsteps gaining from behind. His foot snagged something in the darkness and he tripped, landing on his hands and knees in slimy garbage. Lost his gun as it went skittering into the gloom.

Gunshots erupted at his back and he lurched up, stumbled on, shards of brick exploding to his right. Sweating, breathing hard, he reached the end of the alley—a corridor that ended in a tall, high fence.

Panting, he braced one hand on the fence and laid the other on his jeans, over the wound. His pants were soaked with blood and now he could feel the warm liquid squishing in his shoe. Dizziness assailed him, and he knew the bullet had probably nicked an artery. He was trapped.

It was over.

Putting his back to the fence, he leaned against it, determined to die on his feet. Tio jogged up and stopped a few feet away, gun pointed squarely at Bastian's chest, crooked smile glinting in the scant light.

"Where's your traitorous boss?" Bastian asked.

"Close. Not that it will matter to you in a moment."

"Figures, since you two are practically married," he taunted. "Do you scream his name when he fucks your ass raw?" His hope was to incite Tio to deliver a quick death.

The taunt backfired. The big man crossed the space in two strides and slammed the butt of his gun into Bastian's head.

The night shattered around him and he fell. Hit the ground and rolled to his side, instinctively trying to protect himself. A boot connected with his stomach and he gagged, tried to scramble away. Another blow caught his ribs, another his chest. They rained down until he stopped moving, strength gone, floating somewhere above the intense pain.

As though conjured from his worst nightmare, Tio's silhouette loomed over him. Slowly, he raised his arm, aiming his gun at Bastian's skull.

"*Adios*, Chevalier."

Distantly, Bastian heard a shout, the deafening explosion of a gunshot.

Then nothing.

Thank God he hadn't sent the team home when Bastian called an end to the op.

"Hang on, buddy," Michael said, as Ozzie whipped the surveillance van in a sharp turn toward the motel. "We're coming."

They'd listened just a while longer, grumbling but respecting Michael's sixth sense. His crazy instinct not to call it so soon. To wait. The kid's confession had chilled their blood, and when he said Dietz's men were on the way, Michael and his team had burned rubber.

Four minutes. That's all the time it took to reach the motel, but it was four fucking minutes too long. He'd listened to Bastian's message on the way, having just missed the call. God help him, he hadn't heard it ringing because they were already roaring toward the motel by then. As they skidded to a stop at the back of the place, behind Bastian's car, Michael spotted a man lying on the sidewalk.

"One of Dietz's."

"I'll check him," Willis said, climbing out and walking over. Two fingers to the man's throat, and he shook his head. "Dead. I'll check the room, too, and get a cleanup crew here."

Michael climbed out and ordered Ozzie to keep the van running. Quickly, he walked over to where an exchange of gunfire had obviously occurred. "From the way this guy is positioned, Bastian had to be standing close to the door of his room." His gaze followed the path from the dead man to the spot where his friend might've stood. Crimson droplets were scattered on the walk near the motel-room door, and led from the scene to the corner of the building. "He's been hit and he's running."

Jumping back into the van, he slammed his fist on the dash. "Go!" he yelled at Ozzie. "That way!"

The van squealed through the parking lot, and as they came to the front of the building, he caught sight of a huge man ducking into an alley across the street. "Shit, I think that was Tio," Ozzie said. "I'll take the next street and try to intercept them."

If Tio had Bastian on the run, the situation was dire. The Mexican was a stone-cold killer. Michael willed himself not to panic as Ozzie wheeled the van onto the next street—only to be blocked by white construction sawhorses and a big hole in the pavement where the city had made yet another mess to impede traffic. In front of them, a few businesses down, Tio was just disappearing into another alley.

"Goddammit! I'm going on foot." Michael flung the passenger's door open. "Call for backup and get McKay and his medical team here, fast."

"Got it."

Michael ran. Gaining the mouth of the alley seemed to take forever. When he got there, he entered cautiously, listening. Shuffling noises, maybe footsteps, drifted from the far end. He heard voices. Pulling his weapon from his holster, he moved forward as quietly as possible, sticking as close to the wall as he could.

Wasn't easy with all the boxes, crates, and rancid garbage strewn everywhere.

Drawing closer, he could make out the hit man standing. Kicking a form on the ground, over and over. And then his arm angled downward, the glint of metal in his outstretched hand.

"*Adios*, Chevalier."

"Tio!" Michael shouted, bringing up his own gun. The man spun, and Michael did on pure, honed reflex what he was trained to do.

He blew the motherfucker's brains out.

Lowering the weapon, he reholstered it and jogged to Bastian, avoiding the human feces that used to be Tio. He dropped to his knees. Even in the darkness, he knew his friend was in bad shape.

One leg of Bastian's jeans was saturated with blood, as was his face. He wasn't moving or making a sound. Reaching out, Michael placed two shaking fingers to his neck and found a weak pulse.

"Oh, my God." He ran a trembling hand over his friend's hair. "Bastian? It's me. Christ, please don't leave me. Hang on, help is coming."

And it was taking too long. Fishing in his jeans, he retrieved his pocketknife, flipped it open, and used it to split the seam of Bastian's bloody pant leg as far as he could without cutting flesh, then used his hands to rip the material all the way to his thigh. Peering at the wound, he saw a dark stream of blood pouring steadily from the hole. Not pumping in a full-fledged arterial spray, but losing too much all the same.

Working fast, he cut the torn denim into a long strip and cut it free. Then he wrapped it around Bastian's thigh, tying it as tight as possible in a makeshift tourniquet. It wasn't nearly enough, but it was all he could do.

A sound had him reaching for his gun, but it was just Ozzie sprinting toward him. "How bad is he?"

"Pretty bad," he said, voice rough. His throat burned, but he had to keep it together in front of his men. "I think the bastard got an artery. What's McKay's ETA?"

"Seven."

"That's too long."

"I know, but the nearest hospital is fifteen, even if we took him to the van and drove him in ourselves. And with the gunshot wound, there's the mandatory reporting."

"I don't care about the red tape with the cops if it means Bastian survives," he snapped.

"Our way is still quicker. McKay is bringing the helicopter and setting it down about a mile from here. One of our men is meeting him, driving him here. They'll stabilize Bastian, take him back to the copter."

Michael nodded. The helicopter would whisk his friend back to the compound, shaving off crucial minutes. Time Bastian didn't have to spare.

He wanted to pull Bastian into his arms, but didn't dare risk moving him. He longed to tell the other man just how much he meant to him, beg for forgiveness, and now it might be too late.

At last, a vehicle stopped at the mouth of the alley. Four men came into view; one was an agent, and the other three were McKay, a male nurse carrying a backboard, and another doctor named Rhodes.

"Come on," Ozzie said, tugging Michael's sleeve gently. "Let's get out of their way."

Reluctantly, he stood and moved back, half-frozen. Katrina was half of his heart . . . but the other half was pouring his life

onto the filthy pavement, unaware that Michael's soul was screaming in agony. That he'd give anything for Bastian to survive, smile
at him again. Give him another chance.

Give the three of them a chance.

"I can't do much for him here," McKay said grimly. "We need
to transport *now*."

The doctors transferred him carefully to the backboard,
strapped him down. They lifted their burden and headed back to
their vehicle at a steady clip, the nurse holding the IV bag aloft.
At the mouth of the alley, Michael started to climb into the van
with them, but McKay shook his head.

"There's no room for you in the helicopter. I'm sorry, Michael.
Follow us, and I'll let you know something as soon as I can."

"I understand," he murmured. "Take care of him, Taylor."

"I will."

And then the vehicle roared away, leaving him staring after it,
a ragged hole in his chest where his heart should be. Was this how
Bastian had felt after Michael had been shot? Like his whole world
hung in the balance, as though he'd been plunged into hell?

"Michael," Ozzie said softly. "Come on, man. He'll be in surgery by the time we get there, and I'm sure we'll know something
soon after that. I'll have someone from the cleanup crew give Willis a ride back from the motel."

He shook himself. "Okay."

On the interminable ride to the compound, Michael's phone
rang. It was Willis.

"Boss, we got that kid, Cory. Kelly picked him up and is taking
him to the compound. We figured he wasn't safe going home with
Dietz still out there."

"Good," he said numbly. "You guys did exactly right. Take

him to one of the empty living quarters and let him get some sleep. We'll figure out tomorrow what the hell to do with him."

Michael knew what he'd *like* to do to him, especially after listening to the little shit service Bastian—enthusiastically—for hours on end. And then the naive brat almost fell for Dietz's trick. Even though the kid had wised up in time to redeem himself, he might have cost Bastian his life, anyway.

"Got it, boss." Willis ended the call.

Immediately, Michael placed a call of his own. Katrina answered on the third ring.

"Hey, you! Is the stakeout over? This was the last night, right?"

"Yeah. Um, listen, baby. Bastian . . ." To his horror, his voice broke.

"What is it? What's happened?" she demanded in alarm.

"One of Dietz's men got to him. Can you meet me at the compound's hospital?" His teeth chattered and he started to shiver. Delayed reaction.

"Oh, Michael," she breathed. "I'm on my way. Hang in there, honey."

"Yeah."

Ending the call, he stared at the blur of lights whizzing past and prayed harder than he ever had. Which was saying something, because he'd never been a praying man.

Tonight, he was making an exception. On his knees, if necessary. *Please, God, don't take him from me. From us.*

Katrina grabbed her purse and keys and hit the door, uncaring that she wore only a pair of well-loved sweat pants, a T-shirt that stated YOU CALL ME "BITCH" LIKE IT'S A BAD THING, and running shoes. She'd gone for a walk earlier and was just about to take a long, hot bath when Michael phoned.

One of Dietz's men got to him.

The heartbreak and terror in his voice got her moving, fast. She'd paused only long enough to make sure she had her ID badge for entry to the compound.

All the way there, she wished she'd asked for a few more details. Her mind was spinning with all of the possible scenarios, each one more horrible than the last. Three weeks, and not a single appearance from Dietz. The guys were ready to scrap this op. What the hell had gone wrong?

Okay, enough. No use speculating. She had no choice but to be patient and get the story later. One thing was for sure: tonight effectively put an end to her argument with Michael over her moving to his estate. She'd claimed that such a move would clue in Dietz as to their relationship. He'd countered that the asshole might know already, and she'd be safer at his place. Now Michael would get his way.

She wasn't so sure she minded. Hell, she was at his place more often than not. Which, if she was honest, was in no way a hardship.

At the compound, she found a close parking spot and rushed inside. Took the elevator to the fourth floor, vibrating with impatience. The second the doors slid open, she sprinted down the corridor to the hospital and pushed inside. As she approached the receptionist, she tried to be calm and polite though she felt anything but.

"Could you tell me where Mr. Ross is waiting? He's expecting me."

"Through those doors, dear. He's in the private waiting room, second door on the right."

"Thank you."

She forced herself to slow her steps, to project calm strength despite her fear. If she barged in panicking, that wouldn't do Michael any good. Pausing outside the door, she took a deep breath and pushed inside.

Michael was sitting in one of the padded vinyl chairs, elbows on his knees, face buried in his hands. As she approached, her serene facade evaporated.

Michael was crying.

Tears dripped off his chin and his shoulders shook. He was pulled into himself so tightly, as if afraid he'd fly apart. "Michael?"

His head jerked up and it took him a couple of seconds to process that it was her. His face was ravaged, eyes red. Dark stains were drying on his shirt, the knees of his jeans. Blood. He rose, visibly attempting to pull himself together, and then his face crumpled, his arms reaching out.

"Katrina . . ."

Launching herself into his arms, she enveloped him in her embrace, held on. He clung to her and she stroked his back, rubbing in soothing circles. "Shh, I'm here. Right here, with you."

She kept talking, mostly nonsense. She'd never been good at this sort of thing—comforting another person in a terrible situation—but this felt right. Natural. Michael was hers, and she wanted more than anything for Bastian to be, as well.

"He was shot and beaten," Michael said, unsuccessfully trying to stifle a sob. "The bullet hit his thigh and he was bleeding out. They're in there trying to save him."

God, no. "They will. We have to believe that."

"Rhodes came out a few minutes ago. They had to restart his heart, give him lots of blood to replace what he lost."

"He's strong. He'll make it." *Please.*

"I don't know what to do."

"Just let me hold you."

"This must've been how he felt. When it was me, in there. And I didn't understand what he went through until now." He paused. "Do you think he knows?"

"That you love him?"

"Yes."

"Deep down, he probably does. But you'll tell him when you're ready."

"I swear I will." Pulling back a bit, he gazed into her eyes, more serious than she'd ever seen him. Even for Michael. "I love you, too, baby. It's newer, but it's there. I want you to know that, because it seems time is so short. . . ."

"I do know," she assured him, soul lightening some in spite of the agonizing wait. "I feel it, too."

"Why have I been so stupid? So stubborn? I've wasted all this time, and now he might—"

"No. We're not going to think the worst," she said firmly. "Let's sit down, and I want you to tell me what happened." Maybe if she got him into agent mode he'd have something to grab onto, be able to pull it together. A scattered, devastated Michael frightened her more than she'd ever dreamed possible.

"That kid, Cory. The one Bastian has been seeing. Dietz got to the kid, fed him a story about how Dietz was FBI and Bastian was a criminal they were after." Michael gave a bitter laugh. "Can you believe that shit? Our Bastian, a fugitive? But the whelp bought it and agreed to get Bastian to the hotel tonight so the FBI could collar him. Dietz had promised the kid five grand for his cooperation."

"I'm sure Dietz made it sound legit. He likely even had authentic-looking FBI identification."

"Probably. Anyway, we kept listening after Bastian said to call off the op. A gut feeling on my part, I guess. We heard Cory get suspicious of the story he'd been fed, and finally confess his role to Bastian. They got out of the motel room, but Dietz's men arrived. Cory got away and called our private emergency number. Bastian killed one of the two men Dietz sent, but was shot in the thigh. He ran, and Dietz's main henchman, Tio, pursued. He cornered Bastian, beat the hell out of him, and was about to shoot him in the head when I got there."

"And you stopped him."

"I blew the bastard's fucking brains out."

"Good," she said fiercely. "I'm glad."

He nodded and fell silent, but kept a tight hold of her hand. Relating the story had done the job, giving him the chance to compose himself. She didn't have to be told how important appearing strong was to a man like Michael. Even if she knew the truth.

He was a kind man with a huge capacity for love. For hurt and grief. He might not want anyone to know, but Katrina did.

And that just made her fall deeper in love with him than ever.

Ten

Almost three hours with no word. Ozzie and Willis had arrived a couple of hours ago, and all three men had finally succumbed to exhaustion and were dozing in their chairs.

Next to Michael, Katrina was listening to his even breathing when McKay walked in and gave her a small smile. "Shall we wake up these guys? I have some news that will put their minds at ease."

"Thank God," she said. Turning, she gently shook Michael's shoulder. "Hey, sweetie? Wake up. Michael?"

He stirred, blinked. "What?"

"Taylor has news." She nudged Ozzie's foot with her toe. "Guys, wake up."

The three men straightened, coming instantly awake when they saw McKay standing there. Michael gripped Katrina's hand.

"How is he?"

McKay's gaze swept them all. "Barring any further complications, he's going to completely recover." His tone was guarded but optimistic. "He's critical but stable. I expect to be able to move him out of intensive care tomorrow."

Collective relief sucked all the tension from the room like a giant vacuum. Now that the main fear was behind them, Katrina imagined they were all like balloons deflating. Terror had been their air, and now there wasn't much to hold them up, tired as they were.

"Thank Christ," Michael whispered, running a hand through his hair.

"Bastian was very lucky," McKay continued. "He was beaten, but sustained no serious internal injuries. He does have a concussion from a blow to his temple, but no sign of swelling on his brain. The nicked femoral artery was the life-threatening injury, and it has been successfully repaired."

"How long until he's recovered?" Katrina asked.

"A couple of weeks. He's going to be sore as hell for a few days and he'll need to take it easy on that leg, but he's in great physical condition, which will speed healing." McKay paused. "My main concern at this point is who will see to his care once I release him. I believe Bastian lives alone."

"He'll be coming home with me," Michael said firmly. "He'll have all the care he needs."

"All right. He'll be on pain meds and antibiotics. I'll make sure he has plenty of both when he leaves here, which should be in a couple of days."

Michael stood. "Can we see him?"

"For a few minutes—just two people at a time. He won't know you're there, anyway. After that, go home and get some rest. I'm here all night and I'll keep a close eye on him."

"Doc, thanks for everything." Michael stuck out his hand and McKay shook it.

"That's why you pay me the big bucks." He nodded at the others. "See you all later."

After the doctor left, Ozzie spoke up. "Why don't you two go first?"

Michael didn't argue, just led Katrina out of the room and down the hallway toward a set of double doors marked INTENSIVE CARE UNIT. Katrina had never been back there before, and after Bastian was released, she hoped she never had cause to visit again. Especially when they walked into their friend's cubicle and she got a good look at him.

She didn't know how it was possible for anyone to be that pale and still have a pulse. The ugly purple knot on the side of his head stood in stark contrast to the surrounding white skin. The bruises hidden by his gown must be just as bad. His breathing was so shallow, his chest barely moved, but at least he was managing on his own.

"God," Michael rasped, moving to his friend's side. "He looks . . ."

"I know. But he's not." She went to stand on the other side of the bed and laid a hand on Bastian's, careful to avoid the IV needle. "He's going to be fine."

"He almost died." His jaw clenched, rage warring with love as he gazed down at Bastian. "I haven't made good on my promise yet, but I will. I swear I'm going to find that foul piece of shit and I'm going to kill him. Whatever it takes."

"He knows," she said softly. "But what he needs most is TLC. I vote we make sure he gets plenty of that."

Michael raised dark eyes to hers. "I couldn't agree more."

A knock interrupted and Ozzie strode inside, a clear plastic bag in hand. "Boss? I've got something to show you." He thrust it at Michael, who took it.

"A motel card key," he said, peering at the object inside. "From the Rest Right out on I-35."

"The cleanup crew found that in Tio's wallet."

His entire body stiffened and his eyes hardened. "Are we ready to roll?"

"Damned straight. You coming?"

"Try to stop me."

"Wouldn't think of it."

Michael started out, pausing long enough to give Katrina a quick kiss. "I'll have Simon send the car for you. You'll go to my place and stay there, and we'll worry about your stuff later. I don't want any more arguments about this."

"You won't get any," she assured him. "I'm stubborn, not stupid." She wasn't about to make herself a target for Dietz because of foolish pride.

"I'll see you at home."

He walked out with Ozzie and she stared after him, the word "home" making her feel fuzzy and strange, but good. Great, actually. She was about to share her life with two exciting, dynamic men, if Bastian was willing to give it a shot.

She, for one, was going to do her part to convince him.

"Save your strength, handsome," she told his sleeping form. "With any luck, you'll need it."

The cold rage twisting Michael's insides needed an outlet. One in the shape of a tall, sandy-haired, average-looking man who was really Satan in disguise. For months, he'd done nothing but dream of creative ways to kill Dietz, prolonging the torture indefinitely. In reality, he'd probably have to settle for a method far quicker and less satisfying, but at least the vermin would be out of everyone's misery.

At the motel, Michael and a handful of agents converged on the room registered to Tio under a false name. Surely they'd catch a break this time.

Michael nodded, motioning to Kelly with his gun. Inside, a light was on, but there was no movement. The two of them positioned themselves on the other side of the door, and Michael held up a hand, starting the count on three. *Two. One.*

It took two solid kicks to break in the door, and then he was in, Blaze and four more agents trailing right after them. Nothing but an empty room greeted them, bed made, the place neat as a pin. The only evidence that anyone had been there was a white sheet of folded paper lying on top of the cheap desk. Michael stalked over, saw his name printed on the outside, whipped it open, and began to read.

You're always one step behind, aren't you, Ross? Did you honestly think I would be politely waiting here when Tio failed to return? I hope he killed your Bastian, and made him suffer before he pulled the trigger. If not, he'll die yet, screaming in agony—and so will you.

Crushing the paper in his hand, he stood fighting the overwhelming urge to destroy everything in sight. But that wouldn't help find the bastard, and it wouldn't make Bastian recover faster.

"Michael?" Blaze ventured.

"It's a taunt, of course. The one useful thing to glean from it is he doesn't know for sure whether Tio was successful in killing Bastian, and we're going to keep it that way. I want a tight lid kept on that information, at least for now."

Blaze looked thoughtful. "That's just good common sense."

"Which means Bastian is going to be bound to the estate for a while, even after he recovers. No going out, period."

Blaze rolled his eyes. "And he's going to *love* that."

"He doesn't have a choice."

After the other men had left the small room, Blaze clapped a hand on his friend's shoulder. "We'll get him, Michael," Blaze said with absolute conviction.

"Yes. And when we do? He's going to regret the day he fucked with me and my family."

That's how he viewed Katrina, Bastian, and all his agents, he realized. His family. To love and protect.

God have mercy on you, Robert. Because that's His job.

Not mine.

Awareness returned by slow degrees.

Strange silence, punctuated by soft beeping. Weird smells.

Then he realized he was a person. Alive. So there should be a body attached to his floating brain, right? He tried to wiggle something. Anything. With no results for the longest time. He wanted to cry out, but his mouth refused to work. Where was everyone? Had he been abandoned?

Or worse . . . was he dead? Was this the afterlife? Was he doomed to have only a consciousness drifting aimlessly in space, unable to cry out? No. He couldn't bear that. Give him heaven or hell, but not this *nothingness*.

"Bastian?"

Frantic, he tried to find the voice. *Where are you?* he shouted, but just in his mind. Or so he thought.

"Easy. I'm here. You're okay."

No, he wasn't. If he was, he'd be able to—

A touch, just there. On his arm. Arm? And a gentle hand stroking his hair. So good.

The touches seemed to spark his nerve endings, and a tiny thread of light awakened his body from his head to his toes. *I'm not dead! God, what's wrong with me?*

With great effort, he concentrated on forming a question. "Wh-what . . ."

"It's me, Katrina. You're at the compound, honey. In the hospital. Do you remember getting shot? Can you open your eyes?"

He worked at opening his eyes. Remembering could come later, when his body was functioning better. His lids were heavy, but after a few moments, he found himself wincing at bright light, squinting to relieve the pain in his head. To focus.

"Head hurts," he informed her. Was that where he had been shot?

"Oh, sweetie. I'm afraid that's only the beginning." A soft hand caressed his face. "Can you see me?"

Clouds of dark red hair swam in his vision. A beautiful face came into focus. A face dominated by worried blue eyes.

"Katrina."

"Yes." The blue eyes crinkled in a smile.

"Don't . . . remember."

"You will—don't worry. You had surgery and you're on good drugs."

"Tired."

"Then sleep. You're okay now."

"I am?"

"Yes."

He must've slept, because the next thing he knew, he awoke for real, fully aware, with a vague recollection of Katrina being there and talking to him in soothing tones. Had he dreamed her presence out of wishful thinking?

One thing he hadn't been dreaming, then or now, was the throbbing agony in his head, torso, and thigh. Three spots of pounding misery, shouting the news to the rest of his body that something awful as fuck had happened. Car wreck? Bar brawl?

No, wait. Something about Cory.

He'd been with Cory. In a motel room.

Shot. Bastian had been shot, and ran. What happened? It was all a jumble in his mind.

With great effort, he opened his eyes and waited as his surroundings came into focus. Hospital room. Probably at the compound. His gaze strayed to his bedside, where a familiar man was sprawled in a chair, snoring lightly. Bastian had never beheld a more welcome sight.

"M-Michael." Jesus, his throat sounded like he'd gargled with asphalt. "Michael?"

Dark lashes fluttered open, and the man's eyes widened as he bolted upright. "Thank God you're awake. How do you feel?" His friend scooted his chair closer, laid a hand on Bastian's arm.

"Chewed up and spit out," he managed. "Hurts."

Michael's expression softened. "I know it does, buddy. I can give you a hit of morphine if you'd like."

"Please."

The other man picked up a device and punched a button on it. In seconds, Bastian felt the stuff flow through his veins, wrapping him in a nice layer of cotton. With the receding of the pain, the memories returned.

"Tio," he gasped. "He was going to kill me."

"That's one asshole who won't hurt anyone ever again," Michael growled.

"He pointed his gun at me, and I heard a gunshot. I thought I was dead."

"That was me blowing his head off. And you're going to be fine."

"Thanks," he said quietly. "I owe you."

"Cut that shit out. If I had protected you better, he couldn't have gotten to you. That's a mistake I won't repeat."

Bastian started to shake his head and instantly regretted the movement. After the bed stopped spinning, he said, "You can't protect me. You won't always be around, and—"

"Listen to me. I'm going to do a hell of a lot better job because when McKay springs you, you're coming home with me."

"I—what?" He blinked at Michael in confusion.

"I'm moving you to the estate. I've already taken the liberty of moving most of your clothes, and the other stuff you can sort later."

His heart stuttered, joy and trepidation surging through him at once. With a dash of irritation joining the party. "Wait. I didn't agree to this."

"Yes, you did, the second I saw you bleeding out and beaten half to death," he said, voice catching with emotion. "When I realized I could lose you and I knew real, honest-to-God fear for the first time in my life. When I finally understood that you own part of my heart and if I did lose you, I'd never recover."

Stunned, Bastian stared at the man who meant more to him than any other and was so afraid he was misunderstanding. Making more out of Michael's words than his friend intended. Strong fingers enclosed his own, and he looked down at them, wondering if the morphine was tripping him out.

"I think . . . you're going to have to spell it out."

Michael nodded, expression earnest. "Okay. First, I'm so sorry from the depths of my soul that I hurt you. But I was scared of the fact that I was capable not only of wanting a man sexually, but of having real feelings for him."

"Any man?"

"No. Just you. I set out to prove what a big stud I am with the ladies, thinking my thing for you was a strange curiosity that would wear off. But that's the thing about love—it won't be denied and it doesn't care about gender."

"I—You love me?" he croaked.

"Yes, dammit! Shit, I suck at this." He sighed.

Bastian couldn't help but smile a little. "You're doing all right."

"There's something else, though. Or some*one* else, I should say."

"Katrina." Closing his eyes, he waited for the ax to drop. "Of course, if you two have feelings for each other, it would be the easier choice for you."

"What if I don't have to choose? What if none of us did?"

That got his attention again. Fired his imagination. He opened his eyes and studied Michael, wondering how many more surprises the man would bestow. "Meaning we all try to make it work together? Katrina mentioned the possibility, but I never thought you'd go for it."

"Me, either, but we were both wrong." Enthusiasm lit his voice. "That's what I wanted to talk to you about the other day, when you all but threw me out. Not that I blamed you."

Well, hell. If he'd just heard the man out—but that was in the past. "And?"

"I know Katrina has feelings for you, and that you two have been getting close. I know that you fucked her in her office."

He couldn't help but flinch. "Should I apologize?"

"No. She loves you, just as I do. She's been here, right at your side, for most of the past twenty-four hours. I had to make her go home."

They both loved him. He tried to wrap his mind around it. Slowly, happiness began to bloom. "And where's home for her?"

"At the estate." He held Bastian's gaze.

All at once, Bastian remembered. "She asked me not to give up on the three of us. But when I asked her who she'd pick if she had to decide between you and me, she couldn't answer."

"Because she *couldn't* choose. She told me after. It's both of us or neither."

"I feel the same way," he said. "Once, I could've chosen between you and her, but not anymore. Somehow, she worked her way into my heart and stayed there."

"Mine, too." Michael paused. "What about Cory?"

"What about him?"

"You kept seeing that twink," Michael pointed out, a little sad. "You fucked him even though it wasn't necessary to go that far for the op, and you kept him around."

"I was still raw and I thought I needed to get over you. I figured Katrina was just wishing for a relationship between us all that couldn't happen. Can you blame me?"

"No. There's no point in hashing over that. Just tell me you're going to stop seeing him and I'll be happy. And don't forget the dumbass almost got you killed."

"I'm not going to see him anymore, but I did like him." Michael curled his lip, and Bastian reveled in the man's unguarded moment of sheer jealousy. Nothing on earth had ever made him feel higher than that single outward sign of possessiveness.

Definitely not the morphine.

"How is Cory?" he asked in sudden alarm. "He got away, right?"

"Yeah. He's staying in one of the extra living quarters until we get Dietz."

"Oh. Good."

"Enough about the twink."

"Okay."

In spite of all the happy revelations, he yawned. Damn, he was scared he'd wake up later and realize he'd dreamed this conversation.

"Go to sleep, buddy. You've earned the rest."

"Michael?"

"Hmm?"

"I love you."

"I know," he said gruffly. "Sleep."

Bastian smiled and let exhaustion pull him under.

Katrina walked into Bastian's hospital room on the third morning following his shooting. His face immediately brightened on seeing her, and her pulse did a funny tango. The man was a jade-eyed, golden-haired god sporting an engaging grin that never failed to make her feel cherished.

"Hey, beautiful! Is McKay letting me out of here?"

"Soon. Probably this afternoon." Leaning over, she gave him a slow, lingering kiss and then took a seat by the bed. "And only because we promised to make you take it easy at home."

"I don't care, as long as I'm out of here. I know I can't get in yet, but I want to sit by the pool. And drink a beer," he said, practically drooling.

"Not until you're off the pain meds."

"Okay, I'm officially off."

She laughed. "Doesn't work that way, champ. If you don't take your pill, you'll be crying in that beer in a few hours."

"Damn," he pouted. He squirmed a little, plucking at the sheet on his lap.

"What's wrong?"

"Nothing. I'm just uncomfortable."

"Why, do you need to use the bathroom?" The catheter had come out yesterday, and he had to use crutches to go anywhere. He still needed help getting on his feet, and the action caused his leg a lot of pain.

"No." Two red spots appeared on his cheeks.

"Are you going to make me play guessing games? What's wrong with you?"

"I'm having a slight *problem* if you must know. Jesus, is nothing sacred?"

"What kind of—Oh." Noting the rigid outline under the sheet, she smiled. "I can help you with that, you know."

"How? We're in a hospital."

"A private one, owned by Michael. What's McKay going to do—throw us out?"

"Yeah, but . . . what if a nurse walks in?"

"She'll walk back out in a hurry, I suppose." She made a face. "If it's the same one from yesterday, it'll be the most exciting thing that's happened to her all year."

His eyes rounded, and she could tell he was getting on board with the idea. "You're serious."

"Very. Here, let Nurse Brandt make an assessment of your condition." Tugging the sheet from his grasp, she pulled it down and folded it over his knees. The thin gown did nothing to hide the erection making a tent at his groin. Lifting the material, she exposed his rosy cock, the tip weeping tiny pearls. He smelled manly but clean and soapy, and she knew he must've had a sponge bath.

Grasping the base, she bent and licked the droplets, eliciting a swift groan from him. "You're my captive, you know that?" Another lick. "You can't go anywhere or do anything to stop me from taking what I want. And make no mistake, I've been wanting to taste you again, badly."

"Yes." His eyes rolled in pleasure.

"Does this turn you on? Knowing we could be caught?"

"Fuck, yes! Suck me." He tried to thrust his hips, but winced in pain.

"No, let me do the work," she scolded. "Can't have you aggravating those injuries."

She suckled the bulbous head first, tonguing the sensitive slit, catching more drops. She began to take him deeper, making him wet and slippery. Pumped him some at the base as she sucked, driving him insane. Then she swallowed him to the root and manipulated his balls, relishing the velvety sac rolling in her fingers. Loving his moans of pleasure.

She knew he was close when his balls tightened and his breath came in sharper bursts. He buried a hand in her hair and urged her on, moving his hips as much as he could despite her telling him to be still.

"Close, baby," he panted. "Christ, yes! So good."

Laving and sucking, she bobbed up and down on him faster, pulled harder. Apparently he liked it a shade rough, because he stiffened and gave a couple of seconds' warning.

"Coming!"

His cock jerked in her mouth and she drank the hot, salty-sweet cum down, not wanting to miss a drop. She continued to work him, bringing him down. Then she licked him clean, released his softening shaft, and replaced his gown.

"Better?" She grinned at him and licked her lips.

"I think you sucked my brains out through my dick." His head flopped back on the pillows. "Kinda disappointed we didn't get caught, though."

"I knew it! You're a thrill seeker."

"And maybe a bit of an exhibitionist."

"There's always next time," she suggested. "We can make certain we're seen, if you want."

He looked intrigued. "And who would we let see us? Not Simon or Mrs. Beasley, because eeww."

"What about Michael's head of security at the estate. What's his name?"

"John. Yeah, he's hot—and kinky, I've heard." He said the last on a teasing note.

"Honestly, does Michael surround himself with any other type than hot and kinky? Besides Simon and Mrs. B."

Bastian closed his eyes, and a comfortable silence descended. He was prone to drop off to sleep and would until he regained his strength. She didn't mind. In fact, she loved sitting with him, keeping him company. In a few minutes, however, he opened his eyes.

"Can I ask you a question?" He did sound tired, but he was fighting it.

"Sure."

"How is it that you show such a cool, classy exterior and secretly have the soul of a sensualist? Where does that come from?"

"You mean the soul of a wanton slut?" she countered.

His lips turned up. "Was trying to be nice."

"Don't knock yourself out on my account." This was good between them, she decided. There was something about Bastian that made her feel as though she'd known him much longer than she had. They'd been working together for a while now, but lots of people shared a work environment without getting close. But once she and Bastian had really begun to interact on a personal level, the connection had been there, ready and waiting to be nurtured.

He was still looking at her, waiting for an answer. Watching his reaction, she said, "I have three parents."

"You mean your folks divorced and one is a stepparent?" His brows furrowed.

It was always fun to see people figure out the truth. "No, I mean that I have three parents. One mother and two fathers. Really spiced up those PTA meetings, I can tell you."

"Oh, my God! No way," he said, incredulous. "I've never actually known anybody who was raised by parents in a ménage relationship. Christ, I'll bet you were teased unmercifully as a child."

"Kids can be cruel," she agreed. Some of those memories were deeply painful. "That's why they eventually decided to homeschool me. I guess that's why I sort of hold myself apart from people until I get to know them. You and Michael were exceptions."

"I'm glad you trusted us enough to let us in," he said with feeling. "So your parents are still together?"

"Yes," she said, smiling. "And so in love it's nauseating. They are proof that it can work, despite the crappy odds and the stigma attached by society."

"You want what they have."

She looked down at their hands, which had somehow become entwined. "I thought I did have it, once. Things didn't work out."

"From your voice, I'm guessing that's an understatement," he said quietly. "Want to talk about it?"

She shrugged. "I don't mind. We were in our early twenties, and when you're pushing forty, that seems like a lifetime ago."

"No kidding," he agreed. "You had two male partners?"

"One man, but the other was a woman." Surprise registered on Bastian's face. "I loved them both and I thought they loved me, but the dynamic was doomed from the start. Our downfall began when Brenda wanted to get pregnant."

"Uh-oh."

She nodded. "You'd think I would've seen this one coming a mile off, wouldn't you? But no, I was so excited. I thought I should get pregnant next so our children could be close in age. Joe thought it was a good idea to wait until after Brenda had her baby before we tried for another one. You can probably fill in the ending."

"Let me see." He pretended to think hard. "Joe and Brenda bonded over the pregnancy and changed their minds about raising their child in a ménage relationship. They broke your heart."

"You get the prize." God, she'd been devastated at the time. "Getting over it took years. But I've always believed I could have what my parents do and that someday I'd want to try again. Just not with another woman involved, ever."

"I can certainly understand that." He grinned at her. "You won't have to worry about me or Michael wanting to get pregnant."

"Idiot." She leaned over and brushed his lips with hers, then deepened the kiss. He tasted sweet, minty, and the man knew how to use his tongue. She couldn't wait to learn its other talents.

Breaking the kiss, she laid her head on his shoulder, careful not to hurt his healing bruises. His arm came around her, held her close against his solid body, and she felt it.

The tenuous thread winding between them was like a tender green shoot pushing through new soil. Growing stronger with each passing hour. A thought hit her: where the three of them were concerned, Bastian was their glue. Their quiet strength.

One man was forged steel, and the other was the only fire hot enough to make him bend.

Now she just had to make them hers, for keeps.

Eleven

"Are you comfortable?"

"Yes, thanks."

"Need anything before I go?"

"No, thanks."

"More coffee? A bagel?"

"I'm good."

"I don't think so. You're not eating enough, and—"

"Michael," Bastian growled. "Go. To. Work! Because if you don't, so help me, I won't be held responsible for where I shove this crutch."

Michael eyed his grouchy friend. "I've been hovering too much, huh?"

"For the entire past week since you brought me home! You're both driving me crazy!"

"Hey!" From her spot at the breakfast table, Katrina scowled at Bastian over the top of her newspaper. "Before lunch, you'll be bored out of your mind and wanting us to come home."

"Fat lot of good it'll do me when neither of you will touch me. And blow jobs don't count," he grumbled. "I even have to sleep by myself because you guys are afraid one of you will bump my thigh in the night."

Katrina's eyes narrowed. "What do you mean, they don't count? The last time I checked, 'Oh, God, suck harder. Take it all' wasn't a complaint."

Oh, boy. Time to make a tactful retreat. "Well, since you're all set here, we'll give you some peace and quiet. If you need anything—"

"I know. Simon and Mrs. Beasley are here. Have a nice day." Their lover went back to moping over his cold coffee.

He raised his brows at Katrina in a signal to get moving. She folded her paper and followed him out through the living room. Simon met them in the foyer.

"The car is waiting, sir."

"Great."

"Sir, if I may be so bold?"

He stifled a sigh. "Go ahead."

"Sir, if you don't take matters in hand, I shall be forced to seek other employment." Simon sniffed, looking down his regal nose at Michael. "There's nothing wrong with that lad that a sound buggering won't remedy."

Michael choked, and beside him, Katrina giggled. "I'm sure your resignation won't be necessary. Bastian will be better than new in no time."

"Very good, sir."

He beat a retreat out the front door and headed for the car. "Jesus."

As they climbed into the back, Katrina said, "Simon's got the problem pegged, you know. Our guy is craving some attention that has nothing to do with his injury."

"I know. He's like a grumpy porcupine."

"If this is the way he gets when he has to go without for a few days, it's a good thing there's two of us."

For some reason, he felt it necessary to defend his own libido. "I have just as many needs as he does. I'm just as sexually active."

She gave him a knowing grin. "Yes, honey. You're a virile He-Man beyond compare."

"See that you don't forget it."

They enjoyed the rest of the ride together, the mood lightened some. So what if they'd been forced to delay consummating their relationship? Bastian was alive and healing, and the three of them were together. His friend would be smiling soon, his grumpiness a thing of the past.

And when Michael caught Dietz and sent him to hell, their lives would be perfect.

At the compound's gate, the day guard waved them through. When the car stopped, he got out first and gave a hand to Katrina, pointedly ignoring the stare of one curious agent who glanced back and forth between them. He didn't give a rat's ass what his employees were saying and knew Bastian would hold his own, but he worried about the effect on Katrina.

"Does it bother you that they're probably talking about us?" he asked as they disappeared inside.

"No. Remember, I was raised in a nontraditional environment and I have a thick skin when it comes to those who don't understand."

Earlier in the week, she'd told him about her parents' loving three-way partnership. It had made sense to him then, how she could be so accepting of alternative lifestyles. She was a wonderfully sexual woman, open even to exploration and play with other partners, and he felt like he'd won the fucking lottery.

"But I'm willing to bet your parents don't work together," he pointed out. "And one of them isn't the boss at work over the others."

"True. But I still don't give a shit what anyone thinks."

"That's my baby."

He'd worried about the work angle, but if any of his people didn't like it, they could hit the road. SHADO didn't even officially exist, for fuck's sake, so who were they going to complain to? The president?

At the corridor that led them in opposite directions, he gave her a kiss and went to tackle the pile of crap waiting in his office. The stack was twice as big as normal with both Bastian and Michael out for the past few days, and Bastian's return on hold indefinitely. Common sense would dictate getting a temporary replacement to handle Bastian's load—either Ozzie or Blaze would do a fine job—but he couldn't bring himself to make the call.

Cursing himself for going soft, he dove into the pending cases on his desk. Checked top secret status reports from the FBI and CIA on some of America's most-wanted criminals, spoke to the agents in charge for updates. Three of the fugitives had been captured by SHADO, two more busts were imminent, and the president had phoned to check on Bastian's recovery and praise Michael again for "neutralizing" Tio. All of which heralded a good day in store.

He'd worked through half of his 146 e-mails when Blaze walked into his office without knocking. He peered at his friend around his computer monitor and immediately tensed upon seeing the man's serious expression. "What's up?"

"Randall Burns wants to talk," he announced. "He's decided our accommodations aren't up to his standards."

Michael snorted. "Poor little felons just don't get a fair shake these days. I assume he has a sad story to share in hopes of improving his future?"

"So he says, but he won't spill it to anyone but you."

"Fantastic. I knew this day was going too well." Leaning back in his chair, he crossed his arms over his chest. "And I suppose he wants a golden ass wiper installed in his cell in exchange for this tidbit? Maybe a steak dinner thrown in?"

"He wants to walk."

For about two seconds he stared at Blaze, then burst out laughing. "Sure. Right. I'll put that on my agenda, right next to launching my 'Hit Men Are People, Too' campaign."

It took him a few more seconds to realize Blaze wasn't laughing. And that he'd closed the door.

Cold washed over him and he sobered, studying his friend. "Okay. You know more than you're saying. Tell me."

Blaze remained standing, one hand gripping the back of the guest chair in front of him. "He claims he can give you Maggie's killers."

The breath left Michael's lungs with the force of a blow from a sledgehammer. He sagged in his chair, one palm pressed to his chest. Maybe then he could hold his heart together, keep it from finally falling apart. His voice emerged as a hoarse whisper. "He's a fucking liar."

"Could be. But you're the only one who can find out because he won't say jack to us. We've tried, believe me. Nobody wanted to come to you, upset you, if he was spouting a load of bullshit."

He took a few deep breaths, tried to compose himself. "I appreciate that. You guys did what you could. Where is he?"

"In the interrogation room."

"All right. Let's go hear what this asshole has to say." He stood on shaky legs.

"Michael . . . what are you going to do if he's telling the truth?"

Wasn't that the million-dollar question? He had no answer, and Blaze didn't press him as they rode the elevator down and strode through the maze of corridors to reach the small, sterile space where Burns was waiting.

The man was sitting at the sole table, hands folded on top. To Michael, he looked like any average man—a coach, a car salesman, a teacher, your next-door neighbor. There wasn't much remarkable about him, save for the fact that he'd been hired by Dietz to kill Bastian and had attempted to follow through. Burns was an amateur, and as Michael slowly approached the table, flanked by Blaze and Ozzie, he got the impression that's all the man would ever be. A loser looking for a quick buck.

Michael took a seat at the table, folded his arms on top. He stared dispassionately at Burns for several long moments, letting the man sweat. As most dogs do, Burns looked away first, unable to hold his stare. Michael took grim satisfaction from the telling body language.

"Talk," he ordered Burns.

"What are you going to do for me?" The man's attempt at bravado was spoiled when he wiped the perspiration from his upper lip.

"Doesn't work that way. You're at a disadvantage. You want something from me, not the other way around. You want to deal, give me what you've got and I'll see what I can do. Otherwise, you can rot in your cell for the rest of your miserable life—where nobody can hear you scream."

Burns licked his lips nervously. He seemed to consider, but must've known his captor wasn't bluffing. "You had a wife who got mugged last year. Stabbed to death for her purse."

He longed to crush the man's throat in his bare hands. *Wait for the correct target.*

"Tell me something I don't know."

"How about this—it wasn't no mugging. It was a *job*."

The statement blasted through him, left a ragged, bleeding hole. Old grief and helplessness washed over him, through him. Rage. Some shred of the steely agent clung to the necessity of finishing this interview. Because now he had a chance to learn what had really happened to Maggie.

"Don't you think I considered that possibility? No evidence of a higher plot was ever found."

"That's because you weren't *supposed* to find it. There's proof." He paused, appearing a bit more confident. "Did you know the gas station next door to where she was killed has a security camera pointed at the parking lot?"

Michael shook his head. "Already checked. The manager at the station claimed the camera wasn't working during the week in question. The tapes were blank."

"That's what the manager, Gene, told you and the cops. Funny how he ended up dead four days later, killed during a home burglary. Bet nobody told you that."

Nobody had. Michael's hands clenched into fists. "Go on."

"Gene's place was torn up, but hardly anything was taken. Hell, he didn't have nothing worth stealing, 'cept one thing. Three guesses."

"A tape. With my wife's murder on it."

"A tape showing *somebody's* murder, but I never saw it. Just know what he told me."

"Why the hell should I believe you talked to this Gene guy about this tape? How do you know him?"

"Gene is—was—my cousin." Burns leaned forward and lowered his voice, as though there was a reason to keep quiet. "He told me a woman was killed right next door to the station and that the deal smelled dirty to him. Turns out he was right. Some scary dude came to him, demanding the video that night before the cops even thought to talk to him. He didn't want no part of that, see? To the scary dude and then the cops he says, 'No tape.' He takes the thing home, hides it good, and tells me all this the day before he's whacked. Me, I don't want no part of it, either, and I decide it's healthier to forget all about it."

"And at what point did you connect any of this to me?"

"Your guards were talkin' about you. Ain't shit down here to do but listen. I heard them sayin' you seemed happier, and how worried they was about you when your woman got mugged and knifed to death last year over on Holland Drive. Couldn't be two different women who done got killed over there in the same way."

The blood was rushing in Michael's ears. He was vaguely aware of a steadying hand on his shoulder. "Where is the tape now?"

"I expect it's still in my cousin's house someplace. I don't think the scary dude found what he was lookin' for."

"Have you ever killed anyone, Burns? Don't bother to lie, because I'll find out within the hour."

"No. I took the job on Chevalier because I needed the money, pure and simple. But I fucked it up like I've done most everything else."

That, he could believe.

"Mostly I provide a little weed, some blow, to a few clients to make ends meet. Or I did. I won't do nothin' like that again if you let me go."

He seriously doubted that. "I'm going to need your cousin's address."

Burns rattled it off. "Gene's sister lives there now." He flinched as Michael stood. "What do I get if the tape has what you need on it?"

With a cold smile, he said, "You get to live, Burns."

He walked out, his men on his heels.

Mae Burns was a thin woman in her mid-thirties with stringy, unkempt hair who looked like life had beaten her with a hammer, then shit on her for good measure. She granted them entry into the house with a minimum of fuss, considering she'd initially demanded to see their warrant. When Michael presented her with ten crisp one-hundred-dollar bills and a promise not to disturb so much as a dust bunny, she'd pocketed the cash, stepped aside, and offered them all a beer. Which they'd regretfully declined.

"Miss Burns, the item we're looking for is most likely the same one your brother's killers were after the night they broke in. We believe it could still be hidden here, and if so, you could be in danger."

"What's everyone so hot to find? My brother led the most average, boring life imaginable," she said doubtfully. "He was hardly the type to inspire intrigue or passion."

"Sometimes they find us." Quickly, he related her cousin's tale about the tape allegedly showing a murder, her brother being visited by dangerous men who wanted it, and his lie that the tape was blank. He left out the part about the victim being his wife.

"Randall claims your brother was frightened because of what was in his possession. I speculate he kept it from the cops partly out of fear of reprisal from the men who'd come calling. Though in the end, his silence didn't buy his life."

"Gene never said anything to me about any of this, but he wouldn't have."

"Why's that?"

"He was a card-carrying member of the good-old-boy system. What women don't know won't hurt them and all that."

Michael checked the urge to curl his lip in disgust. Maybe the man's prehistoric attitude had saved his sister. They'd never know for sure. "If it's all right with you, we'll get started and be out of your hair in no time."

She regarded them, head cocked like a bird. "Just out of curiosity, what will you do with this tape if you find it?"

"Hopefully identify the men who murdered the woman." *And make them pay* hung in the air, unspoken.

"That would be nice, wouldn't it? Go ahead," she said with a shrug. "Never have seen any strange tape, but knock yourselves out."

Michael, Blaze, Ozzie, and Willis spread themselves throughout the small house and began a methodical search. Michael started in the kitchen, opening every drawer, peering into the pantry. He looked in the cereal, flour, and sugar, knowing that it could be stashed inside a container, sealed in a plastic bag. He even searched in the freezer and refrigerator. Any nook or cranny of the appropriate size to hold a security video was fair game.

Next was the living room. Their searches would overlap, but that was okay. One person could see something another missed. On it went. The hall closet, the two small bedrooms and one bathroom, and the rest of the closets. Boxes and drawers were checked. The mattresses. They were out of options and standing in the deceased brother's bedroom when Ozzie blew out a frustrated breath and tilted his head back, staring at the ceiling.

"Damn, what a waste of . . ." Ozzie trailed off, brows rising.

"What?" Michael and the other two men followed his gaze. Straight to an air-conditioning vent high on the wall, near the ceiling. Ozzie fished a pocket knife from his pants and flipped out a blade.

"No way," Willis said.

Ozzie grabbed a chair from a small desk and positioned it under the vent. "Why not? Nobody ever thinks to look *up*."

He climbed on the chair, reached up, and used the blade to work at the screws, dropping each one into Michael's hand. Then he used it to pry the vent frame from the wall and lifted it out, handing it to Blaze.

He stuck his hand in the hole and made a face. "Nasty. They need a duct-cleaning service."

"They need to bulldoze the place and start over," Willis suggested.

"They need—wait." He twisted his arm deeper into the hole, and something rattled. "Hey, what do we have here?"

The rattle came from a plastic grocery bag. As his hand emerged, they saw it was wrapped around a small, rectangular object.

"Bingo," Ozzie crowed, climbing down from his perch. After putting away his knife, he unfolded the bag and drew out the object.

The black videotape seemed to glare at them all, daring them to learn its secrets. Michael's stomach did a slow roll. Very soon he might well learn the truth of what had happened to Maggie the night she never came home.

Ozzie studied the tape. "Jesus, the camera at the gas station must be, like, fifteen years old or more. Do we even have anything that will play this?"

Michael nodded. "Katrina will have the necessary equipment to get this on digital. She can probably get a better picture than these old things have, too."

The question was, now that he had the tape in his hand, could he stand to watch it?

On the way out, he thanked Mae Burns and handed her another four thousand. "Do you have other family, Miss Burns?"

The woman's eyes bulged at the unforeseen extra windfall. "I got a cousin in Seattle; she's been wanting me to come out for some time."

"Go visit her," he said. "Indefinitely."

Her mouth tightened in understanding. Beaten down she might be, but not stupid. "I'll do that. But . . . why so much money? I didn't ask for any."

"The woman on that tape was my wife, Miss Burns," he said quietly. "And she would've given you the shirt off her back if she could have. To catch her killers? It's a small price to pay."

Her wary expression softened. "She was one lucky lady. I hope you get them."

Michael nodded, though he knew Maggie hadn't been lucky at all. She'd loved him and had died knowing she didn't own Michael's heart. Nothing he ever did could make up for the pain he'd caused her.

But maybe, if he caught and punished her killers, he'd finally be free to love with his whole being. Without any lingering reservations.

And maybe he'd deserve for the two people he loved most to love him back.

Katrina was peering at a pinhole camera, wrestling with the tiny device to get it properly installed in a ballpoint pen, when her cell phone chirped a greeting from its spot on her worktable. Gingerly, she laid down the small parts of her project and bit down on a spurt of annoyance. Why did the phone always ring when she was in the middle of the most delicate tasks?

Looking at the display, however, jump-started her pulse. *Michael.* Wasn't he out of the building on a job? She hurried to pick up. "Hello?"

"It's me," he said shortly. "I'm bringing in an old VHS tape of questionable quality that supposedly contains important footage. Can you transfer it to digital and enhance it?"

"Of course I can. You're bringing it now?"

"Yes."

His tone was off. Something was wrong. "What's on the tape?"

"When I get there."

With that, he disconnected. Scowling at her phone, she did the same. Sometimes working with a boss who was also your lover wasn't all fun and games. She was just reaching for the fake pen again when the phone rang a second time. "Dammit. Hello?"

"It's Blaze," he said. "Has Michael called you?"

"He just did," she said in a tone that betrayed her irritation. "He wants me to copy and enhance some old tape. Where are you?"

"I went with them to find this tape. I'm riding in a different car than Michael, and we're on our way back. Has he given you any details about it?"

"No, and I'd appreciate if you let me know what the hell is going on."

"The footage is from a security camera positioned outside a gas station and allegedly shows his wife's murder."

Stunned, Katrina fell back in her chair. "How did you guys get this tape?"

"Long story. The thing is, one of our prisoners downstairs

tipped us off, and he claims Maggie's death was a hit, not a random mugging, and that the film will support his claim."

"Oh, my God."

"Yeah. Michael's putting up a badass front, but I know the man. He's one thread away from completely unraveling the sweater."

"And if it's true . . ."

"He's gonna lose his shit."

"I hate to say this because Michael's going to be pissed, but I think Bastian needs to be here," she suggested.

"As long as he's well enough to come, I agree. Besides, he's going to be ticked if he finds out Michael had to see what went down on this tape and we didn't tell him so he could be there."

"True. Okay, I'll call him. I know he'll come."

"Good. See you soon."

Quickly, she placed another call. Bastian answered on the second ring. "Hey, are you busy?"

He made a noise. "Sure. I'm sitting by the pool watching John swim naked, after which he's going to rise from the waves like a sea god, come over here, and have his nasty way with me. Not."

Any other time, she would've laughed at his apparent boredom and teased him about the fantasy scene. "Are you feeling well enough to take a ride to the compound?"

"Are you kidding? I'm about to fossilize here. When do you need me?"

"Now." After she finished explaining what was going on, he reacted pretty much the same as she had.

"Oh, Christ. I'll be there soon. Don't let them start that tape without me."

"I won't. I've got to transfer it to digital, anyway, so there's plenty of time."

"Okay. 'Bye, sweetheart."

Michael and his three top agents arrived minutes later, her lover handing over the tape. His eyes were anxious, haunted. She couldn't work with him and the others hovering, looking like accident victims, and she waved a hand at the group.

"Wait here if you want. I'm going to take this to my office, and I'll call you when I'm ready."

Without waiting for their protests, she disappeared into her office, praying Bastian was there by the time she was ready. No sense in prolonging this more than necessary.

At her desk, she stuck the tape into an old VCR and prepared to work her computer magic. Transferring the film wasn't really difficult, though. No, that part came when she had to enhance the images of Maggie Ross's murder in cold blood.

A hit. Not a mugging. Just as they'd been told by the prisoner below.

This was going to kill Michael. Grabbing a tissue from the box on her desk, she dabbed her eyes. She had to be composed before she went out there again. Not only for Michael, but for all three of them. Michael's seeing this would either tear them all apart or bring them closer than ever. A turning point.

With the video saved to her computer, there was nothing left to do but bring them in. Standing, she went to get them. To her relief, Bastian had arrived and was sitting, holding his crutches, next to Michael. Michael's expression was closed off, and everyone else's anxious.

"I was just telling Bastian how good he's getting around, hardly needing those anymore," Blaze remarked, trying to lighten the mood.

"I'm doing a ton better, ready to come back when the doc clears me. I'm hardly sore at all."

Bless his heart, he was trying, too. Unfortunately, their efforts fell on deaf ears. Michael stood and gestured toward the office.

"Are we ready?"

"Yes, but . . . this footage is very rough. Graphic. I wanted you to know before I play it."

"I figured it would be." Holding her gaze, he softened his tone. "But thank you."

They trailed into her office like a funeral procession and crowded around the monitor. Willis produced a chair for Bastian, which he gratefully accepted. She sat down and laid her hand on the mouse, cursor hovering over the PLAY button. The one small thanks she could give was that there was no sound, only video.

The film began with Maggie walking to her car about thirty yards from the camera, a purse over one shoulder, and carrying a sack of Chinese takeout. Since the camera was positioned under the eave of the gas station's roof, the angle was good, giving a bird's-eye view, but not so high that faces and other details couldn't be seen.

As the woman reached her car and pointed the little black box on her key ring to unlock it, two men approached from the right of the screen. One was a big man, holding an equally big knife.

"Holy fucking God," Bastian breathed, face pale. "Is that . . ."

No one moved or responded to his unspoken question. On the screen, Maggie turned briefly to see the men and dropped the sack of food, then scrambled for the door handle. She managed to jerk it open, but the shorter of the two men slammed it closed and spun her around, her back against the side of the car.

"We never knew there were two of them," Michael said, voice low. Strained. "Muggers don't work in pairs, or stop to taunt their victims. They grab and run."

And these two were definitely terrorizing her. The shorter man yanked away her purse, and the big one stepped close, holding the tip of the knife just under her sternum. It was clear he was speaking to her, but from the distance and at the angle he was standing, it might not be possible to get a transcript of the conversation.

Maggie shook her head rapidly, replying to him, her body language clear—she was begging for her life, terrified. She lunged to the side in an attempt to run, but the bigger man yanked her arm, slammed her into the car. His arm thrust forward and he plunged the blade into her stomach. Withdrew, stabbed her again in the side, as she twisted in his grasp.

"Mother of God," Ozzie whispered.

Maggie crumpled to the asphalt like a rag doll and writhed, dying, as the men walked off. Katrina closed the video. "That's basically it."

Michael didn't need to see his wife's struggle to phone for help, or watch her life drain away as she stopped moving. The woman was pronounced dead on the scene, the camera dutifully recording all of the sadness that came afterward with the paramedics, police, and eventually the coroner.

Without saying one single word, Michael rose and slowly walked out.

Bastian broke the silence first. "The big bastard was Tio, Dietz's lapdog."

"Dietz had Maggie killed," Blaze said hoarsely, running a hand down his face. "My God. He cold-bloodedly arranged a woman's death. Why? So he could take over SHADO while Michael was out mourning her?"

Bastian nodded. "I think you nailed it. Her murder was the first step of his big, insane plan to run his own little kingdom here. But he failed."

"But who's the other man in the video?" Ozzie wondered aloud. "Does he look familiar?"

"I wasn't watching him as much as I was her and the other one," Bastian admitted. The others agreed.

"I'll play the beginning, just until he comes into the picture." She ran the video again. When the man approached, she paused it. She didn't recognize him, but then again she didn't often come into contact with their targets. She just provided the surveillance equipment. "Any ideas?"

Blaze moved closer to the screen, frowning. "Go a little farther ahead. There's a spot where he faces the camera more." When she came to the place, he said, "There. This is the—Oh, shit!"

"What?"

"That's the guy who gunned down Michael a few weeks ago! He's the one I caught, who's been in the cell down below, cooling his heels."

"And if Michael recognized him just now?" Bastian asked.

They all shared a look filled with fear.

"Oh, fuck! Let's go."

Blaze took off running, followed by Ozzie and Willis. Katrina hung back with Bastian, frantic for Michael but not wanting to leave her other lover behind.

"Go ahead. I'll catch up."

"No, we'll go together. The others will get there first and he'll be fine."

She hoped. The two of them made good time, Bastian moving fast despite the crutches. She worried he'd aggravate his injuries, but that thought flew out of her head when they approached the cell and she got a look at the horrifying scene in front of them.

The cell was open, the three agents standing in a half circle around Michael and the suspect. The man was kneeling at Michael's feet, eyes crossed, staring at the muzzle of the hand canon pressed in the center of his forehead. He was babbling in terror.

"Please! I didn't kill her! It was Tio!"

The feral snarl transformed Michael's face into that of a man she'd never seen before.

"You're just as guilty, you worthless piece of shit. You went along with Dietz and Tio. You watched her die." He pressed the barrel harder into the man's head. "How does it feel to know your life is about to end? Will it hurt to have your brains splattered all over this cell, do you think?"

"No! Please. I didn't do it!" he shrieked. A dark, wet stain quickly spread across the front of his drab trousers.

Bastian maneuvered into the cell and the others moved to give him room to try to talk his friend down. "Michael, you don't want to do this."

"Oh, I think I do." His chest heaved with emotions raging out of control. The hatred in his eyes as he gazed at his prey was a truly frightening sight. "I blew off Tio's head a few days ago. Did you know that, worm? He looked shocked as fuck when the back of his head sprayed all over that dirty alley."

The man on his knees started to sob.

Balancing himself, Bastian slowly laid a hand on Michael's gun arm. "You killed Tio in my defense, to save my life," he said calmly. "Killing this scum, with him begging on his knees, drenched in his own piss, is not honorable. It would be murder, and you're not like him. You're not like Dietz or Tio."

"He stood there and did nothing while she died." His voice broke and the gun shook.

"Yes, and he has to face justice. But not this kind. You pull that trigger and you'll become everything you hate. Your life will be over and it won't be only yourself you've destroyed." Bastian paused to let that sink in. "Put the gun down, Michael. Let the Feds take custody of this creep. Choose life. Choose us."

Katrina held her breath, so scared for him. Bastian was right. If Michael did this, he'd destroy himself in the process.

One long minute passed. Michael's arm lowered, the weapon pointing at the floor. All of the rage seemed to drain out of him, leaving him spent. Hollow. He turned and left the cell, pausing only when Katrina took his hand.

Their entourage continued on, leaving the weeping prisoner alone again. In the elevator, Katrina whispered in Bastian's ear. "We need to take him home."

"Good idea."

Michael didn't protest, didn't speak a word as they led him straight from the building and climbed in the limo. Her eyes met Bastian's and she knew they were on the same wavelength.

Their tough, strong man needed them both tonight. This crisis had been a long time coming.

And together they would love him through it.

Twelve

*I nearly murdered a man in cold blood. I don't deserve to lead SHADO.
I don't deserve two wonderful lovers who look at me like I'm their world.*

He hadn't deserved Maggie. And she was dead.

He'd known her death was horrible, agonizing. But to see it played out in front of his eyes, to know she'd been murdered because of him was more than he could take. Too much. His mind had snapped, and when he'd recognized the other man on the video, he'd wanted only to torment and kill. How Bastian had gotten through the crimson haze to him was a mystery. He still felt disconnected. A stranger in his skin.

During the ride home, his lovers let him be. While he appreciated the silence, he didn't believe it would last. He wanted to crawl into a hole and never come out, but doubted they'd let him, especially after he'd completely lost it.

Or maybe they would pack and leave. He wouldn't blame them if they did.

"Come on, let's get you inside and upstairs," Bastian said, his tone brooking no argument.

They were home already? Simon met them in the foyer, his wrinkled face a study of concern, but Bastian shook his head and the old butler retreated. In a daze, Michael allowed himself to be hustled to his room—their room, if they still wanted to stay with him—and pushed onto the bed. He moved to the middle and they sat beside him, each one touching him, saying nothing for a long while. Katrina stroked his hair and Bastian untucked his dress shirt, pushed a hand underneath to rub his stomach.

The touches were soothing, and after a while, he realized they weren't going to lecture or barrage him with questions. They weren't offering sympathy, pity, or false cheer—all of which he would have rejected in an instant. They simply offered comfort, and he drank it in big gulps, like a man dying of thirst, while they waited. So patient with him.

"It's my fault," he said at last, the words like razor blades in his throat.

Katrina's voice was soft. "No. She was the victim of Dietz's power play, and you had no control over what he did. You couldn't have known his plans. He was good at putting on his mask of respectability when it suited him."

"If anything, it's *my* fault," Bastian interjected. His eyes were shadowed. "If I had accepted your job offer in the first place, he wouldn't have been in the position to—"

Michael cut that bullshit off. "If I can't claim fault, neither can you. We both know the reason you turned down the position back then was because I broke your heart by marrying Maggie. You couldn't stand the thought of working side by side with me after what I'd done, and I didn't blame you. By the time I knew I'd screwed up, it was too late. Or I believed it was. I didn't know what to do to fix things between us."

"What are you saying?" his friend asked.

"I loved Maggie as a friend, but not like you should love your wife—like she's your next heartbeat. Like you can't breathe without her. She deserved to be loved like that, and I took that chance from her," he said wretchedly. "I was selfish, and she paid for loving me. So did you."

"Michael, if Dietz had never hatched his plan and Maggie was alive, do you think you would still be married to her?" Bastian watched him carefully, as though waiting for his friend to realize something.

And when it came to him, the answer was simple.

"No," he said. It was like a curtain opening, showing the future behind door number three, had it ever been opened. After her death, he'd never paused to follow his relationship with her to its logical conclusion. "We couldn't make each other happy. We wouldn't have stayed together."

Bastian leaned over him, palm skimming up to his chest to rest in the center. "You see? She would've been free to find her special person and be happy, and I have no doubt it would have happened. Dietz is the one who took away her future, not you."

He considered that, and eventually gave in. "My brain knows that, but it's hard to let go of the guilt. I've carried it so long, I'm not sure how."

"By letting us love you," Katrina said. "What happened isn't your fault and you can't change any of it. Let go and embrace what you have now."

"And what you have now is pretty darned good." Bastian gave him a small smile, full of hope.

Michael glanced between them, a strange feeling building in his chest, right underneath Bastian's hand. The glow spread and seemed to envelop the three of them, vibrating with promise. And something more.

They were so beautiful, inside and out. He was a damned lucky man to be presented with a second chance, and he'd be a fool to let it pass by. "Touch me. Don't let me go."

Take me away from death, sadness, and pain. Make me feel worthy again.

"We've got you," Bastian whispered.

And then he bent and lowered his lips to Michael's, muffling his "mmmph" of surprise. He stiffened at first, then gradually gave way to the expert mouth claiming his. Bastian's lips were soft but firm, his tongue probing gently, seeking entrance. Michael didn't think twice, opening for him to allow the other man to taste and explore. He'd never dreamed it could feel so right, or that he could be aroused by kissing his best friend and be eager to do more. Much more.

But it was better than good, and he returned the kiss, their tongues dueling, Bastian enjoying his friend's spicy taste. The musky smell of his cologne, manly and clean, teased Michael's nose. His strong, hard muscles pressed Michael into the mattress. His cock responded, filled, wanting in on the action. He didn't want the kiss to end and when it did, he and Bastian were panting, proof of the other man's arousal rubbing against his thigh.

"My God, that was hot," Katrina said.

Bastian chuckled and reached around to playfully slap her on the ass. "Skin, honey? Pretty please?"

"Michael first. I want to drive him crazy until he begs for mercy."

"Mmm, let's make him scream. Does he know what he's gotten into, I wonder?"

"He'll find out soon enough."

Bastian started on the buttons of his shirt while Katrina pulled off his shoes and socks, then went to work on his pants. Michael raised his hips to allow her to whisk down the pants and underwear, and then shrugged off the shirt. In all his naked glory, he'd never felt so exposed . . . and despite the number of lovers he'd had, never so excited.

The evidence jutted from between his thighs, flushed and hard. Irrefutable. No more hiding from the truth. His search for completion and the endless loneliness was done, but he had to hold it to himself a bit longer. Savor it like a decadent secret and let it sink in that this was real, not some product of his fevered dreams.

But even in his dreams he'd never conjured two mouths—one male, one female—nibbling his skin. Working together, they teased his nipples with teeth and tongues, shooting little bolts of joy to his nerve endings. After a few moments they moved south, nipped his ribs and belly. He squirmed, urging them to get to the prize, and Katrina laughed.

"Patience, big guy."

Was she kidding? He needed more. Burying his hands in their hair, he grumbled and nudged them lower still, making his wishes clear. Playfully they complied, nipping his hip bones, the hollow of his groin.

And finally, two hot tongues twirled around his cock, starting at the leaking tip. They fought over the little droplet, but he wasn't sure who was the winner, or that he cared. Hissing between his teeth, he stabbed the air with his cock, unable to help thrusting as they gave him a thorough tongue bath from head to root. Then Katrina swallowed his entire shaft, pretty lips working it, head bobbing. Bastian settled between his legs and mouthed his balls, sucking in one, then the other.

They were driving him insane and he loved every second, but he could hold out against the delicious assault for only so long. "I'm going to come too fast if you two don't let up."

Bastian raised his head. "I have an idea. Katrina, lie on your back so our man can eat that pretty pussy. I'm going to be occupied with something else." He leered at Michael.

"Like what?" He wasn't sure whether to be scared.

"You'll see. Just go with it," his friend encouraged.

He arched a brow. "All right. You heard the man, pretty lady."

His lovers undressed and he drank in their long limbs and toned bodies. The swell of Katrina's creamy breasts, trim hips, and long thighs. The glistening pussy awaiting his attention. Bastian's nicely muscled chest, lean torso, strong thighs, and the thick, eager cock straining and full with heavy balls underneath.

Bastian suddenly appeared a bit anxious. "Like what you see?"

"I do," he said without hesitation. "I thought I'd feel weird about being with you this way, but I don't."

His anxiety drained away. "It's called making love. You can say it, you know."

"Making love." There. He'd tested it and the sky hadn't fallen. "I've fucked plenty, but I can't recall when I've made love to anyone. Until you two."

Katrina crawled in and lay beside him, opening her arms. He went into them, pressing close, kissing her deeply. He liked how her breasts pushed into his chest and decided to show his appreciation. Moving lower, he plucked one to a peak with his fingers while suckling the other. She arched into him, practically purring.

After he'd plumped them to attention, he moved down her belly to the warm, damp place between her thighs. Crouching, he licked the slick lips of her pussy, getting every drop of dewy moisture. With two fingers, he opened her and probed into her channel, giving her a good tongue fucking. Grabbing his hair, she squirmed and whimpered her appreciation, especially when he shifted his attention to her clit.

A hand patted his rear. "Up on your knees," Bastian ordered. "I'm going to show some love to this fine ass like I've been dying to do for ages."

He did as he was told, too goddamned horny to be alarmed. He was in this for the long haul, so he figured why worry about something that was sure to be pleasurable? He knew Bastian would never hurt him. He trusted his friend implicitly, and that realization was very freeing.

As he continued to eat their woman's cunt, his ass cheeks were spread, making him feel shy and more than a little vulnerable. No matter his level of trust, he was still not prepared for the questing tongue that circled his hole—or the jolt of lust it inspired, rocketing to every limb.

"This okay?" Bastian asked.

"Y-yes. Jesus Christ, I've never . . ." He had no words to put to what his lover was doing.

Bastian chuckled. "It's called rimming, and it's extremely enjoyable. For both parties."

He had to agree, even if the intended words came out as a grunt. Never would he have imagined he'd allow anyone to do this to him, but it was as though every nerve ending in his body was centered right where the firm, hot tongue licked and probed. Ate his ass until he was making helpless noises, pushing back into the other man's face. His cock was ready to explode without anyone having touched it, and he couldn't let that happen.

"Condom," he told Katrina breathlessly. "Nightstand drawer."

"Get two, and lube."

A shiver of fear ran through him, and more than a little excitement. He knew what Bastian was planning and was surprised that he didn't want to stop him. Maybe that was partly because he'd taken the dildo really well when he'd played with Katrina and Jeri, and being filled, the phallus hitting his sweet spot, had felt so fucking fantastic. He'd wondered whether the real thing would be as good, and now he'd find out.

Katrina retrieved the items from the drawer and handed them to Michael. "I want you to fuck my ass while he does you," she informed him in a sultry voice.

The visual nearly made him come. He pitched a condom to Bastian and focused on the pale globes of Katrina's pretty rear as she knelt in front of him. If he couldn't get control, this could be the shortest lovemaking session on record. But this was only the beginning for them, which made him smile. He could always look forward to more.

Parting her cheeks, he squeezed a generous amount of the gel onto his fingers and began working the slick substance into her channel. This wasn't his first rodeo when it came to anal sex, though he'd always been with women and he'd always been the giver. He knew to prepare her so she'd feel nothing but fullness and pleasure, and trusted Bastian would do the same.

Pausing, he coated his cock with lube and passed the tube to his friend. Working his fingers in and out of Katrina's channel, he tried to relax as cool gel hit his asshole and was spread around, worked into his hole in the same way. The initial strangeness soon gave way to whirls of wicked delight spiraling from his ass to his balls and cock. Firm lips kissed the spot where his spine met the curve of his butt and his friend's voice caressed him.

"Do you like this?"

"Yes."

"You look so gorgeous, all those muscles flexing under my hands and that beautiful ass waiting for me to take it. Do you want me?"

"God, yes," he rasped.

"Get inside her first, then I'll take you."

"As long as the strain won't hurt your thigh." He didn't want to stop, but he worried about Bastian's healing.

"No, it's doing much better. I promise."

"Okay. Coming in, baby."

Katrina pushed back as he breached her with the head of his cock, wanting more of him. He didn't want to hurt her so he went slowly, watching his dick disappear an inch at a time. "Shit, that's so good. So goddamned fine, baby."

"Oh, Michael," she whispered. "In me, all the way."

At last, he was seated to his balls. Christ, his cock was lit like a blowtorch. Every bit of friction propelled him closer to the razor's edge and he knew he couldn't tread the line much longer.

Especially with Bastian's cock spearing his hole the same as he'd done to Katrina's, opening him wide and filling him deep. "God, that's good," he groaned. "The real thing *is* way better."

Bastian sounded amused. "Oh? Been experimenting, have you?"

"It was all Katrina's fault."

"Boys, stop talking and move," she begged.

"Yes, ma'am." Grasping her hips, he started a slow rhythm, sliding out and in again.

Behind him, Bastian held steady, letting Michael set the pace, fucking their woman, then impaling his ass on Bastian's cock each time he withdrew from her. The double stimulation was so decadent, so naughty, it was nearly impossible to hold on to his impending release.

His balls tightened and he thrust faster, determined to take his lovers with him when he flew. He increased the tempo until he was pounding in time to their cries, the three of them soaring higher, higher—

His orgasm burst, his cock on fire as he pumped into Katrina's ass. She tensed underneath him and keened her pleasure, grinding into him. Behind him, Bastian drove to the hilt and shouted with his release, his cock jerking, pumping his load into the condom. The three of them remained together, twitching and breathing hard, until finally Bastian gently disengaged and Michael did the same.

They collapsed into a sweaty, sated pile, Katrina tucked against his right side, Bastian his left. Each of his lovers laid their head on his shoulders, hugging him tight, rubbing his belly, and placing little kisses on his heated skin.

"If I'd known you had the makings of a submissive, I'd have plowed your ass a long time ago," Bastian said, a hint of humor in his voice.

Michael looked down at him, eyes widening. "*Submissive?* In your rainbow dreams, boy toy."

Katrina snorted. "Guess that settles the question of who's top dog around here."

"Yep, me." Bastian snuggled in with a happy sigh and began to breathe deeply, already drifting off.

Katrina laughed softly and settled in, too. Michael tried to recall when he'd ever been so content. At peace with the world. Holding safe in his arms the two people that he . . . loved.

Yes, loved.

This wasn't conventional, wasn't what he'd expected to find, and some people wouldn't approve. But he didn't give a damn. They were his and he wasn't about to give them up for anyone. No one, not Dietz or even Satan himself, was going to take them away from him.

No matter what he had to do, no matter the price, he would keep them safe.

And that meant finding Dietz, ridding the earth of that scum once and for all.

"What's he doing in there?" Bastian frowned at the closed office door and listened to Michael yelling, and felt sorry for whomever he was talking to on the phone.

Katrina crossed her arms over her chest, causing her breasts to plump over the cups of her swimsuit. "Three guesses."

"Sorry, stupid question."

For the past four days, their lover had been driving himself—and everyone else—crazy searching for the slightest hint of Dietz's whereabouts. No one had escaped Michael's wrath. The man was a fucking ghost, vanished into thin air since SHADO had converged on his abandoned hotel room.

"Finding out that bastard was responsible for Maggie's murder has really done a number on him," Katrina said, eyes shadowed with worry. "I wish I knew how to help them find him."

"Me, too. I have a few contacts, but some of them are street people, and communicating with them means I have to go out. There's only so much I can do from here, and when I proposed that I leave to get in touch with some of them, he freaked out."

She cupped his face. "He just worries about you. So do I. You're not completely healed, even if you want us to think otherwise. And, anyway, there's no sense in making yourself a target again. Do you really want to do that to Michael or me?"

"No, baby. I wouldn't." She didn't have to remind him of his disastrous sting operation. He carried the reminders with him every day when he struggled not to let them see that his body still ached some, that his limp was worse when they weren't looking.

"Should we try to go in?" he asked. Mostly to get her mind off his injuries.

"All he can do is growl and tell us to get lost." She shrugged.

"Okay, let's do it."

He pushed in, with her trailing him, and took in Michael's ragged appearance. The man was sitting in his rolling chair, bare feet propped on his desktop. He hadn't shaved in a day or two and wore a pair of old, torn jeans that sat low on his hips. His faded blue T-shirt had the sleeves ripped out, showing off the bulge of his biceps. Bastian might have appreciated the sight if it wasn't for the circles under his eyes and the fatigue etched on his handsome face.

"Yeah, I've heard that before, so start singing another tune for me or life is going to get unpleasant for you, Lenny." Pause. "Shit flows straight downhill, you know that. Get me a lead on this cock-sucker, or I'm going to have to switch to a more reliable snitch."

"Reliable snitch? Is that an oxymoron?" Katrina whispered in Bastian's ear.

Michael looked up and saw them standing there. "Listen, I gotta go. Call me soon." Hanging up, he took in their gloomy expressions. "What?"

Katrina waved a hand at him. "Have you eaten at all today? Something more than a bar of that cardboard granola, I mean."

"Sure. I had a banana." His jaw was set stubbornly.

"When?"

"Earlier."

"Like, yesterday, I'll bet." When he didn't deny the charge, she regarded him with a mixture of love and exasperation written on her face. Walking over to him, she sat in his lap, and his arms went around her. Linking her arms around his neck, she nuzzled his ear. "If you don't eat right and get some sleep, you're not going to have any fuel for the fun stuff."

"I will *always* have the energy to play, sexy, so don't worry. But I also want the three of us to feel safe stepping off the property, and in order for that to happen—"

"We know, the asshole has to be caught. Might go faster if you'd let us help," she pointed out.

Their lover shook his head. "No. I went that route once before and look how it turned out," he said, gesturing to Bastian. "No way is that happening again."

Bastian struggled not to take it as a slap against his ability as an agent or an affront to his masculinity, and failed. He knew Michael's heart was in the right place, but the man's attitude was tough on his bruised ego. "I'm not a child. I'm a man, a trained agent, and in spite of the last fiasco, I'm damned good at what I do." Anger crept into his tone. "I'm almost healed, so let me do what I can. What you hired me for."

"Believe me, I know you're all man." When Michael's teasing didn't produce the smile he'd hoped for, he relented. "Okay, I'll compromise. You oversee my office from here, take over this list I've got going with leads from some of our contacts. *I'll* hit the street and see what I can learn from there. That's the deal—take it or leave it."

Bastian returned his arch stare. "That doesn't sound much like a compromise. But I'll take it *if* you take Blaze with you and promise to at least wear a disguise. And if you swear you'll book it home at the first sign of trouble."

"Done."

"When will you go?"

"Tomorrow night. I'll call Emma and get her to come along and bring some simple things, like street clothing and a wig."

"That should work. Anything we can do now?" he asked, including Katrina in the question.

"Not at the moment, thanks."

"Take a break and come to the pool with us?" she asked hopefully.

"Later, okay? I'm going to chase a few more leads and then see what Mrs. Beasley has to eat. I'll be along as soon as I can."

She exchanged a knowing look with Bastian. Their guy was running himself into the ground. Sliding off Michael's lap, she stood and poked a finger in his chest. "You've got two hours, or we're coming to drag you away from here. Got it?"

His lips quirked. "Yes, dear."

After giving him a slow kiss, she turned and marched out. Bastian smirked at his partner. "Better listen. I wouldn't want to be on the receiving end of her temper when she's pissed."

"We will eventually. We're guys," his friend quipped. "But I won't risk bringing her wrath down on my head any sooner than necessary."

"Good plan. See you later." They exchanged a smile that went straight to Bastian's cock. God, the man was like a piece of chocolate—smooth, tasty, and hard to resist.

"Definitely." He made the one word seem like a delicious fact.

Bastian sauntered out, his mood much improved with the headway they'd made with their lover. Michael had said he'd share the load and take a break, and he wasn't a man to go against his word. The day was beginning to improve.

At the pool, he joined his lady, and things took a definite turn for the better. They dove and splashed for a while, chasing each other and generally horsing around. When Katrina decided to swim a few laps, he gave in to the temptation of enjoying the warm day. Venturing onto the patio, he spread his towel in the grass off to one side, and, removing his trunks, sprawled on his back. Gloriously naked, he basked like a lizard for about five minutes before a shadow loomed over him.

"You're going to sunburn the important bits, and then where will we be?"

Opening his eyes, he squinted at the beautiful redhead. "I don't suppose you have any suggestions on how to provide me with shade, do you?"

"Oh, I believe I have just the thing."

Bastian's cock thickened as Katrina peeled off her bikini bottoms and top, tossing them over his discarded trunks. She stalked him like a graceful cat until she stood over him, one foot on either side of his hips. The position gave him an unrestricted view of everything the woman had been blessed with, which was quite stunning indeed.

"Bring yourself down here, baby."

She lowered herself to sit straddling his thighs, his turgid cock poking up in front of her insistently. Her fingers found his sac and kneaded. Manipulated his balls with delicious pressure. She moved to crouch between his legs and grasped his aching shaft with her other hand, squeezing. He moaned low in his throat, his shaft throbbing. His entire body was strung tense as a bowstring from wanting this pleasure with her for the past four days.

Fisting him, she pumped his length from head to base. Slow and excruciating. Building the heat of silken friction. Bending, she flicked out her pink tongue and tasted the broad head. Licked a drop of pre-cum, causing mini shocks to zip down his shaft.

Out of the corner of his eye, a movement caught his attention. Turning his head, he got another shock—John, Michael's hunky security man, standing frozen at the edge of the patio, a big erection tenting the front of his khaki slacks. Katrina followed Bastian's gaze and smiled invitingly.

"Well, hello. Like what you see?" she purred.

The man nodded in mute fascination, eyes wide.

"Why don't you pull up a seat and enjoy?"

With that, she took Bastian in her mouth. He was certain he'd die from the sheer ecstasy of her expert sucking, not to mention the arousal they'd caused in their voyeur. He groaned, lifting his hips, granting her better access, and the man a better view. Silently pledged his body to her wishes. Fascinated, he watched his cock disappear between her sensual lips, loving the warm, slick sheath sucking him, her shiny red hair pulled to the side in a way that ensured his view. Did John like what he saw?

A quick glance gave him the answer. John was sitting on a lounger, pants opened and pushed to his hips, and he was fisting his own gorgeous cock with enthusiasm.

"Sexy," Bastian whispered, and the man groaned.

John was a captive audience, observing Katrina kneeling between his splayed thighs, eating him like a stick of candy. Enjoying the show. The idea torched Bastian from head to toe, and he hissed, grabbing a fistful of the towel underneath him. He nearly lost control, so close to shooting down his lover's slim throat, and was forced to urge her gently from his sensitized cock.

"Easy. I want to last." He pointed to the towel. "On your hands and knees?"

"Mmm, with pleasure." She knelt, ass in the air, making sure John would see everything from his angle.

Bastian inhaled, loving the rich scent of her arousal as she spread her legs. The sun played on her sleek skin, illuminated the pink, glistening slit so wet and ready for his cock. The animal in him snarled, demanding that he fuck her hard and fast in front of the handsome security man, show him what belonged to Bastian.

He got into position behind her, laying one hand on the firm, round globe of her rear as he used the fingers of his other hand to rub her moist folds. She moaned, arching her spine as he spread her cream, teased her tiny clit. Next, he parted her folds and plunged two fingers into her channel, driving her to near insanity.

"You want it? You need me to fuck you right here in front of John, so he knows who belongs inside you?"

"Yes," she whispered, backing into his touch. Opening herself wider.

"Beg me."

"Please fuck me!"

Her broken plea nearly sent him over the edge for good. Every muscle trembled with the fierce urgency to take her. Withdrawing his fingers, he grasped her hips and guided the broad head of his cock between her folds. Nudged her entrance.

And then he pushed inside by inches, savoring her cry of joy. Relishing the sensation of her slick heat surrounding his dick. She opened for him like a flower, taking all of him. Seated to the hilt at last, he held himself deep and let the decadence of their fucking in front of a virtual stranger wash over him.

"God, it's so good," he rasped.

"Bastian! Fuck me now!"

Shaking, he withdrew to the tip, hovering at her entrance. She whimpered in protest. Growling in triumph, he slammed home, burying himself to the base. Filled her, grinding his balls against her juicy pussy. Then he pulled out and lunged again. And again. Hard and deep. Faster and faster.

Pounding into her relentlessly, he rejoiced in the dark, heady feeling of riding her to their satisfaction. There was nothing but the fire between his thighs as she met his thrusts. Suddenly, she cried out, her pussy convulsing around his thick shaft. Release tore through him and he pulsed his cum into her. On and on, spilling more than he'd ever thought possible, his eyes rolling back in his head, it was so damned good.

Even when he was finished, he remained inside her, coasting on the echoes of their lovemaking. A strangled sound from behind made him turn his head just in time to see John spurting white cum onto his flat belly, head thrown back, eyes closed.

"I'd say that was a success." Bastian kissed her spine before pulling out and sitting cross-legged on the towel, and pulling Katrina onto his lap.

"I hope I don't get fired for this," John said cautiously, tucking himself into his pants.

"No worries, John," Bastian assured him. "I imagine you're going to see lots of interesting things around here from now on. I assume you don't have a problem with that?"

John's lips quirked. "No, sir. Not in the least. Any time I can make sure your person is safe, let me know."

"We will. Thank you."

John was a smart guy and heard the polite dismissal. He nodded and disappeared down the path between two hedgerows.

After he was gone, Bastian took Katrina's chin in his hand. "I owe you an apology."

"For what?" she asked in surprise. "I wanted him to watch, too."

"No, for not using protection. I got caught in the moment and lost all common sense."

"Oh. Well, me, too. But I'm healthy and I trust that you and Michael are also."

"Honey, you should never take other people's health for granted. I'm clean and I'm sure Michael is, too, but it's something we should have discussed before we did it bare."

"I know. I agree. I'm just saying I trust both of you. I've always used protection before."

"Okay. We'll talk to Michael about this later, then. Maybe we can forgo the condoms altogether, unless we're playing with others."

"What others?" She frowned. "Because I'm not too keen on the idea of any of us straying on our own, like you did with that kid Cory."

He grimaced. "I screwed around with him because I didn't think I had a chance with either of you. Now that we're all together, I would never play with anyone we didn't approve of as a threesome. You have to believe me."

She kissed him sweetly and smiled. "I do. I just needed to hear you say it. Think Michael will feel the same? The man has an insatiable sex drive."

"I'm positive he will. And knowing his appetites the way we do? We'll just make sure he stays happy."

Now if they could only get their lover to slow down before he collapsed from exhaustion. He needed a break.

And Bastian thought he might have the right solution to his sexy lover's problem.

Thirteen

D ietz pushed through a sea of bodies and took a seat at the bar, hoping nothing unsavory stuck to his pants. This was the sort of place where the lower-class blue-collar types hung out after a long, sweaty day at wherever the fuck they toiled. They flocked here in grimy droves, drank beer and whiskey, listened to Hank Williams or some other awful shit, and bitched about wives they ought to be grateful were willing to put up with their smelly carcasses.

Doing his best to ignore them, he focused on the bartender. A better-than-average-looking guy named Lenny who slung drinks and made small talk with practiced ease. He worked his followers like a pro, and Dietz waited with false patience until the man finally stopped in front of him.

"What's your poison tonight?"

"Beer—whatever's on tap." What he really wanted was a single-malt scotch, but he figured he already stood out enough in this crowd. The bartender nodded and went to pull the brew.

Finished, he pushed the beer across the bar. "Three fifty."

Digging in his wallet, he handed the man a fifty and waved off his change. The man paused, then palmed the money and stuffed the bill into his jeans. "Do I know you?"

"Why don't you tell me, Lenny?" The man's eyes narrowed, and Dietz stared back. "Has it been that long, or are you just off your game?"

Lenny huffed an irritated breath and began wiping the bar with a white cloth. "You. I shoulda known." The bartender eyed the customers around them and decided none were paying attention, then addressed him again. "A certain mutual acquaintance has feelers out all over the city, looking for you."

"That's what I'm counting on."

"What do you want from me?"

"For you to make certain our friend finds me."

Lenny slung the little towel over one meaty shoulder and cupped a hand around his ear in blatant pretense. "I'm sorry, it's a bit loud in here. Want to say it again?"

Mercenary son of a bitch. Then again, Dietz could respect a man's instinct to look out for number one. He slid another fifty across the polished wooden surface. "Can you hear more clearly now?"

The second bill vanished. "I sure can. Where and when can our friend find you?"

"First of all, I was never here and you never spoke to me. Respond to our friend's inquiries tomorrow afternoon. You heard from a reliable source that I'm holed up in an abandoned house in Cranville, at the address on one of the bills in your pocket."

"Easy enough." The man started to turn away.

"That's not all."

Cocking a hip, he leaned against the bar. "Of course not. Hope you're feelin' real flush tonight."

He'd anticipated this, but it didn't grate on his nerves any less. This time, a Ben Franklin found its way into the man's pocket. "After you make that call, you'll get one from me. Could be one hour or four before you hear from me, so be ready. You'll follow my instructions then. Should my evening reach a satisfactory conclusion? A hundred more of those Franklins will find their way into your savings account."

Lenny froze, no doubt calculating all he could do with ten thousand dollars. Buy a car that actually ran or pay the rent for a few months, maybe even have some left over to buy something nice for the girlfriend. He nodded, and Dietz resisted the urge to outwardly gloat.

"Very good. Until tomorrow."

Draining his beer, he disappeared through the crowd the way he'd come. A surge of dark anticipation hummed in his veins. In a little more than twenty-four hours, the loss of all Dietz's plans and dreams would be avenged.

And Dietz would be on a plane to the Caribbean to liberate his money from the numbered account. A plastic surgeon waited on the other end, his new life bought and paid for.

He'd live with the hand dealt him. But not before doing some dealing of his own.

Lenny stared at Robert Dietz's retreating back, heart thudding against his ribs. *Holy shit. Ten fucking thousand dollars.* Jesus, the things he could do with the cash.

But the green would be dripping with dark red. He wasn't stupid. Dietz and Ross were circling each other like a couple of ravenous sharks, and if he went along with Dietz . . .

Ross would die. Simple as that.

But what do I owe him, really?

Plenty. The man had been good to him. Paid him fair and square for good tips.

But not ten thousand. Nothing ever close. And Lenny was hurting for the money, bad. Would Ross double the amount if he brought him in on Dietz's scheme? Maybe.

But if Ross failed, Lenny was a dead man for pulling a fast one on a rabid animal like Dietz.

Fuck, fuck! What to do?

In the end, he worked his shift, bided his time. And tried not to think about how he had to betray a good man so that a really nasty motherfucker would walk away free.

Michael found Bastian sitting alone on the sofa in the darkened den off the formal living room, swirling a glass of amber liquid. Moonlight caressed his lover's hair, gilding it in silvery gold and playing over his fine features.

Does he have any idea how beautiful he is?

A stupid question. Michael knew he didn't, which made the man all the more desirable. He moved into the room, not bothering to hide his presence. "I woke up and you weren't in bed with us. Can't sleep?"

His friend looked up from his glass. "No. Sorry if I woke you."

"You didn't." He sat on the sofa next to the other man. "Bad dreams?"

"Something like that."

"Tell me."

Silence stretched out for a long moment. When he spoke, his

voice was barely a whisper. "I woke up crying. I never do that, but I felt such despair. Stupid, huh?"

Michael laid a palm on his friend's pajama-clad thigh. He couldn't help but note the man had on no shirt, and the drawstring pants were oh, so thin. "Fear is never stupid because it often has roots in reality. The dream was just feelings? Nothing specific?"

"Not really."

"What does that mean? Tell me what you remember," he said firmly.

"You were dead, okay?" His voice broke. "You were dead, and I knew Katrina and I were next, and nothing else mattered. I was suffocating and I welcomed death because you were gone and . . ."

Michael took the glass from Bastian's hand, set it on the coffee table. Then he pulled his friend into his arms and held him tight, lending his warmth to the chilled skin. "I'm not going to die," he said, and willed it to be true. "I'm not leaving either of you, and we're all going to be fine. I'm not going to allow Dietz to win the war, Bastian. Know that, and trust me."

The other man shuddered. "You know I do."

"Good." He kissed the side of his friend's head. "I think I have just the plan to help us both blow off enough steam so that we'll sleep like babies. It involves some role-playing and it might get intense, though."

Bastian gave a shaky laugh. "Are you kidding? Count me in."

"You don't even know what I'm going to do to you."

"Doesn't matter. I trust you." He paused. "Can we go bareback?"

A thrill shot to every cell in Michael's body. "I'm clean. You?"

"Yes. So is Katrina." Pulling back, he looked Michael in the eye. "Earlier, she and I didn't use anything. We should have discussed it together with you first, but we got carried away. I'm sorry."

"I wouldn't trust anyone else except you two," he said seriously. "I'm in this for the duration, so if you want to go natural, I'm in— as long as it's just that way between the three of us. If we play with others, we glove up. And we don't play outside our trio without us all being on the same page," he added with a sudden spurt of jealousy. Bastian's fling with sweet little Cory still rankled.

"Agreed."

Happy with this development, he stood and pulled Bastian to his feet. "Come on. I have another room we can use so we don't wake our sleeping beauty."

Bastian's eyes locked with his, filled with longing. Need. Heat spread through his limbs, familiar yet new at the same time. As incredible as the fact seemed to him, he'd never been alone with Bastian this way. Not once, excluding when Bastian had blown him in the limo. And he suddenly couldn't fathom why.

Michael arched a brow, lips turning up in a sensual smile. "This way."

Bastian followed him through the den and down a short hallway. At the end, they turned right and walked into a spare bedroom that Michael had obviously prepared before coming to get him.

Eyes wide, he studied the scene. This room was as gorgeous as any other on Michael's estate, done in dark chocolate tones. A huge king-sized bed provided the centerpiece, a mirror on the ceiling above it. Four massive oak posts were adorned with leather restraints. Secured to the headboard was a new addition to the room: a length of silver chain attached to a leather collar.

Oh, shit! He jerked his gaze from the bed.

"I'm not a Dom, like Blaze, but sometimes I like a dangerous edge to sex. Like when I fucked Katrina in the alley behind the club, no matter who might be around. This could get rougher. Is that going to be a problem?"

"N-no." His cock was already making a large tent in his pajama bottoms to prove his eagerness.

"Good. Remember, no matter what happens in this room, it's just me, and I won't really hurt you—at least not more than you can handle. Okay?"

"Yes." *God, yes. Take me!*

"Safe word? Because 'no' sometimes means 'yes,' and we need a word that means 'stop.'"

"Sable."

"Sable?"

He flushed. "The color of your hair."

Michael looked pleased. "All right. *Sable*, and I stop."

"I trust you."

Michael seized his arm, abruptly flinging him against the wall with enough force to drive the air from his lungs. The man pressed close, resting his palms on either side of Bastian's head. His lips hovered near, whispered a dark promise.

"I'm going to make you scream."

"No." He slipped into his part easily, caught up in this wicked side of Michael. So frightening, yet exciting.

"Oh yeah."

Michael kicked his legs apart and settled between them, fitting every hard contour of his perfect body to his own. The huge bulge in his friend's boxer briefs evidenced his desire, and Bastian was helpless to stop the answering fire beginning to consume him. The other man ground his hips in slow circles, teasing.

His breath caught as Michael buried one hand in his hair, cupped his face with the other. Slowly, he lowered his head and brushed his lips against Bastian's, sipped. Their tongues touched, licked, deepening into a kiss. With a groan of pent-up longing, he melted as Michael ate his mouth, devouring him.

Michael pulled back slightly, panting, his dark eyes glittering dangerously. "You know better than anyone what I want, what I *need*. I *am* going to make you scream. I own you now."

"Oh, God." His dick jerked in response. He'd waited for too long for this.

Michael laughed, a purely sexual sound. One palm skimmed over Bastian's muscled chest, then to his straining crotch. "You're mine. I'm gonna tie you down, make you beg for mercy. Pop quiz: who do you belong to?"

Bastian could barely speak. This was the man who turned him on like no one else. Predatory, with wicked tastes that made him a little afraid, and who he was sure would take his experiences to heights no one else ever had, not even Blaze.

"Don't make me repeat myself," Michael warned.

"You, Michael. I belong to you," he rasped. Strong fingers plucked at the drawstring on his pajamas, worked down the fabric. Jesus, Michael smelled so damned good.

"That's right. In this room, I'm your master, and when you're desperate for mercy, screaming my name, I'll show you none." He slid the sleep pants down Bastian's legs, face darkening as his cock sprang free. Pressing close again, he breathed another promise into his captive's mouth. "No mercy, baby. Make no mistake—I'm going to punish you until you submit to my will. Fuck the hell out of that beautiful body. There's no turning back now."

Pulse hammering, Bastian watched as Michael stepped back and removed his boxers. Totally naked, he was a pagan god, and never failed to make his mouth water.

"Get on the bed," he ordered. "Facedown."

Bastian did as he was told and lay on his stomach, his dick like a steel pipe squashed between him and the mattress. His wrists were jerked behind his back and bound with a piece of rope, tight enough to give him pause. But Michael said he wouldn't truly hurt him, and he trusted his lover.

The other man's weight pressed him down, stiff cock sliding along his rear. One hand grabbed a fistful of his hair, jerked his head back. Then the padded leather collar was worked over his head and tightened, as well. Belatedly, he realized that the device was a choke collar, a chain looped through it, and a ripple of real fear shot through him. Along with a mad craving unlike anything he'd experienced before.

"You're my prisoner, my sex slave. Have any idea what I do to them?" his captor growled.

"N-no."

"You'll find out. On your knees."

Michael moved off him and stood at the side of the bed, waiting. Insides shaking in anticipation, Bastian went to him on his knees. The man reached behind him, wrapped the chain around his wrist for leverage, and gave a vicious yank, causing him to gasp in pain—and pleasure.

"Suck me."

Bastian bent to him, desperate to wrap his fingers around Michael's hot, thick shaft, to touch his body. But his submission, his punishment, was part of this evening's rules. As a bottom, his role was to give his master as much pleasure as possible, to surrender his body with complete trust. Allow his master to do whatever he wished. Michael would tolerate nothing less. A thrill knotted his stomach.

Bastian licked the wide, pearly head, then took the cock into his mouth. Sucked deeper, deeper. Cherished the silky skin between his lips. Michael groaned, hands pushing his head down in rhythm to his strokes.

"That's my boy. Jesus, yeah. Suck it."

He took the entire length down his throat, lips grazing the very base. He might be bound, but he had power over his master at the moment and it filled him, aroused him. Michael must have sensed this, and pulled out.

The man laughed. "No, you don't. Lie on your stomach again, feet at the headboard."

He did, turning his head to the side to rest his cheek against the bedspread, and the position stretched the chain to its limit. The collar exerted enough pressure to completely subdue him, remind him of his submission, but not enough to harm him.

His legs were spread wide, his ankles placed in the restraints. He craned his neck to look around at Michael, and saw him holding a riding crop, tapping it against his palm, eyes black with lust.

"Now, babe, you'll start begging."

"No," he whispered, wiggling to get away. But there was nowhere to go, and he knew he didn't really want to escape. Still, he begged. "Please don't."

The blow landed across his buttocks, sending shock waves of stinging pain and erotic gratification to every cell in his body. Especially his cock. Raw hunger washed over him, fusing with the sweet torture.

"Please, no!"

Whack. "Are you going to cause me another second of worry, like you did when I found you in that filthy alley?"

Probably. "I'll try not to."

Whack. "You'd better not! Who's your master?"

He twisted, unable to move. "You! No more, I'm begging you!" But the blows intensified.

"You know how to make this stop. Say the word."

"No," he murmured. His cock was a lightning rod for this torment.

Whack, whack, whack.

No mercy, he thought, and tears seeped from his eyes. Several more blows fell and his voice broke, along with the last shreds of his resistance. He was lost to this. "Master, please, I'm begging you."

He was barely aware of Michael's movements as the crop was tossed aside and the other man lay beside him. A hand burrowed in his hair and then Michael's mouth captured his, licking away the tears.

"You did well, but I'm not through with you—not even close," he said softly. "Tell me again—who owns you, body and soul?"

"Y-you. No one but you." He tried to still his thundering heart.

"And what am I going to do to you?"

"Punish me."

"That's exactly right. And you're going to love every minute. Isn't that so?"

"Yes, sir." Tremors shook him as he waited. The whipping had stung, but Michael had never truly hurt him. He wouldn't. He'd said so. But just the hint of the unknown, that thrill of fear, nearly made him come.

Michael sat up and moved between his splayed legs. Bastian tried to see what he was doing, but couldn't. Cool liquid was

smoothed over his heated ass, easing the slight pain. His tormen-
tor worked the oil over his skin, between his thighs, and rubbed
his balls. Then his cheeks were parted and two big fingers plunged
into his hole.

"Ohh."

"Very good. That's it, relax. Give yourself to me completely."

Michael's fingers stroked, working in the lube, stretching him.
When his wet tongue joined his fingers, Bastian gasped as the fire
surged again.

"You're so tight. When I fuck you, you're gonna scream." He
leaned over to the bedside table to get something. Bastian started
when he saw that it was a rolled-up strip of black silk. "Wouldn't
want to wake the entire household, would we? Open your mouth."

"No!" But Michael slipped the gag into place and tied it firmly
at the back of his head.

"I've been in hell for so long, needing you this way. Dying to
fuck you, but denying it to myself. You're so damned gorgeous.
Since you can't speak, two fingers means 'sable,' okay?" Bastian nodded, and Michael moved to pick up something. "Remember this?"

Michael held the riding crop where he could see the rough
crisscross weave of the leather handle. His eyes widened. It was
shiny, slick with the oil.

"Let's see if this end can make you beg, too."

Bastian's pulse tripped in alarm, half afraid Michael meant to
go too far, and half afraid he didn't. Walking the line between
carnal pleasure and agony was a risky proposition.

His cheeks were spread and the handle probed his hole, inching inside, then out. In and out, delving deeper with each slow
stroke. Exquisite little shocks radiated to every part of him. He
whimpered into the gag, raising his hips.

"Like that, do you, my slut?"

A low, rumbling laugh, charged with lust, echoed in his ears. The handle worked faster, deeper. Treading the razor's edge of pain, and still he silently begged for more. Didn't know how far his lover would take this dangerous game, or how much he could stand. Suddenly the handle was removed, but he had no chance to recover.

"Scream, boy. No one will hear you. You're mine!"

The weight of Michael's body pressed him down, covering him like a blanket, the tip of his swollen cock pushing at his tight entrance. Teasing, tormenting. With a powerful thrust, he buried himself to the hilt.

Sensitized as he was by now, the cock owning his ass was pure agony and pleasure rolled into one. He screamed, thrashing, fighting against the restraints, but it was no use. His master rode him, strong thighs gripping his hips, heavy balls slamming against his. The collar compressed his throat as Michael wrapped the chain tighter, slowly cutting off his air as he fucked him. Bastian wasn't afraid. He was riding high on euphoria, secure in the knowledge that Michael had him. Would never let him go.

At that moment, he knew what it was like to be totally owned, under another man's complete command. Wild and forbidden.

Oh yes, yes. Don't stop. Please ride me, fuck me. . . .

His muffled screams turned to cries of helpless passion and mingled with Michael's. Tears streamed down his face as he reveled in his lover's big cock filling his ass, pounding him, splitting him in two. So ready to explode—

"Ahh! Fuck, yes!" Michael fell against his back, rocked with his release, spewing hot cum deep inside his channel. Shuddered again and again until he was spent, and then pulled out. Without allowing Bastian to come.

Bastian's ankles were freed from the restraints. Then Michael flipped him on his back, hands still bound. He removed the collar, but made no move to take off the gag or untie him. Instead, he gave Bastian a sultry look.

"I'm going to feast on you, boy. Devour every drop you have to give, and there's nothing you can do to stop me. Do you understand?"

He nodded, knew he couldn't have spoken a word, gag or not. The other man placed a pillow under his hips, elevating him. His shaft strained, eager and pulsing.

"Spread your legs." He did. "Wider."

Dazed, he gazed up into the mirrored ceiling for the first time. His body lay sprawled before his lover like a decadent, tasty offering. He shivered, watching the bird's-eye view of Michael's dark head dipping low, moaned as his tongue licked away the warm juices streaming down his ass.

"God, we taste good." Then he worked upward, laving Bastian's balls, licking the ridge of his cock.

Bastian squirmed at the sweet torture of it. Michael grinned, took Bastian's cock into his mouth. Sucking, eating him. Bastian arched his hips and began to pump, mindless with lust. Oh, he had to have this man's hot mouth working him. Had to have all of him, and give all to him.

The pressure built, molten fire. His cock exploded, and he screamed in ecstasy, viewing the scene through a haze. With only a slight hesitation at first, his master drank, throat working, his satisfaction apparent as their eyes met. Bastian shuddered, coming again and again. True to his word, his lover didn't stop until he'd wrung every last drop from his body.

Spent, Bastian went limp, unable to move. His eyes drifted closed and he was vaguely aware of the gag and the last of the bindings being removed. Being pulled into the circle of Michael's arms, tender kisses being pressed to his brow. The musky scent of them entwined together, slick with sex, sweat, and their natural, earthy scents, enticed his senses. He loved how good Michael smelled.

"God, Bastian, did I hurt you? Because if I did, I'd never forgive myself."

He managed to pry open an eye, and gazed up into his lover's anxious face. "No—well, not much, and it was in a good way. That wicked side of you scared me a little, but it sent me up in flames, too. You'll notice I didn't use my safe word."

"Did you like it enough to do it again sometime?"

"Are you kidding? I came so hard I thought I'd turn inside out! I'd love to." He thought a second. "I think this sort of scene would be a little rough for our girl, though."

"Maybe not. She likes naughty toys, and she likes it rough sometimes. She sure liked the scene behind the club, not to mention when you two performed for poor John. But right here and now? This is ours."

Ours. Another word he never thought he'd hear from Michael. His insides hummed in happiness. "Sounds like heaven."

"Bastian, I want you to know something." His arms tightened. "I love you. Always have."

His lover had said the words in the hospital, but Bastian had been recovering from a grave injury then. Hearing them now, when wrapped in the afterglow? Nothing could ever be more perfect.

"And you've known for a long time how I feel. I love you, too. Even though it hasn't been that long, I feel the same about Katrina."

"Me, too. About us . . . I'm sorry it took me so long to wake up, but it's the truth. I may not say it enough, but you'll always know it." He paused. "After we're recovered, I'm going to make love to you."

He smiled. "You just did. That's what *we* did, even if the loving had an edge."

"Make love *again*, then."

"I thought you'd never ask."

Michael grinned, his dark eyes feral. "I wasn't asking."

Fourteen

Katrina met Emma and Blaze in the foyer just as Simon shut the front door behind them. Blaze was carrying a large duffel she assumed held the stuff he and Michael would need for their disguises.

"Hey guys," she said, moving forward to greet them. "The terrible twosome is upstairs. This way."

"Are they still arguing about tonight?" Blaze asked as he and Emma trailed her.

Glancing over her shoulder, she made a face. "Like a couple of old women. Bastian had a bad dream last night that's got him freaked out and he's begging Michael not to go. Of course, our resident leader is committed to this no matter what, because he wants to put an end to Dietz as quickly as possible."

"He's got even more reason to want that now," Emma observed. "He's got you and Bastian to protect."

"That's what scares us," she admitted. "He's so obsessed with Dietz, we're afraid he's going to ruin his health." Or make a critical error, though she'd never say that to two of his employees behind his back. Besides, she had a feeling their friends were thinking the same thing.

In the bedroom, they found the two men arguing, clearly at a stalemate, as they stood facing each other.

"Why do *you* have to be the one? We've got at least two dozen agents available right this second who could go with Blaze to poke around and ask a few simple questions!" Bastian glared at his friend.

"Exactly!" Michael shouted. "It's just a few questions, and there's no need to bring anyone else in!"

"Are you forgetting I'm your CEO? I don't work in the fucking mail room, and I get a say in this!"

"That can be remedied," Michael snarled, and his partner paled.

Blaze dropped the duffel and stepped between them, placing a hand on each man's chest, pushing them apart. "Whoa! Hey, guys, time out. Both of you shut up and breathe. In and out—there you go."

The two combatants stared at each other, chests heaving in anger. Gradually, however, cooler heads prevailed and they glanced away, both appearing sorry for the argument. Michael, in particular, was ashamed.

"Bastian, I'm sorry. I didn't mean that last remark," he said with remorse. "You're my right hand, and I believe we've already established that I couldn't do without you."

"Forget it." Bastian still wouldn't look at him.

Michael persisted. "I swear I'll be careful."

"Fine. Do what you want, like you always do. It's not like I or anyone else can stop you."

From Michael's expression, that wasn't what he wanted to hear. But it was all Bastian had left to say.

Blaze glanced between them and lowered his hands. "So, we're good here? We're gonna get down to business?" Both of his friends nodded, and he picked up the duffel, sitting it on the bed. "Great. Emma, show them what you brought for us to wear."

The woman stepped forward, eyeing her bosses warily. "Right." Unzipping the bag, she pulled out several articles of clothing, a wig, and a baseball cap. "I know I'm preaching to the choir here, but the main thing to remember when going incognito is that people see what they want to see. For this outing, we're going to do some basic alteration, no heavy makeup or anything elaborate."

They all watched as she sorted the outfits into two specific sets. Even Bastian moved closer, interested in the process.

"These are for you," she said to Michael, gesturing to the clothes. "When I'm done with you, all anyone will see is an average street person who's maybe a little down on his luck and could use a shower."

"Great. I'm supposed to get my contacts to talk, not run them off," he muttered, and everyone laughed.

Well, everyone except Bastian.

Emma shook her head. "You won't run them off, because they'll no doubt look just like you. Here, go put these on." He took the clothes and disappeared into the bathroom. She turned to address her lover. "Since you're already wearing the jeans, all you need is the rest. Take off your shirt and put these on." She indicated the black T-shirt and matching leather jacket adorned with silver rivets.

Obediently, Blaze stripped off his shirt, and Katrina couldn't help but admire the view. The man was ripped with muscle, more than two hundred pounds of mouthwatering male perfection. She wanted to run her fingers through all that silky black hair falling to his big shoulders. Yum.

She glanced at Bastian, and from his smirk, she realized he'd caught her looking. His grin said, *Look all you want. I've had some of that!* Impulsively, she stuck her tongue out at her lover, which only amused him more. Dammit, she was jealous.

Michael emerged from the bathroom, wearing ratty jeans with holes in the knees, a stained, yellowed T-shirt, and a plaid flannel shirt worn over it as a jacket. He went to stand beside Blaze, who'd donned the studded jacket. "How come he gets to wear the cool stuff?"

"Because it fits his persona," Emma explained. "He's too big and brawny to come across as a poor, little street waif, so he gets to be the badass, don't-fuck-with-me guy."

"I think I just got insulted." He scowled, which made the ladies giggle. "Hey, I've got your *little* right here."

Emma rolled her eyes. "*Any*way, let's get this wig and the ball cap on you." Working quickly, she covered his short sable hair with the wig, transforming him into a man with shoulder-length, dirty-brown locks. With the whole outfit, topped off with the ball cap, he looked like a different man. Walking the street tonight, even his friends would be hard-pressed to spot him.

"Oh, and don't smile," Emma said. "Your teeth are too white and perfect for a street rat. They'll give you away in a second."

Standing in front of the mirror over the dresser, Michael studied himself and tried an experimental smile. "You're right. No smiling—not that either of us will have a reason."

"Now you." Emma combed back Blaze's hair and tied a black bandana over his head, gang style. A pair of silver stud earrings capped the outfit, and she stood back, eyeing him critically. "Crap."

Blaze looked at himself. "What?"

"That getup makes you look even sexier than when we started. The idea is for you to blend, not attract every male slut and biker bimbo within twenty miles who's looking for a hard ride." She did not appear pleased at the prospect.

"Aww. I'm not giving rides to anyone but you, sweetness." He gave her a smooch on the lips, which seemed to placate her.

"He won't blend, but I seriously doubt anyone's going to mess with him," Bastian pointed out. "Not if they don't want their asses kicked."

"I think we're ready." Michael looked at Blaze. "Which car did you bring?" SHADO had a garage stocked with cars they used for undercover ops. Most of them had been confiscated from criminals during busts.

"The old blue Chevy. Looks like a rattletrap, but she's a beast under the hood."

"That'll do. Let's get out there and see what we can learn."

Blaze busied himself with giving Emma a heated good-bye. Michael walked over to Katrina and Bastian, held open his arms. She walked into them, but noticed that their other lover stayed off to the side, face turned away. Michael kissed her thoroughly, giving her a promise of delights to come. He pulled back and gave her a small smile, eyes shadowed.

"I'll be home before you even miss me."

"Too late. I already do." She stroked his cheek with one finger. "Be careful."

"I will." He turned to their lover. "Bastian?"

"Good luck." He limped from the room.

The curt dismissal cut Michael to the quick. Katrina saw the hurt in his eyes before he covered the raw emotion by giving her another quick kiss. "See you both soon, baby."

Then he and Blaze were gone, leaving her and Emma standing

in the huge vacuum created by their departure. Her friend's husky voice was quiet.

"Love isn't all fun and games, is it?"

"I wish. Those two are both so hardheaded, they rip each other to shreds before one of them finally gives."

"And I thought *one* stubborn alpha male was a challenge. Good luck, girlfriend."

"Gee, thanks." She paused. "Would you like a glass of wine or two while we wait up for the guys to get back?"

"I'd love one! Maybe we can convince your blond stud to stop fretting and join us."

"We can try."

As they made their way downstairs, she attempted unsuccessfully to squelch some worry of her own. A queasy feeling settled into her gut, making her wonder whether Bastian had been right to fight Michael on tonight's outing.

An uncomfortable inner voice whispered, *Just maybe, Michael should have listened.*

"Where to next?" Blaze turned the key and the Chevy roared to life, then settled into a throaty purr.

Michael rubbed his tired eyes as his friend pulled out of the parking lot next to the latest club they'd hit. Two hours, and nothing. It wouldn't have seemed like a long time if he'd gotten any sleep lately. "Let's see. We've talked to Skeeter, Dog, Snake, and Skunk. Who's left in the zoo?"

Blaze snorted. "Lions, tigers, and bears?"

"All accounted for."

"Then I guess that leaves all the dudes with normal names."

"That's a really short list. There's Dave, Pat, and Lenny. Pick a name."

"Pat's hangout is the closest from here. But of the three, his tips aren't usually as reliable," he added thoughtfully.

"Then let's save him for last. Let's try Lenny. I was kind of harsh with him on the phone and I'd like to follow up in person."

"You know, of all the snitches we use, he's the one I don't mind paying. That guy works hard and he's really trying to make a go of getting out of that neighborhood." Blaze made a right and drove down a darkened street toward the bar. "The money doesn't go up his nose."

"If anyone can make it, he can," Michael agreed. In his pocket, his iPhone sang a greeting. Pulling it out, he peered at the number and blinked in surprise. "Speak of the devil." He answered as Blaze glanced over curiously. "Lenny, what's up? Me and a buddy were just on our way to see you, incognito."

The younger man gave a nervous laugh. "Yeah, incognito is real good. Listen, I got something for ya. Just as well we don't discuss it over the phone."

"We'll see you in ten."

"I'll take a break. Meet me at the employee entrance in the alley."

"Gotcha." Ending the call, he placed the phone back in his pocket and checked the gun hidden in the waistband of his jeans. "Lenny's spooked."

"How so?"

"Said to pull around back, employee entrance. He doesn't want to be seen talking to us." They shared a significant look.

"He's never done that before?"

"Nope."

Silence hung heavily in the car as they rode the rest of the way to the bar. Pulling up to the seedy establishment, Blaze steered the car around back as instructed. The alley, which accommodated regular deliveries from trucks carrying beer and liquor, was plenty wide, so he was able to pull right next to where their contact leaned against the wall.

He and Blaze got out and Michael circled the car, his gaze sweeping the entire area. A nervous contact was not a good thing, and an agent never took even the best of them for granted. When he had discerned that no one else lurked nearby, he addressed Lenny.

"What do you have for me?"

The other man pulled a scrap of paper from his jeans pocket and passed it to Michael. Who noticed how badly his hands shook. He gave Lenny a long, hard look, not liking how the man flinched under his gaze, unable to meet his eyes. The sinking sensation in his stomach was a feeling he knew all too well. Turning his attention to the paper, he held it up to catch the light from the dim bulb near the employee's door.

"An address?"

Lenny was fidgeting with a thread on his jeans. "That guy you're looking for? That's where you can find him," he said, voice quavering a bit.

Michael fought to keep calm. "Says who?"

"Just a guy. Someone who knows someone. That's how it goes."

"Is it?"

"Yeah."

He let the man stew for a long minute, exchanged another glance with Blaze. His friend's skepticism didn't escape him. He felt the same, but what else did they have going for them?

"All right. I'm going to check this out because you've always been straight with me. But I'm warning you now, if you're setting me up, you'd better pray I'm dead before this night is over. You got that?"

"Y-yeah, but I'm not. I swear." A bead of sweat rolled down his temple.

"And if I am dead," he continued, "you'd better pray that whatever amount of money you get paid is enough to ease your conscience for the rest of your life. You got anything else to say, Lenny?"

"N-no. I don't know what you're talking about."

Pulling out his wallet, Michael dug out a hundred, grabbed Lenny's hand, and slapped the money in his palm. "For your trouble. Take a good look at it, Lenny." The younger man stared at the bill. "The only blood on *that* money will belong to the monster who killed my wife, the same bastard who's trying to kill me and the people I love. And if I'm gone, he'll off you, too, no matter what lie he spins for you. Remember that."

"That's real interesting, but you're off base. I-I don't have anything else, okay? See you around."

They watched as he disappeared inside, and then returned to the car. Inside, Blaze drummed his fingers on the steering wheel. "You're right, he's scared. But that doesn't mean the tip isn't legit."

"Do you honestly believe that?" he asked dryly.

"No. Let's plug this address into the GPS and see what we get."

Michael read it off while Blaze punched the information into the small, handheld unit. After a moment, the map popped up, along with the mileage. "Hell, that's all the way across the county from here."

"Do we check it out?"

"I don't see what other choice we have."

But as they drove, the tension in the vehicle increased with every mile. About twenty minutes in, Blaze pulled over in the parking lot of a fast-food place and shook his head.

"I've got bad vibes about this."

"Me, too." Michael tugged at the ball cap, wishing he could tear off the wig and scratch his scalp. The damned thing was hot and itchy. "Turn around. We'll send a team out there at daybreak if necessary. But something tells me that we got sent on a snipe hunt."

Blaze whipped the car back in the direction they'd come and hit the gas. "Snipe hunt?"

"Means being sent on a search for something that doesn't exist. My dad used to send me on snipe hunts when I was little, until I found out there's no such thing as a snipe."

"Never heard that one." He laughed. "Kinda mean, though."

"No kidding. He—" The phone in his jeans buzzed again. Pulling it out, he raised a brow. "Guess who?"

"Lenny."

"Bingo." He answered the call. "Ready to level with me?"

"Michael, don't go to that house," Lenny rasped. "I'm pretty sure it's just a diversion."

He squashed the anger rising in his chest. "We figured as much. Tell me who gave you that address."

"Robert Dietz," he said, his misery clear. "Came by in person last night. Said I was to give you the address and wait for his call. Said he'd tell me what to do next."

"You completed the first part. So did he call?"

"Yeah, a few minutes ago. He instructed me to wait three hours before I called you, but I can't do it, man. I know he's planning something bad and I don't want no part of it, no matter how much I need the cash."

"How much cash?"

"Ten grand."

Michael swiped a hand down his face. "You never would've lived to see that money. Believe that. What's the message he gave you for me?"

"He said wait three hours, then call and tell you that he has what's most valuable to you."

The blood drained from his face. "Oh, my God. My house. Hurry," he yelled at Blaze. "Lenny, what else?"

"He gave me another address, for a warehouse. You ready?"

"Yes, give it to me." He memorized the information. "Is that all?"

"He said come alone and unarmed, and then he hung up."

Right. Dietz must be totally mental to think he'd follow that last instruction.

"Okay. Lie low until I can get by to see you."

"You gonna kill me? I'm dead, anyway, if you don't get that fucker."

"No, I'm not going kill you, though it's a good thing your neck isn't in my hands right now. Talk to you soon." He laid his head back on the seat, trying not to be sick. "Hurry, for God's sake."

"I am. Emma's with them," he reminded his friend, his face a mask of rage.

"Dietz was counting on having three hours' head start. Maybe we'll get there before he does." Quickly, he placed a call to the house. The phone rang and rang, and cold fear gripped him. "Nobody's answering at home."

"Try their cell phones."

He did. Bastian first, then Katrina and Emma. There was no way *none* of them would answer when they knew he and Blaze were out on an op.

The next call he placed was to one of his agents who regularly coordinated emergencies like this one. When Lawrence answered, he ordered two teams to be sent immediately—one to his estate, and the other to the warehouse. Both were to approach with stealth.

Please let us be in time.

If anything happened to them, he might as well be dead.

But Dietz would die first.

Bastian inspected his third glass of cabernet and mused over how quickly the first two had gone down. He supposed he should monitor his alcohol consumption, but for the life of him, he couldn't think why.

Oh yes. That little detail about his lover being out in the city, possibly in danger, and the idea of Bastian suddenly getting an emergency call and having to rush off—that's why.

With regret, he set the glass aside and tried to focus on the women's conversation. But chatter about every subject from home decorating to which brand of bra was the most supportive gave him the yawns. His assertion that bras should be banned was met with giggles before they went back to talking about girly things.

Emma stood and stretched. "I have to hit the powder room. Would you be a sweetie and get us another bottle of white?" she asked him, smiling impishly.

"Sure. Be right back." He needed an excuse to get up and do something, anyway.

Picking up his glass, he headed to the kitchen for another bottle and to dump the remnants of his wine. Now that his worry about Michael had returned, no way could he take another sip. Ridiculous, because the man had everything under—

Three steps into the kitchen, he froze. Two legs clad in dress pants were sticking out from behind the big island. "What the . . . Simon?" Hurrying over, he plunked down the glass, skirted the island, and crouched beside the elderly gentleman, wincing some at the pain in his healing leg. "Simon? Shit!"

With two fingers, he pressed the side of the man's neck, holding his breath until he found a pulse. It was slow but steady. But his relief was short-lived. "Dammit."

Blood. A small pool of it around the man's head. Had he slipped and fallen, then hit his head on the island? Or had a stroke or a heart attack and then fallen? Christ, he had to call an ambulance. Now. Bolting to his feet, he spun and reached for the phone on the counter.

And found himself staring down the barrel of a gun. A weapon held by a very smug Robert Dietz.

"Don't make a sound," Dietz whispered, a maniacal grin plastered on his face. "Turn around. Any heroics, and I shoot you like I did that worthless security man, then the others."

Seething with hatred, he put his back to the man, keeping his hands visible. "What did you do to Simon? He needs help."

"Gave him a headache. Perhaps he'll recover to seek another employer, since his present one will be deceased." Cold metal pressed into his temple. "Walk."

Slowly, he walked into the living room, fervently wishing he had a way to warn the women. When they came in, Katrina was still on the sofa, waiting for more wine. Emma hadn't returned, and he hoped she saw what was going on before she came back.

Katrina must've sensed their movement, and swiveled in her seat. "Took you long enough to find—" Her eyes widened and she gasped. "How did you get in here?"

"Your security man was good enough to override the alarm system before I put a bullet in him for trying to hit the silent alarm."

As Bastian was forced to move around the end of the sofa, he caught Katrina's gaze and glanced desperately at Emma's wineglass. She nodded imperceptibly to let him know she got the message. Dietz shoved him into a chair, and while the man was distracted, she deftly snatched the empty glass, laid it on the floor, and pushed it underneath the sofa with her heel. Smart girl.

"How do you plan to get away with this? Michael will be back soon, and he'll know something is wrong the minute he arrives," she declared, a little louder than necessary. In his self-important glow, Dietz didn't seem to notice.

"Oh, we have a while yet. I sent him on a couple of fool's errands to buy myself some time. We're going to have such fun together." He laughed at his own sick joke. "What should we do first, I wonder? Shall I tie up lover boy here and make him watch while I fuck his lovely whore? Or just shoot you both in the head and wait to see Michael's reaction before I kill him, as well?"

A furtive movement from the hallway leading to the powder room shot Bastian's adrenaline into overdrive. He had to make sure Emma knew their captor's identity without a doubt, and how he'd gained access to the house. "You're a big man, aren't you, Dietz? Shooting a guard and knocking out a helpless old man? And you had to do it all by your lonesome, since Michael broke up your group of Liberation assholes and, oh yes, blew Tio's brains out."

The shadow in the hallway retreated just as a blow connected with the side of his head. He slumped, gritting his teeth through the waves of pain, riding it out through sheer will. He couldn't pass out and leave Katrina to this lunatic's mercy.

How much longer could he keep baiting the fucker before Dietz made good on his threat and pulled the trigger?

He took comfort in the fact that Emma was, even now, calling in the cavalry.

"For your information, I'm not alone," Dietz hissed. "My men are waiting for Ross. He's going to have quite a surprise in store."

"If you say so."

Hurry, Michael.

As they sped the last few miles toward the estate, Blaze's cell phone rang. Blaze snatched it off the dash and barked a hello. Michael listened anxiously to the one-sided conversation.

"Slow down, angel. What?" Pause. "Dietz? Shit!" Pause. "Okay, you did good. Now get out of the house and—What do you mean you can't?" Pause. "All right. Stay out of sight. We've got a team on the way to intercept them. I love you too, angel." He pitched down the phone. "Fuck!"

"Tell me." Michael could barely breathe.

"Dietz got in the house. Emma said he shot John and knocked out Simon. He's holding Katrina and Bastian at gunpoint in your living room."

"Fuck!" What a nightmare. When would this be over? "Why can't she sneak out?"

"She overheard Dietz say he's got a handful of his former Liberation flunkies guarding the grounds. Dietz doesn't know she's there, so she's better off staying in the house, out of sight."

"I agree—if she'll actually stay hidden and not try to play the kick-ass heroine."

"She does, and I'll put her over my knee and spank her so hard she won't sit without a foam donut for a month."

Michael knew the Dom wasn't kidding. "I'll call Lawrence and let him know the situation, have him pull the team that he sent to the warehouse and send them to my estate instead. Since Lenny was supposed to wait three hours before calling to give me the false lead on the warehouse, Dietz will believe he's got time to move. Hopefully that will make him overconfident and he'll be slow."

"True. But I think we should still dispatch teams to both addresses Lenny gave us, in case Dietz has men there. We can catch them all in one swoop."

"You're right." Damn, he wasn't thinking straight. "I want Lawrence's team with us, though."

"And phone McKay so he can bring extra medics for the injured."

He placed the calls to both men, and warned Lawrence that Dietz's men would be waiting. They'd have to go in quiet, dispatch the soldier wannabes, then sneak into the house and take Dietz by surprise. Nice and simple.

Right. By the time they parked about a mile from his house on a side road, his nerves were jumping like he was hopped up on crack. Lawrence and his team of six agents were waiting, making a total of nine of them. Those were good odds. At least that's what he told himself to take his mind off his gut-wrenching terror of something happening to the people he loved.

It didn't work, but he showed none of his fear as he ripped off the horrid wig and ball cap, leaving them behind in the car. He and Blaze approached Lawrence and the others, who waited for instructions.

"How many men does he have?" Michael asked without pre-amble.

"We've spotted a dozen, so we're nearly even number-wise," Lawrence said. "In reality, we have a big advantage over those Liberation dumb-asses, who are so poorly trained and lack any real military experience."

"But they're dumb-asses with guns, so they're still dangerous," Blaze cautioned.

"Point taken. And although they lack experience, they have a good positioning around the house. There's one stationed on each corner. The other eight are spread in a rough circle on the outer perimeter of the property. Take them soundlessly if you can, and if the worst happens, have your NVGs on so you know who the fuck you're shooting at. Closer to the house you might not need them, since the area is lit, but that's your call."

Blaze wouldn't wear the goggles, Michael knew. He claimed they screwed with his field of vision. Everyone else took a pair and Michael fixed his in place, then palmed his gun. They started off, and when they reached the edge of his wooded property they began to fan out. Blaze stayed about thirty yards to his left as they stepped as quietly as possible through the foliage. Until now, Michael had never realized that the wooded area that gave him privacy also provided cover to his enemies. When this was behind them, he'd have to see about thinning out some of the trees.

To his right, a soft grunt sounded and he looked to see one of his agents lowering one of Dietz's flunkies to the ground. His men knew countless ways to kill with their bare hands, in the proper situation. *One down, eleven to go.*

Well, twelve. Counting Dietz, the bastard.

Eventually they'd spread out enough that he could only see

Blaze, but as they reached the edge of the trees and came to the sculpted lawn, the continued silence meant the op was going as planned. It might even have gone flawlessly . . . had he not stepped on a branch that gave with a loud snap, alerting the soldier twenty yards ahead to his presence.

The man spun and opened fire. Michael hit the ground, cursing as bullets pelted the scant cover around him. Propping himself on his elbows, he returned fire and took the man down, but the damage was done.

Gunshots erupted all around the perimeter, an all-out battle now.

Taking off in a sprint, keeping as low as he could, he began to fight his way to the house.

Fifteen

Bastian's face throbbed and blood dribbled from the corner of his mouth. He was running out of insults to hurl at Dietz as he tried to stall for time. Any minute, the asshole was going to put a bullet in his brain and be done with it. If only there were a diversion. He needed a split second with the man's attention focused somewhere else, and he'd make his move.

"Do what you want to me, but Michael's going to kill you for this," he taunted. "He's going to fillet you like a stinking fish."

"Shut up."

"Just sink his knife in and watch your eyes pop out of your head—"

"Shut the fuck up!" he snarled.

Another blow whipped his head to the side and he thought, *This is it. I've pushed him too far and now he'll kill me.* Dietz's face was twisted into an ugly mask as he slowly raised his arm.

Just as gunshots split the air from somewhere outside.

Dietz spun in surprise at the noise, and Bastian launched himself from the chair without even thinking twice. He tackled his enemy and they crashed onto the coffee table, rolled to the floor.

"Katrina, run!" he yelled. She did, and he hoped she didn't look back.

Half on top of Dietz, he pinned the man with his weight and struggled to wrest the gun from his outstretched hand. But Dietz bucked, knocking him sideways, and jammed the gun between them. Panting, Bastian grabbed his arm and fought for control of the weapon. When the tide began to turn in his favor, the bastard used his free hand to slam Bastian's head into the floor, twice in rapid succession.

Stars glittered in his vision and Dietz's weight was gone. He was sure the man would shoot him now, but heard footsteps instead. Blinking, he realized the man had fled.

Katrina!

Pushing to his feet, he staggered to the dining table, where he'd discarded his shoulder holster with his weapon in it. If only he'd had it on. But, then, Dietz would have taken it.

Weapon firmly in hand, he ran, heedless of the pain in his leg, in the direction his nemesis had gone, out the front door. Into hell.

Flashes of gunshots punctuated the night. Ahead, Katrina was racing across the lawn, toward the relative safety of the trees. But she wasn't going to make it—Dietz was on her heels.

Bastian ran, shouting.

"Katrina, run!"

Heart tripping, she did, with one goal in mind: getting help for Bastian. Bullets flying meant Michael was here, and she had to find him.

Outside, however, she paused at the bottom of the steps. She couldn't run out into the middle of the battle like an idiot. Breathing hard, she peered into the darkness around the perimeter of the house, beyond the area illuminated by the security lights. She listened to the gunfire, noting where the sounds were coming from. Much of it was happening to the sides and rear of the property, it seemed.

There was nobody close to the house, so she figured the men Dietz bragged about had gone to meet the threat of Michael and his agents. Seizing the opportunity, she struck out across the lawn in a zigzag pattern, going from tree to tree. Pausing first, then continuing on.

She'd gotten about a third of the way to her destination when she looked over her shoulder and saw Dietz barreling out the front door, weapon in hand. He flew straight for her at a full-out run, exercising none of the caution she had in crossing the open space.

With a frightened cry, she shot from her hiding place in a deadly foot race she knew he was winning. Footsteps pounded behind her and then his heavy weight slammed into her back, driving her into the earth. She couldn't stop her skid, barely registered the sting in her hands and knees before her forehead smacked the ground.

And consciousness faded away.

Michael saw them, and his heart stuttered.

Dietz was after Katrina, bearing down on her. Michael ran, but he wasn't close enough to stop the bastard from catching up, taking her to the ground. Where she lay unmoving.

The man was lying on top of her. Michael couldn't shoot without the risk of hitting her instead. So he sprinted the remaining distance and launched himself at Dietz in a flying tackle, just as the man started to rise.

He hit hard, and his gun went flying as they struck the ground together. Grabbing Dietz's shirt, he drew his fist back and delivered a punishing blow to the monster's face. A satisfying crunch of bone and a scream from his enemy were music to his ears, and he struck again.

"I'm going to fucking rip your lungs out, you son of a bitch," Michael hissed.

"You'll try."

Dietz rallied, pushing up, and rushed him. Bowled him over backward, got in a few good licks to Michael's ribs. He grunted, aware the man had lost his gun, as well, and was glad. A fair fight, then, if there was such a thing.

A fight to the death.

They rolled over the earth, punching and kicking, each trying to gain the upper hand. Michael almost had him—right up until the man aimed a well-placed kick to his stomach, laying him flat on his back. Dietz pounced, and the speed with which he wrapped his hands around Michael's throat left him stunned.

"Now who's going to die?" The face above him was stark with madness, the grip unbreakable.

Michael tried. Every self-defense trick he knew, to no avail. He couldn't move, couldn't breathe.

"Good-bye, Ross."

Precious seconds ticked and the world began to fuzz at the edges. He was in complete disbelief that he was going to die this way, the life choked from him by the man he hated.

Sounds faded. Sparks burst in front of his eyes, and then he saw nothing.

The ground disappeared and he fell into a black void. Wind rushed past him, and he ceased to be. All that he was, forgotten.

And then he simply vanished into mist.

They were too far away, near the tree line.

Bastian saw her go down, and fear pushed him faster. Michael and Dietz were fighting, out for blood. His lover seemed to have things under control.

But that's the nature of a disaster: it happens so quickly. Before a man can blink, the fickle bitch called fate steps in and turns the tables.

Destroys lives.

In a blink, Dietz had Michael pinned, hands around his throat. Strangling him. Bastian closed the distance, half limping now, and the scene took on a horrible clarity. Suffocating, just like in his nightmare. Only it was Michael, not him, who couldn't draw a breath.

Screaming. Someone was screaming as Michael went limp, head falling back. Dangling from a monster's hands. "Noooo!"

Dietz jerked upright, releasing Michael. He bolted to his feet, eyes wide, and scrambled backward as Bastian's arm went up. The man was fucking dead, and the knowledge was etched on his face as Bastian pulled the trigger. Over and over.

As the bullets plucked his clothing, Dietz's body jerked, doing a macabre sort of marionette dance before finally crumpling to the ground. He didn't move again.

Bastian was hardly aware that the other gunfire had stopped, or that his agents were jogging toward them. Part of him registered profound relief to see Katrina sitting up, rubbing her head. But Michael wasn't moving.

Dropping to his knees, he shook his friend. "Michael?"

Too still. He placed his hand under the man's nose. No warm puff of breath. No life.

"Oh . . . Oh, God, no." Gathering his lover in his arms, he worked to position him, used a finger to part his lips. Then he placed his mouth over Michael's and gave him air. "Come on, breathe. Don't do this to me."

"Bastian?" Katrina whispered.

"Help me," he begged her. Or was he begging Michael? She scooted up to sit to one side and pushed on Michael's diaphragm.

"Give him another one."

Another breath. And she pushed again. In and out, breathing for him. His face was so pale, his lashes dark against waxen cheeks.

Clutching him tightly, Bastian began to sob. "I killed him for you, just like I promised I would. Remember? I got him for you. For all of us. Please come back. Michael, *please*."

He looked at Katrina. Tears streamed down her face and she held one of Michael's hands between hers, rubbing as though she could warm life into him. How could this happen? How? His body was numb, but his mind all too aware of the horror.

Bending, he gave another breath. Another.

A hand on his shoulder. "Bastian, you have to let him go," Blaze said hoarsely.

"No."

"This isn't—"

"Wait!"

Under his hand, Michael's chest heaved. And his lover sucked in a huge breath and began to cough. All around them, the men exclaimed in excitement and relief. But he and Katrina didn't pay attention to anyone but Michael, who at that moment opened his big brown eyes. It was the most beautiful sight Bastian had ever seen.

"Welcome back," Katrina said through her tears.

Michael stared up at them and blinked slowly. "Dietz . . ."

Bastian stroked his hair. "Dead. I got him for you."

"Like you promised," he rasped through his injured throat. "I heard you."

"Good. Now I want you to rest. McKay is coming and you're going to get checked out, okay? So is our girl."

Michael's gaze found hers. "Baby?"

"I'm fine," she assured him. "Just a bump on the head when he tackled me. Nothing to be concerned about."

"But she's still getting a scan. I'm not leaving a damned thing to chance with either of the people I love. Never again."

That was his word, and if he was a little overprotective from now on, they'd have to live with it.

Somehow, he didn't think they'd mind.

Katrina basked in the sun with her two handsome men, Emma, and Blaze. If there was anything that topped a beautiful day, margaritas, and her friends' company, she had yet to be introduced to it.

"More refreshments? I'd be happy to refill the pitcher."

Cracking open an eye, she smiled at Simon. "I think we're good, thanks. Guys?"

"There's still plenty, but if we run out we can get it ourselves," Michael said. "Why don't you take the afternoon off?"

"And remain far from this area, lest my virgin eyes burn from their sockets?"

Michael grinned. "You're a smart guy. Which is why I keep you around."

"Indeed. Enjoy the rest of your day. I know I will." Nose in the air, the old man glided away.

"I'm so glad he recovered without any complications," Emma said fondly. "I really like the stuffy old fart."

"Me, too." Katrina glanced at Michael, heart swelling with love. They'd come so close to losing him, but the bruises on his neck had faded almost completely.

"How's your security guy? John?"

"He's still healing, but he should be back on the job in a few weeks. He got really lucky."

"We all did," Emma said.

Katrina knew Emma felt bad about not doing more when Dietz broke into the house, but there wasn't anything she could have done other than phone Blaze. The events had unfolded so fast that by the time she joined them outside, Michael was breathing again and everything was over.

"Yes. That's why we're celebrating," Katrina said happily. "Dietz is gone, his dirty money has been seized, most of the Liberation soldiers have been rounded up, and Mr. President is ecstatic. I, for one, am feeling like doing something a little wild and crazy."

Three pairs of male ears perked up at that statement.

"Oh?" Bastian's brows rose over his sunglasses as he sipped his drink. "Do tell."

"Well, for example, I'm feeling way too clothed." She looked at Emma. "You?"

"Me, too! Isn't that amazing how we were thinking the same thing?"

"What should we do about it?"

"Strip, of course! How else will we get comfortable?"

"Now we're talking!" Michael said, laughing. The other two joined in, egging them on.

Performing for their rapt audience, they set their margaritas aside and stood, facing the guys. They peeled off their swimsuit tops, doing a little shimmy, letting their breasts dangle enticingly. Next they hooked their thumbs in their bottoms, slowly drawing them down and stepping out of them. Bastian's straw fell from his mouth, and all three adjusted themselves in their swim trunks to accommodate their growing discomfort.

"Okay, your turn," Katrina called to the guys.

Immediately, they scrambled to get naked and recline on their loungers, waiting excitedly to see what would happen next. Katrina studied all three of their cocks pointing at the sky, like exclamation points in a sentence, and giggled.

Emma laughed, too. "Now what? Do we take our own men? Or maybe . . . just this once we could . . ."

"Swap partners?"

Emma's blue eyes lit. "Could we?"

"Like, all the way? You'd let Blaze fuck me?"

"Just this once, and only because it's you. What about you? You'll let your guys fuck me, and you won't come after me with a hatchet afterward?"

"Yes to the fuck. No to the violence." She smiled, gesturing to the men and their poor, beleaguered erections. "But we forgot to ask them if they're game. Boys?"

Three enthusiastic responses sounded in a chorus of "Hell, yes!"

Excited, Katrina walked over to her bag sitting beside her lounger, and brought forth the items she'd hoped they would be able to use: three condoms. "Here's your team uniform, guys. Let's play ball!"

Tossing two condoms at her lovers, she took one for herself and Blaze and sauntered over to him. As much as she loved her two men—and she loved them more than life itself—she'd been wanting this big, delicious man for some time. The fact that she could have him without guilt was a wonderful bonus. There was nothing wrong with playing, as long as everyone was on the same page, and Katrina knew they all felt that sex was to be enjoyed with no boundaries. Sex was a connection that should be celebrated.

He made room for her on his lounger by spreading his legs and putting his feet flat on the ground on either side. Sitting between his thighs, she admired his ropy muscles. A gorgeous chest and washboard abs. Flowing black hair. And he sported a huge cock, one of the biggest she'd ever seen.

"Want a taste?" he asked, his voice a low rumble.

"God, yes." Taking the invite, she bent and swiped her tongue across the head, marveling at his salty taste. She sucked, enjoying the plum-shaped head, the smooth texture of him as she took him deeper.

Burying a hand in her hair, he pushed her head down, exerting control. It was scary but thrilling, so she let him set the pace, guiding her in giving him pleasure. Soon she was deep-throating him, using her inner walls to massage his length. He made an inarticulate noise and thrust faster for a minute, then gently pulled her off.

"Put the glove on me, beautiful."

Fumbling for the packet she'd dropped, she tore it open, happening to glance toward the others. Her lovers were entwined with Emma, Michael behind her, eating her pussy, while Bastian fucked her mouth. They were lovely together and the sight fired her blood, made her so hot for the man next to her, she could hardly stand it.

After she rolled the condom over Blaze's flushed cock, he sat on the side of the lounger and said, "Stand in front of me and spread your legs, honey. I'm going to eat that sweet pussy like I've been dying to do for weeks. And then I'm going to fuck you until you can't stand."

She did as she was told, hoping she didn't come at the first touch of his tongue. It was close, but she managed to ride the waves as he licked her folds, teased her clit. He suckled the little nub and she almost lost control again.

"Spread wider."

Bracing one hand on his shoulder, she put her feet farther apart. He dove in and really ate her, feasted in naughty slurps that had her hanging right over the precipice, ready to rocket out of control. A few more licks and he pulled back, took her hand.

"On the grass, over there." He snagged his beach towel and led her to a nice grassy spot, and spread it out for her. Grinned in anticipation. "On your back."

As she got into position, glad cries reached her ears. She and Blaze looked to see Bastian fucking Emma with enthusiasm, Michael doing the same to Bastian. All three were nearing climax.

Blaze knelt between her legs, cupped his big hands under her ass. "Does that make you wet, gorgeous, seeing them fuck?"

"Yes," she whispered. She needed him so badly.

"Good. Does me, too. I need my cock in your pretty pussy."

"Please fuck me!"

Lifting her as though she weighed nothing, he impaled her on his thick rod. Slid deep, parting and filling her. *Yes! It's so good.*

"Yeah," he moaned, closing his eyes. "So sweet."

He began to thrust, impaling her again. And again. Harder and faster, until she began to come unraveled. Finally, she exploded, hurtling over the edge, convulsing around him. He came right after, jerking inside her, spurts of heat pumping on and on. At last they stilled, sated and happy.

He kissed her lips, smiled, and murmured, "Thank you."

"Thank *you*. That was wonderful, and so are you. Emma's very lucky."

"So are your guys."

Disengaging, he tied off the condom and tossed it to the edge of the towel to dispose of later. They looked to their lovers to see them tangled in a sweaty heap, in much the same state of euphoria as she and Blaze.

After a few moments, Emma got up, her signal to switch places. Katrina rose and met her halfway, and they shared a hug.

"Just once?" Katrina whispered in her ear. "You sure we can't ever do that again?"

Emma laughed. "Well, I'd say we can keep our options open. If that works for you."

"Oh yeah." She kissed her friend's cheek and joined her men on their towel, which had also ended up in the grass. "Have fun?"

"Christ, that was hot!" Bastian enthused. "Not just us, but seeing you with him."

"Not that I want to swap so you can be with him *all* the time," Michael said with a hint of possessiveness. "But, yes, it was fun."

"How did I get so lucky?" Leaning into them as their arms came around her, she soaked in their love.

Michael kissed her hair. "I think we all did. It's not too often people get another shot at love or life. I don't intend to waste a second of loving you both."

"Neither will we," she promised.

"Damned right," Bastian said.

"I've got something to ask you both," Michael began, suddenly sounding unsure. "I'm not very good at this kind of thing, but . . . will you two do me the honor of celebrating our commitment in a private ceremony? It would be here, with just a few of our friends. And I'd want you both to move here permanently." He faltered, uncertain.

Twisting around to see his worried expression, she and Bastian shared a smile, and Bastian nodded for her to answer for both of them. "Yes, yes!"

They shared a group squeeze, and Michael sighed in contentment.

"Then there's nothing else in the world I'll ever need. Welcome home," he whispered.

Pulling them down to rest in his arms, he proved there was, however, at least *one* more little thing he needed.

And they gave it to him, more than once that lazy afternoon. With love.

About the Author

Jo Davis spent sixteen years in the public-school trenches before she left teaching to pursue her dream of becoming a full-time writer. An active member of Romance Writers of America, she's been a finalist for the Colorado Romance Writers Award of Excellence multiple times, has captured the HOLT Medallion Award of Merit, has been nominated for the Australian Romance Readers Award in romantic suspense, and has a book optioned for a major motion picture. She lives in Texas with her husband and two children. Visit her Web site at www.JoDavis.net.